The Shadow Man

Gordon Wallis

TABLE OF CONTENTS

PROLOGUE

January 15th, 1946, 60 nautical miles off the east coast of La Digue Island, Seychelles, Indian Ocean.

Sixty-year-old Egyptian Captain Mahmoud Salah gritted his teeth and widened his stance as he fought the wheel of his beloved ship, The Pearl of Alexandria. The night was pitch black and the driving rain and howling wind pounded at the windows of the bridge from every direction. Underfoot, the great ship rocked and yawed as it crested the swells and ploughed through the terrifying waves that crashed into the bow sending countless tons of seething, frothing water cascading over it. The storm was by far the most violent he had encountered during his 30-year career as a captain. But this was cyclone season, and although he had expected rough weather, nothing could have prepared him for the ferocity and sheer power of the freak storm he found himself navigating. Built in Hull, England in 1910, the 1600-ton, 265-foot cargo and passenger vessel had plied this route since it had been commissioned by the wealthy Egyptian company owners. The journey had started as always, in Portugal and had progressed with stops in France, Italy and Greece, before crossing the Mediterranean, travelling through the Suez Canal and on to the Indian Ocean. From there the vessel would make port at Bombay India, the Seychelles and Mombasa in Kenya before making its way down the east coast of Africa towards Cape Town. The subsequent journey north would see stops in every major port along the west coast of Africa before finally arriving back at the starting point in Portugal. It was a long and arduous journey, but one that Salah had made hundreds of times. His long-suffering wife in Cairo had often joked that he could do it with his eyes closed. But at that moment his eyes were as wide as plates and filled with only one thing. Fear. The same could be said of the first mate who was being violently tossed about as he frantically gathered fallen instruments and other items that had been dislodged from their rightful places in the bridge by the savage storm. It had been known well in advance that they would be travelling through the cyclone. The passengers and crew had been informed, that very afternoon, to be sure to secure their cabins and check on the cargo in the holds.

However, nothing could have prepared any of them for the astonishing brutality of the squall they had found themselves in. The captain's powerful arms bulged as his sun-bronzed hands gripped the wheel, his knuckles turning white as he fought to keep the ship on course. It was a battle he feared he was rapidly losing and one which would have devastating consequences if he did. A hard-working family man, his worry was not only for his beloved ship but for his passengers. All had been told to lie low in their cabins until they had passed safely through the storm. *What would they be thinking now?* This massive weight of responsibility played repeatedly through his mind as he clung to the wheel during the sickening rocking and plunging. There were women and children aboard as well. By now they would all be terrified.

It was then, strangely, that he thought of the mysterious passenger bound for Walvis Bay in South West Africa (Namibia) who had boarded in the dead of the night in Italy 3 weeks beforehand. The first mate had joked and dubbed him 'Passenger X' because his boarding had been carried out in such a secretive and clandestine manner. This 'Passenger X' had remained in his 1st class cabin ever since then and had not once ventured out. All meals had been delivered to his cabin by the galley staff and left on a trolley outside. It had been stranger still, that his accompanying luggage and cargo, eight small but extremely heavy steel crates on wooden pallets, had been loaded by the sleepy crane operator and crewmen between the hours of 1.00 am. and 2.00 am. while most aboard were fast asleep. It had been only Captain Mahmoud Salah who had caught a brief glimpse of this mysterious man as he climbed out of the black Mercedes in the Port of Genoa and walked up the gangway to the cabins accompanied by three burly escorts. In the mist and yellow glow of the port lights, the passenger had appeared slight of build and tense. Huddled into a thick black overcoat, his short-cropped blonde hair was sparse and his face pale and drawn. The man had disappeared into his cabin immediately and soon after, his escorts had left in the same black vehicle. The Pearl of Alexandria had left port at 6.00 am. that morning and headed east towards Greece. The fact that one man was carrying 8 crates of cargo had crossed his mind as being quite unusual at the time, but this had soon been forgotten with the day-to-day routines of the journey. What Captain Mahmoud Salah had no idea of was the fact that the mysterious 'Passenger X' was an escaped German fugitive. A high-ranking Nazi by the name of Rudolf Baumann.

Also unknown to Captain Salah was the fact that each of the 8 heavy steel crates stashed in the hold was filled with 1000 kilograms of pure gold. Eight tons of stolen gold that had been melted down from jewellery and ornaments and removed from the fillings in the teeth of murdered Jews in the death camps of Auschwitz and Birkenau. Destined finally for Argentina, this gold was intended to fund the lives of other escaped Nazis who had fled to Peron's Argentina after the war. Men such as Adolf Eichmann, Erich Priebke, and the 'Angel of Death' himself, Dr Josef Mengele. These men along with many other war criminals had found refuge there. It was the responsibility of this 'Passenger X' or Rudolf Baumann to make sure this precious cargo arrived in Walvis Bay where it would be securely stored until onward shipping to Argentina could be arranged. The journey was being made in a roundabout way, but this was to reduce any chance of discovery or suspicion by transporting it via more direct routes. An old Egyptian freighter arriving in Walvis Bay via Bombay would attract far less attention than one travelling west from the ports of southern Europe. It was in fact, a carefully and meticulously planned operation that so far, was going very well.

Just then it started to go wrong. Down in the hold several binding straps securing part of the cargo snapped and a huge load of bagged grains lost its footing. The massive weight of cargo slid uncontrollably across the hold and slammed against a side bulkhead causing the ship to suddenly list to port at a dangerous angle. This was immediately felt by Captain Salah and his heart sank as it happened. It was seconds later that he sounded the alarm on the ship. The seven short blasts of the horn followed by one long one sounded eerily in the night. This was the signal to the crew that they were now in an emergency. Captain Salah had never needed to sound this alarm in over 30 years, but he felt it was now necessary. With the ship tilted hopelessly to one side, he glanced at the first mate who stood nearby clutching a wall rail. His face was drawn and his eyes filled with terror. At that moment a rogue wave crashed into the side of the huge vessel. The force of the water smashed the port window of the bridge and instantly both men were soaked to the bone. The deafening howl of the wind was all-encompassing and the rain and spray stung their faces blinding them as they squinted their eyes to stay in control.

"What now?" shouted the first mate in Arabic.

"We must get through it!" replied the captain. "The old girl can make it!"

But in reality, things were not looking good at all. The shifting cargo had damaged the electrical system and burst several hydraulic pipes which were now leaking fluid through the hold.

Very soon, control of the great ship would be lost and she would be adrift in the ocean at the mercy of the storm. But it was at that very moment that the door at the rear of the wheelhouse burst open with a loud crash. Expecting to see a crew member bearing yet more bad news, Captain Salah turned from the wheel and looked behind him. But it was not a crew member. It was the mysterious 'Passenger X'. The man was barefoot and soaked to the bone, wearing what appeared to be full-length pyjamas and a thick black dressing gown. The man resembled a drowned rat. His pale face was green with sea sickness and there was fresh vomit down his front. His dark blue, sunken eyes were filled with terror as he clung to the door to steady himself against the violent lurching and rocking of the deck.

"Was ist los mit, Schweinehund?" he screamed in German, his voice clearly betraying his fear. 'What is going on, pig dog?'

Unable to understand a word of what the strange man had said, Captain Salah turned and continued to battle the wheel. But the man was incensed and furious as well as severely seasick. He lunged forward and began pulling at the captain's clothing while screaming unintelligibly. Seeing this, the first mate ran forward and in the flickering light and maelstrom of wind and spray, pulled the man away causing both to slip and fall. The captain turned briefly and looked down at the two men on the deck. It was then he noticed the thin red lines that ran under the jawline of the passenger. It was as if he had just had an operation of some sort and in fact, he had. Rudolf Baumann had recently undergone plastic surgery to change his appearance. His face was well - known and he was a wanted man. In the confusion and terror of the moment, he turned back to face the storm. But it was then that a freak wave appeared on the starboard side of the ship. In the darkness and spray it seemed impossible. Unreal, even.

A colossal black wall of water rose high above the wheelhouse and towered over the ship. Seconds later millions of tons of water slammed into the side of The Pearl of Alexandria and the old ship instantly capsized. With the hull smashed and ruined and its cargo in disarray, it took less than 15 minutes for the stricken ship to be swallowed by the raging waters of the Indian Ocean and to disappear, taking 150 souls with it.

CHAPTER ONE

Sixty-year-old Maxim Volkov groaned audibly as he stood up from the toilet and flushed. With his stomach still grumbling, he made his way over to the basin and washed his hands with soap and warm water. As he did so he stared at the image in the mirror that looked back at him. In his mind, he still had the rugged looks that had reminded so many of the actor, Rutger Hauer, but in reality, he knew he was bloated, ageing badly and quite unwell. The IBS or irritable bowel syndrome he had suffered for the past 10 years had caused him a great deal of embarrassment and shame. Not only in front of his wife, Ulyanka but from his staff and underlings as well. He grumbled deeply as he dried his hands then walked back over to the toilet bowl to lift the can of air freshener. A liberal blast would take care of the stench that filled the room. The illness had many symptoms. Some more severe than others. Mostly they were abdominal pain, bloating, diarrhoea and constipation. These symptoms were random and could present at any time. Quite often they did at the worst of times when he was under pressure from work in the company of his superiors. It was an affliction that angered him as much as it embarrassed him. And it was not helped at all by his diet. Although his nagging wife, Ulyanka, had set a strict diet for him, sending him to work each day with a bowl of homemade borscht, he regularly dumped this in the waste and ordered his favourite meal from McDonald's. It was a guilty pleasure that he knew did him no good at all but it was one he refused to give up. Maxim Volkov tucked his shirt into his trousers and glanced in the mirror once again. Apart from a slightly green pallor and a few beads of sweat on his forehead, he looked fine. He stepped out of the toilet and into his spacious and ornately decorated office. Situated on the 5th floor of the famous Lubyanka building. A large neo-baroque edifice with a facade of yellow brick it had been designed by the great architect Alexander V. Ivanov in 1897. A bold and imposing structure, it had long been the home of the feared FSB, formerly the Russian KGB until Boris Yeltsin changed its name in 1995. Maxim Volkov remembered that day as clearly as if it were yesterday. At the time he had been a fresh-faced agent rapidly rising the ranks of the KGB and making a mark in the intelligence world. It was a career to which he had given his life and he would not change it for anything.

Still suffering from abdominal pain, Maxim Volkov walked around his huge ornate desk and stepped up to the large window that looked out on a frozen, snow-covered Lubyanka Square below. Out there the temperature was so cold it was physically dangerous to be outside. But still, several pedestrians were making their way about the streets of the capital. Maxim Volkov sighed as he stared out at the bleak cityscape spread out before him. In his mind, he pictured his yacht. The beautiful streamlined machine sat in the harbour of the small coastal town of Zadar, Croatia. That sunny Dalmatian coast was warm even at this time of the year. How he missed it so. How he wished he could simply teleport himself to the deck of that gorgeous vessel. Far from his ugly, nagging wife who by now disgusted him to the touch. Maxim Volkov could not even remember the last time he had found her remotely attractive. Sure, his job with the FSB was highly paid and by Russian standards, he was an incredibly wealthy man. But he was a company man, always had been, always would be. How he envied the oligarchs who had ingratiated themselves with the head of state and made untold fortunes. Yet here he stood, ageing, unwell and waiting for retirement. But that retirement was only six months away. Only six months to go until he put his grand plan into action. The real estate company had already been primed. Once he said goodbye to his beloved bureau, he would sell his country house and smallholding on the outskirts of Moscow and disappear forever. He had already purchased a humble flat in downtown Moscow and prepared it for his hated wife. His wife whom he never intended to see again. Sure, she would be well looked after. There would be a monthly stipend. Some money to ensure she could continue making her disgusting food and watching her insipid soap operas. No, he would have none of it. He would be far, far away, bobbing up and down in the sunshine in a warm climate surrounded by beautiful young women. Good food and beautiful young women. His career and climb up the ranks had not been an easy one. There had been many challenges and problems along the way. But it had been his ruthless streak and disregard for human life that had impressed his superiors and still did. Like all men in his position, he had also gathered a large amount of retirement funds. A nest egg of United States dollars safely stashed away in a Swiss bank account. More than enough to see him through to the end of his days. And one thing was for sure. Maxim Vokov intended to enjoy his retirement. No more routine. No bitching wife. No bosses breathing down his neck. No biting cold winters, and most importantly, freedom. Freedom to roam and drink as much vodka as he wished.

Yes, it will be great. Maxim Volkov grunted and looked at the gold Rolex on his left wrist. It had just gone 4.15 pm and the skies were already darkening heralding the freezing night and treacherous roads he would navigate back home to his wife. Sure, there were the farm animals on the smallholding that brought him much pleasure. Pigs, chickens and two cows. He had cared for them and raised them for many years. They were, in a way, an escape from the horror that was his wife and he would spend many hours cleaning their pens and feeding them. Then there would be the usual tripe and disgusting food and zero conversation. More drudgery and unhappiness. But not for long now. Not for long. Feeling somewhat chipper after his bowel movement, he placed his hands behind his back and rocked on the balls of his feet. 15 minutes to. Tick tock tick tock. At that moment the buzzer on his desk rang. It was an old unit still working from the Soviet era. The loud metallic sound reverberated in his head as he swung around angrily and made his way to his seat.

"Yes?" he barked into the receiver at his long-suffering secretary.

"I am sorry to bother you, sir," said the woman who was sitting outside his large door "I have just received a request from upstairs. They would like to see you urgently and are waiting for you now."

Deep frown lines appeared on Maxim Volkov's forehead as he thought about this strange request. *What could they want from me at this late hour? Could it not wait until tomorrow?* But a request from upstairs was an indication that something important had come up. Something that required his immediate attention. A hollow feeling of gloom enveloped him as he closed his eyes and took a deep breath.

"Tell them I am on my way up!" he barked.

Maxim Volkov stood up wearily and walked towards the full-length mirror at the left-hand side of the office. He brushed the front of his dark grey suit to make sure there were no crumbs from the two Big Mac meals he had consumed for lunch. Finally, he brought his right hand across his balding head to maintain his combover. Satisfied he was looking okay, he made his way across the office and out of the door.

"Wait for me here," he said to the secretary without looking at her. "There may be work to do."

Maxim Volkov walked down the high-ceilinged corridor past the grand fixtures and ornately framed pictures of the great and good of Russian intelligence. He arrived at the lift and pushed the button for up. Presently the doors parted and he stepped inside and pressed the button for the floor he wanted. As the lift rose, he took a deep breath and prepared himself mentally for whatever was to come. With a fake smile as mean as a snake, he stepped out and nodded at the gorgeous young secretary who manned the reception of the hallowed halls above. Halls he had never gotten to in his career. Halls he had so craved to be part of, but never quite made.

"Please step right in, Mr Volkov," said the girl with a wide smile.

It was as if she was torturing him. Every time she saw him she gave him that same smile. It was an inviting smile but it also had a smidgen of ridicule in it. Ridicule that he was ageing and she worked for the big boss. The untouchable director. Maxim Volkov wanted to fuck her and strangle her in equal measure. Stepping forward, he knocked once on the huge ornate doors and stepped inside. There were three men there. Two he recognised and one he did not. Once again he gave his best smile and greeted the three men who did the same and offered him a chair. Cordialities were exchanged before the director broke the moment and spoke.

"Maxim, I'd prefer to get straight down to business," he said "This is Dr Smitzlov of the little-known but very important Marine Intelligence Department. Have you heard of it?"

"No sir," said Maxim. "I have not until now."

"Well," said the director, "I think I will hand the conversation over to him so he can explain the situation to you clearly. It is of importance as I'm sure you know."

Smiling once again, Maxim Volkov felt a rumbling in his stomach and felt a fart making its way down his small colon. Instantly a series of beads of sweat broke out on his forehead.

"Are you all right man!?" barked the director.

"Yes, sir," he replied, "I am quite fine. Please, Dr Smitzlov, go on..."

The young man cleared his throat and sat forward to speak.

"Thank you, gentlemen," he said. "I shall be as brief as possible. Roughly 16 years ago the Marine Intelligence Unit was formed. Our aim as a unit is to monitor the beds of the world's oceans. This is impossible using satellites but it is possible with simple side-scan sonar units. Around that time, our founder invented a small unit that we fitted to the hulls of all major ships manufactured in the motherland. The units are no larger than a suitcase and are permanently fitted on all vessels belonging to the state or Russian companies. These devices, although small, are attached to the electrical systems of these ships and are connected to the Internet. We now have a few thousand of these units on the hulls of our vessels as they make their way around the globe doing trade. Now, should these units pick up any anomalies, or metal structures of a certain size or mass, they are programmed to send these images to our central computers. The images are scanned and compared to data we have and if there is a match, a red flag is raised and we are instantly informed."

"There must be plenty of debris on the ocean floor," said Maxim, moving uncomfortably in his seat.

"Oh yes..." said Dr Smitzlov "There are numerous wrecks, fallen containers, sunken vessels of all sorts. Most of these are completely inconsequential to us and are largely ignored. But our computers are programmed to look for vessels of a certain shape and mass. Vessels that we, as the Russian state, have an interest in."

"I see..." said Maxim. "I take it something has come up?"

"Correct," said the young man, looking proud. "Three weeks ago, a merchant cargo ship registered in Gdansk was making its way down to the Cape of Good Hope from Bombay. Its course took it past Seychelles. While there it passed over a wreck that rang alarm bells. We in the unit have studied these images and concluded that there is a very good chance that it is indeed a vessel of interest."

"One of our lost ships?" asked Maxim.

"No!" barked the director. "A German ship. Lost in 1946. 265 feet long and weighing in at 1600 tons. A ship by the name of The Pearl of Alexandria. Have you heard of this ship, Maxim?"

Maxim Volkov shifted uncomfortably in his chair and responded.

"No, sir," he said. "I have not."

The director took a deep breath and his cold eyes grew impatient. They seemed to bore a hole into Maxim's brain.

"The Pearl of Alexandria was carrying a Nazi fugitive by the name of Rudolf Baumann. This Baumann was making good his escape from Germany and heading to Argentina."

"I see, but..."

"Silence!" barked the director.

There followed a brief pause while the others squirmed in their seats.

"This Rudolf Baumann was not simply escaping Germany. He was accompanied by a cargo of up to eight tons of pure gold. This ship disappeared in a storm and has never been found. That is until now."

Maxim turned to Dr Smitzlov.

"And you are certain this is the ship?"

"Of course not, Maxim," said the director. "How could we possibly be certain? That's why you are here. I am sending you to go and make an identification. If this is indeed the Pearl of Alexandria, there is almost $470 million US dollars worth of gold aboard it..."

CHAPTER TWO

"What is a good beer here in Portugal?" I asked the taxi driver.

"Sagres," he replied, eyeing me in the rearview mirror " Sagres or Superbok."

"Which one do you prefer?" I asked.

"Sagres..." he replied with certainty.

"Good," I said staring out at the pleasant-looking town "I'll be trying one of them within the hour."

I had decided to take a break from the winter in London and escape to warmer climes. I had never been to Portugal and had decided that 3 weeks off exploring the Algarve region would be a tonic for the mind and soul. The 3-hour flight from Gatwick had been a breeze and the airport had been quick and easy. The talkative taxi driver had welcomed me to the small town of Faro and told me that the journey from the airport to the hotel would take 20 minutes at most. Regardless, I was happy to feel the warm sun on my right arm and I took a deep breath as I relaxed. It had been too long since I had taken a holiday and this was something I felt I needed. The insurance company had no objections either. The freelance nature of my work allowed me to dictate the conditions of my work. I planned to spend a few days exploring the town of Faro and then venture out on a hired motorcycle and ride around the Algarve region, stopping in at the small beach towns and taking in the sights. *And the beer, of course*. It soon became apparent that we were entering the old town. Here the buildings were slightly run down and dishevelled. Old Portuguese architecture was something I was familiar with due to my time in former colonies in Africa. It gave me a homely feeling and was comforting at the same time. Far away from the freezing rain and hustle and bustle of London. *Yes*, I thought. *You made a good call here, Green. This is gonna be good.* True to his word, the taxi driver pulled over in a narrow street and pointed to the name of my hotel on a sign up ahead.

He quickly got out of the vehicle and walked around to retrieve my baggage from the boot. I paid him in cash Euros, including a generous tip. His eyes lit up as I handed him the cash and he offered his hand for me to shake.

"Enjoy your holiday, sir," he said warmly.

"Thank you," I replied, "I intend to."

The hotel was situated opposite a motorcycle dealership. The sight of it brought thoughts of freedom to mind and I smiled as I made my way up the cobbled street to the hotel entrance. Once again I was aware of the warm sunshine and the slightly salty smell in the air. The sea was nearby and seagulls were flying and squawking above to confirm this. I walked through the glass doors into a bright reception area. There I found a young Portuguese lady who spoke perfect English. The check-in process took less than 10 minutes, I was handed my key card and made my way to the lift. The room was set on the 5th floor of the establishment. I immediately dumped my bags on the dresser and walked over to the windows to take a look at the view. Beyond a series of streets and ancient buildings, I could see the ocean. There was a table and two chairs on the balcony and I took the opportunity to light a cigarette and soak up the sun. Finishing my smoke, I made my way back inside to do a room inspection. Although small, it offered everything the website had said. Air conditioning, satellite TV and high-speed internet. The bathroom was spotlessly clean and I flopped down on the bed to check if it was comfortable. It was. I lay there feeling pleased with my choice and considered picking the remote and browsing the news channels. But then my mind got the better of me and I decided against it. *Fuck that, Green. Why on earth would you want to do that? You're on holiday here, get out there and enjoy yourself for Christ's sake!* After a quick wash and a change of clothes, I left the room and headed downstairs back to the reception. The young lady smiled at me as I made my way out to the narrow cobbled street. Feeling relaxed, and with zero sense of where I was going, I wandered over to the bike shop across the street and gazed through the windows at the machines on offer. Most were road bikes but there were a few off-road models that would suit my needs.

I made a note to be sure to hire one of those to enable me to reach the more rural and out-of-the-way spots on my trip. I had brought my drone and I intended to get some footage along the way. I took a deep breath and stared up the street. *Now! Enough wandering around and daydreaming, Green. Time to make good on your word and have that beer.* Less than five minutes up the street I found what I imagined was the main tourist boulevard. Cobbled like the rest of the narrow alleyways, it was lined with bars and restaurants on either side and there were holidaymakers of all ages eating lunch in the cafes and eateries. The sun was warm but I felt I would rather find a more out-of-the-way place. Somewhere the locals would go rather than the pricey tourist traps. My sense of direction told me to walk on past and head towards the sea. Up ahead I could see an open area with what appeared to be a green space in front of an old municipal building. I imagined there would be some sort of waterfront and there would be sure to be a small bar or cafe in which to try the recommended Sagres beer. But it was as I was approaching the ever-present McDonald's takeaway that I saw the man. He sat in a tatty-looking wheelchair, opposite the takeaway. His black hair was bushy, long and streaked with grey. His beard was the same and I saw immediately that he was fast asleep in the sun. His right hand was extended in a begging gesture and his blue tracksuit was dirty and stained. Clearly, he was a vagrant and a beggar. But for some strange reason, the sight of him fascinated me. His right leg had been amputated above the knee and he had tied the loose end of the leg of his grubby tracksuit in a knot. Although his face was down in slumber, I could see his skin was a dark olive colour from the sun. I felt a pang of pity, studying him as I walked past and then looked ahead to decide which way to turn at the end of the street. My mind was made up as I arrived and saw the open area I had anticipated spread out before me. On my right was a green lawn with a road surrounding it and a harbour beyond that. Further ahead small boats bobbed up and down in the dazzling sunlight and there was a large and expensive-looking hotel on the right. I made my way along the road towards the harbour until I came across a small bar. There, sitting outside were several people. Most seemed to be locals although there was one man who simply had to be an Englishman. He sat there, dead still, with his face raised to the sun. His skin was burnt to a crisp and peeling on his head. In front of him was a glass of beer. There was a small table near the narrow doorway and I decided to take a seat.

Stretching my legs out and taking a deep breath I lit a cigarette and waited for service. This came soon in the form of a middle-aged Portuguese lady who arrived with a tray.

"Good afternoon, sir," she said, gauging I was English "What can I get you?"

"I'll have a Sagres beer, please..."

She nodded and smiled as she made her way back into the tiny bar. I sat back and basked in the glorious sunshine and sneaked a look at the Englishman who was busy frying himself. He had not moved once and appeared to be in some kind of stupor. It was a strange sight that immediately made me think of the old adage, 'Mad dogs and Englishmen go out in the mid-day sun.' I for one happy to do so and even more when the beer arrived. True to his word, the taxi driver had been right. The beer was excellent and it tingled pleasantly in my throat as it went down. I lit another cigarette as my mind drifted. I spent the better part of an hour sitting there, taking in the sea breeze and 3 more beers as my mind relaxed. I knew then that I had chosen well and I would enjoy the break. There were hundreds of miles of coastline to explore and the freedom of the motorcycle would be an asset. I planned to spend the rest of the afternoon at the bar and then make my way back to the hotel via one of the restaurants I had passed on the street down from the hotel. *Perfect, Green. A perfect day.* But it was then that I saw the tramp I had seen sleeping earlier. He was busy making his way up the street past the expensive-looking hotel. His movements were strained and slow but he moved with the strength in his arms that most wheelchair-bound people have. He looked like he must have been baking in the grubby blue tracksuit and once again I thought about his life as a vagrant on the streets of Portugal. But it was as he drew nearer that I saw he had locked into my gaze and he was in turn studying me. *He got you hook line and sinker, Green. No way you're gonna escape this one. He'll have a few Euros off you sooner than you know.* I took a deep breath and stared out at the harbour once again. It would be a few minutes before the man would reach the bar where I sat and I hoped he might get distracted along the way. But sadly, that was not to be, as when I looked back at him, his dark, friendly eyes were still fixed on my own, despite my sunglasses.

This was a man who was well-versed in his skill. He would have me, no doubt. I did my best to ignore his slow, steady approach, but as he drew nearer I gave up and looked at him. His face was open and pleasant. Once again I noticed his skin was a dark olive colour from being in the sun. He looked Portuguese for sure and his hair and beard were full and wild. He appeared overweight and I wondered then if it had been diabetes that had resulted in him losing his leg. I took a deep draw of beer as he approached the roasting Englishmen and spoke.

"Hello, David," he said.

The old Englishman awoke from his trance and opened his eyes. He grunted and replied.

"Alright, Joe," he said. "How are you today? Lovely breeze coming in from the sea..."

But the man he called Joe was still focused on me and seemed determined to pull up to my table. He had me marked for sure.

"Hello, sir," he said. "Where are you from?"

"I flew in from London today..." I replied, taking a swig of beer.

There was something about the way he spoke. His accent was instantly recognisable. It was the accent of a man from Southern Africa. Much like my own. I frowned as he spoke and it was as if he knew this too.

"Okay..." he said as he arrived near the table. "I'm from Rhodesia."

CHAPTER THREE

"I see..." said Maxim Volkov as he studied the scans of the submerged vessel.

To him, it looked like nothing more than an elongated blurry smudge, but clearly, it had roused the attention of the bureau. That and the obvious value to the state should the vessel be the one they hoped it to be. But the fact that he was to be sent out on yet another mission sickened Maxim. He had been on so many to central Africa and the mines of Senegal and other shitholes. The thought of another one was deeply depressing especially given his retirement was to be so soon. With a brave face, he lifted his eyes from the glossy scans and looked at the director.

"I take it I will be accompanied by some company men, sir?" he said.

"Correct," said the director. "We have chosen two good men, experienced divers and excellent operatives. You will meet them in the morning and will begin preparations. All the equipment you will need has been arranged and you will want for nothing. I expect you back within 2 weeks and I'm sure you agree, we all hope for good news on positive identification."

The company men the director was referring to were of course Wagner operatives. Completely separated from anything to do with the Russian state, theirs was a private army. This anonymity allowed them to carry out operations around the world with nil chance of any connection to the state. There had been instances, recently even, when questions had been asked of Putin if he knew anything about the Wagner Group. He had, of course, denied any knowledge of such an organisation and any further questions had been countered with blank denials. It was and always had been a supremely brilliant operation. With no links to the Russian military, the privately owned and funded group had slipped through borders. They had linked up with crooked governments, assisting them to stay in power in shady corners of the world. By maintaining lucrative mining deals and friendships with dictators in countries such as Senegal and Ghana they kept a military presence on the ground. It was, in fact, a shadow army.

The recent Novichok poisonings of former KGB spies in the city of Salisbury in England had been carried out by Wagner men. Their identities had been established by the UK authorities and extradition requests made. But of course, any knowledge of this was immediately denied by the Russian state and extradition requests were refused point blank. Maxim Volkov had worked with this Wagner Group on many occasions. He had built part of his fortune by doing so. There had been diamond deals in the Congo and other less obvious schemes that he had been involved in to boost his bank account. Of course, he was a minor fish in a very big pond. The owner of the Wagner Group, Yevgeny Prigozhin, was a close confidant of Putin. Outrageously wealthy and completely untouchable, he would never have to move from his villa on the Black Sea. The tight, complicated network of companies that were linked to his own was so carefully guarded, so extremely secretive, that he would never be held responsible for the many atrocities the Wagner group had committed. His shadow army would continue operating with the help of corrupt leaders in Africa and there was very little anyone could do about it. They were, after all, a private entity. Nothing more, nothing less. The fart Maxim had felt earlier was steadily making its way out and he shifted uncomfortably in his seat as fresh beads of sweat appeared on his brow. He glanced at the young man from the Marine Intelligence Unit who smiled at him proudly.

"Very well," said Maxim "I will be ready for the briefing tomorrow morning."

"Excellent," said the director, sitting back in his expensive chair. "It will be at 9.00 am. here in my office. Your men will be present and we will run through everything then."

A frown formed on the director's forehead and he sat forward once again as he studied his clearly uncomfortable underling.

"Maxim!" he boomed. "Are you alright, man? You look rather ill."

"I am perfectly fine, sir," said Maxim as he suppressed a burp. "A little indigestion is all..."

CHAPTER FOUR

I could hardly believe what I was hearing. The accent had been the first give - away but this was beyond bizarre and it felt like a setup of sorts at first. But still, the man trundled towards me on his tatty wheelchair with his warmly gleaming eyes smiling from his sun-bronzed face. His wild, bushy hair and beard were thick and dark with streaks of grey.

"Rhodesia?" I said as if wanting further confirmation.

"Yes, sir," said the man. "Zimbabwe now. I left in the nineties."

I stared at the man as he pulled up next to my table and stopped.

"Well," I said, shaking my head in disbelief. "Me too. I left after the war."

The man frowned as he studied me and then his eyes lit up suddenly. He leant forward and offered me the same grubby hand I had seen outstretched when he had been asleep on the street earlier.

"Jose Fonseca," he said with a wide smile "Rhodesian Light Infantry. Pleased to meet you, sir."

I responded as I had to and shook the man's hand. His grip was dry and strong and the skin of his palms was calloused from propelling himself around in the wheelchair.

"Jason Green," I said, dumbfounded. "Pleased to meet you. Can I offer you a beer?"

Jose frowned and a serious look overtook his face.

"Thank you, sir," he said. "But the drink has caused a lot of problems in my life. I lost everything including my leg, and it's the reason I've been on the streets for the last 6 years."

I watched his eyes brighten up as he saw the pack of cigarettes on the table.

"I will have a smoke if you can spare one though..."

I gave the strange man the packet and offered him a light. It was then that the waiter came out and saw my beer was almost finished. Upon seeing Jose, she greeted him warmly and they spoke a few words in Portuguese. I nodded as she offered me another beer and spoke once again to my new friend.

"How about a Coke?" I asked.

"That would be lovely, sir," he said with another wide smile. "Thank you."

I ordered the drinks and sat back once again to study the man. His dark blue tracksuit was stained and tatty and I noticed a dirty plastic bag tied under the seat of the wheelchair. I had no idea what it contained but I imagined it would be part of his meagre worldly possessions. Our conversation continued after the drinks arrived and I learned that Jose Fonseca had been born in the town of Beira in Mozambique before moving with his family to the border town of Umtali in Rhodesia. He had spent his childhood there and eventually joined the army to fight in the bush war like all young men were required to do. I questioned him further about various landmarks and events during the war. This was in an effort to catch him out on what I had suspected was an elaborate scam. But his answers came back correct every time. There was no doubt. The vagrant I had found on the street of Faro in southern Portugal was indeed a compatriot of mine. Just how he had got himself into such a dire situation in life was still a mystery but I was going to find out for sure. It was a scene as bizarre as it was unexpected and in our short acquaintance I found that I had an affinity for him, his warm kindly smile and open face. Even if it was in the middle of a wild bush of hair and beard. It was a full 45 minutes later, as he was relating a story from the war, that I saw the tears pooling in his eyes. I knew then that he was one of the many casualties of that terrible conflict. Sent out into the world with no counselling or explanations as to why they fought and died, seemingly for no reason. War damages people.

This was a fact that I was well aware of but this particular meeting was gobsmacking in its absurdity. *This is a fucking small world, Green.* Jose Fonseca wiped his eyes and smiled at me once again. The conversation went on for another hour during which he told me he had a brother whom he expected was still alive. He told me he believed this brother lived in Durban in South Africa. I inquired as to whether he was in contact with this family member but he simply shook his head and looked sad. I knew he was not looking for sympathy either. The man was truly a lost soul with very few prospects of getting out of the situation he had found himself in.

"Well, sir," he said finally. "It's been a pleasure meeting you, but I must get back to work."

By 'work' I knew he was referring to begging on the tourist street where I had originally laid eyes on him, asleep with his right hand outstretched. I knew then that I couldn't simply send him on his way with nothing. I reached for my wallet and handed him 100 Euros. He took it from me and pocketed it immediately.

"Thank you, sir," he said. "You're very kind..."

"Less of the sir," I countered, "my name is Jason."

The man smiled through his sadness once again and spoke.

"And my name is Joe," he said. "Goodbye, Jason, and thanks again..."

I watched in dumbfounded silence as Joe Fonseca slowly wheeled himself away in the baking afternoon sunshine. At the speed he was travelling, it would take over 20 minutes to reach the same spot I had seen him begging from earlier. Suddenly I was overtaken by a great sadness. Here was a man who had served his country and gone on in the world only to end up in this awful, hopeless situation. One that he would most certainly never escape. *Where did he live? Who were his friends? Where did he bathe, if at all?* He would surely eventually die on these streets, pleasant as they were. The waitress interrupted my train of thought when she came out and offered me a refill for my beer.

I questioned her, as she was obviously friendly with him. Her reply was simple and frustrating in equal measure. She had known Joe Fonseca for years. On many occasions, he had been offered help by residents and locals. There had been offers of flats and accommodation as well as offers of assistance to find housing through the state. All this help had been politely refused. By all appearances, this was a man who was content with his lot in life. Content to beg on the streets of Portugal until he died. It was a puzzling and tragic story and one which I battled to put out of my mind for the rest of that afternoon and evening. It was 10.00 pm. when I made my way into my room at the hotel. I had walked back up the same street where I had first seen the man but he was nowhere to be seen. I had eaten a steak dinner at a streetside restaurant and washed it down with yet more beer. Feeling full and warm and content, I smoked a final cigarette on the balcony of my room and breathed in the warm salty air with the lights of Faro all around below me. Finally, I lay on the bed and turned the television on. I was tired.

Tired and a little drunk. I tried to concentrate on the programme - about ice road truck drivers, but my mind was stuck on one thing only. One person only. Joe Fonseca had worked his way into my mind and I could think of nothing else. *You have to help him, Green. You have to...*

CHAPTER FIVE

Maxim Volkov arrived as promised at 9.00 am. sharp in the director's office. There awaiting him were his boss, Dr Smitzlov from the Marine Intelligence Unit and two operatives from the Wagner Group. The two were young, in their early thirties and both built like walking mountains of muscle. At 6.4 ft each, they might have been twins, both having short-cropped blonde hair and wide, square jaw lines. The only giveaway that the two were not related was the fact that one had a hooked, aquiline nose, while the other had a small stubby and previously broken one. The men were introduced as Sergei and Yuri and their handshakes were firm, dry and strong. Once all the men were seated, the director began the briefing. The three of them would leave in the next few days on a privately owned jet bound for Dubai. Once there, the cargo and equipment would be transferred to a UAE-registered jet for the onward journey to Mahe Island in Seychelles. Fake passports for all three men had been arranged thus allowing their arrival to be carried out with the secrecy they needed. Their aliases were created for them to look like wealthy businessmen and the purpose of their visit was registered as being for recreation only. Every detail of their itinerary had been pre-planned and it was envisaged that their time on the island would last no longer than 3 or 4 days. Once identification of the sunken vessel was complete and visual proof obtained, they were to return to Moscow immediately where the next stage of the operation would be planned. It annoyed Maxim that there would be little to no chance of any graft on this short trip. No opportunity to loot and steal gold or diamonds from corrupt officials. That and the fact that the trip would be so short meant that in all, it would amount to nothing more than an exploratory venture. There would be no fruits for him as, if it was the actual vessel they were looking for, he would be long retired by the time any salvage operation could commence. There were also international laws to pay attention to. The laws of salvage dictated that any wreck found in open waters is fair game and to the winner go the spoils. The wreck in question was beyond the territorial waters of the government of Seychelles. Still, everything had to be conducted in absolute secrecy. Something Maxim Volkov was quite used to. The briefing continued until 12.30 pm. by which time Maxim was bursting for the toilet and feeling weak from hunger. He knew that his meal from Mcdonald's would be delivered soon and he could hardly concentrate for thinking about it.

It came as a great relief when the director called a halt to the briefing for lunch and Volkov bolted out of the office and down to the sanctuary of his office on the lower floors of the Lubyanka building. The whole thing had happened so fast that there had been hardly time to prepare.

Of course, his nagging, ugly wife had raged at him upon hearing the news that he was to leave on yet another business trip. She had berated him and his inability to call the shots at the offices he had so proudly served. Maxim Volkov had held his tongue and consoled himself with the knowledge that very soon he would never have to look her in the face again. *No, he would be far, far away.* Maxim burst into his office and raced to the bathroom where he fumbled frantically to drop his trousers and sit on the toilet bowl. After an explosive burst of diarrhoea, he went through the motions of washing up before heading back into the office to await his midday meal. It arrived as usual and he sat down to savour the wonderful taste of the junk food that had all but destroyed his health. There would be more hours of briefings that afternoon followed by the short trip home to make further preparations. Then there would soon be a mind-numbing trip on the Citation jet to Dubai. Depending on the arrangements, there would be several hours while equipment was transferred from one jet to another, and then there would be the flight south to Seychelles. Maxim Volkov had never been there and had only skimmed the internet the previous evening while alone and away from the nagging of Ulyanka. By all accounts, it was a beautiful set of islands. But there were constant fears. *Would the toilets be adequate for his illness? Would the company operatives be agreeable?* There was no doubt in his mind that they would be fully trained and efficient, but he was there to ensure everything went smoothly. And Maxim was tired of doing this. All he wanted was to rest. Rest and get away from the job that had swallowed his dreams for so long. Volkov closed his eyes as he took another bite into the soft processed meat of the Big Mac burger while he gripped the large Coca-Cola with his left hand.

CHAPTER SIX

I awoke at 7.00 am. with a pounding headache and a bone-dry mouth. Immediately I stood up and stumbled into the bathroom to fill a glass of water. *Is the water in Faro good to drink? Who gives a shit! You gotta have it, Green.* I stood there in my underwear and stared at the mirror as I downed the warm liquid. It felt good no matter if it was bad for drinking. I made my way back and opened my toiletry bag to search for some headache pills and antacids. Both were swallowed along with another glass of water before I put the kettle on and fumbled with the tiny pod of milk as I prepared a coffee. Apart from the gradually diminishing pounding in my head, my mind was still fixated on the man I had met the previous afternoon. Joe Fonseca. That strange brother-in-arms whom I had stumbled across in the most unexpected way. That kindly-faced man with the burden of a thousand pangs of sadness etched in the lines on his sun-bronzed face. Even turning the television on failed to get him out of my mind and it stayed that way until after I had finished the coffee and taken a shower. By then I was starting to feel half human and I glanced at my watch to see it had just gone 8.30 am. *He should be there, Green. Where the hell else would he go?* Finally, I stepped onto the balcony and lit the first cigarette of the day. The bright morning sunshine stung my eyes but the air was warm and salty and the bustle in the old town of Faro had begun below with delivery trucks and motorbikes plying the cobbled streets. I was hungry but the thought of food would have to wait. There was a sense of urgency. I had to find the man. I had to help in some way. He had mentioned that he had a brother whom he believed to be alive. *Surely he would be in contact? Surely this last family member would not want to know his only brother was set to rot on the streets of the Algarve in Portugal? No way, Green. You can do something here. Fix his situation even if he doesn't really want you to*. Feeling determined, I crushed out the cigarette and made my way back into the room. After gathering some personal items, I made my way out and down the lift to the ground floor. Turning left at the hotel doors, I made my way back towards the tourist boulevard where I had first laid eyes on him sleeping in the afternoon sun the previous day. The image was burned into my mind. Joe Fonseca sitting there in his wheelchair with his right arm and hand outstretched in a begging gesture. For some strange reason, I had a great fear that he would no longer be there - that he would have moved on and I would never have had a chance to help him. With that thought in mind, I quickened my pace as I hurried down the cobbled streets.

Eventually, I arrived on the boulevard with the restaurants where I had first laid eyes on Joe. The day shift workers were busy setting the tables and sweeping the tiles in preparation for the day's trade. With my pace growing faster I hurried past a young waitress who was busy pinning a menu to a sandwich board. I craned my neck as I battled to look ahead towards the spot where I had seen him. But there was no one there. Nothing except a yellow municipal garbage truck collecting bins. Feeling even more anxious, I carried onwards until I reached the main square in front of the harbour. I made a right turn and headed towards the pub I had sat at yesterday. To my amazement, the same British man was sitting in his usual chair with his sun-crusted head facing the morning sun. The peeling skin on his skull was bright pink.

"Excuse me," I said out loud.

The man dropped his gaze and blinked at me with bloodshot eyes.

"Yeah?" he asked with a confused look on his face.

"Have you seen the guy in the wheelchair?" I said. "Joe Fonseca. Have you seen him today?"

The man frowned and a puzzled look came over his face.

"Nah, mate," he replied. "I ain't seen him today..."

Having spoken, he closed his eyes once again and turned back to face the sun once again. At that moment I could have thumped him. *Fuck!* I thought as I looked around for any sign of a wheelchair. But there was nothing. Joe Fonseca was nowhere to be seen.

CHAPTER SEVEN

"You are a weakling, Maxim!" shouted Ulyanka Volkov in her native Russian "In all these years you have never had the balls to stand up to your superiors and tell them no!"

Maxim Volkov swallowed audibly and his face grew red with rage as he stared at his wife. The woman he had hated and wished dead for decades. The woman who had tormented and shamed him so many times. But the one woman he could not kill. And Maxim had killed many women. In fact, he had raped and killed more than he could remember over the years. But Ulyanka was the great untouchable. She was the only person in the world who could get away with talking to him like this. But there was a good reason for this fact. Maxim Volkov was a company man. Appearances were everything in the FSB and upon his retirement, there would be a leaving party and ceremony where both of them would be expected to smile and go through the motions. *Perhaps he would kill her then? Oh God, how he wished he could wrap his fingers around her wrinkled neck and squeeze the vile, disgusting life out of her wretched, sagging body.*

"My darling," said Maxim, his lower lip trembling with rage "You know very well that I must carry out the duties assigned to me. This is how I have provided for us over all these years. You wouldn't have me jeopardise it all, would you?"

"Yes!" shrieked his wife. "For once in your useless grovelling life, you might just stand up and say no. Once! But that will never happen, will it? Maxim will always do the bidding of his masters.

Those powerful men in the upstairs offices! You're nothing but a mouse among them, Maxim! A fucking mouse!"

Volkov turned and as he did so he farted loudly. With his hated wife sniggering behind him, he made his way up the stairs of his modest house to pack his bags for his business trip. The fact that he was leaving seemed good at that moment, even if there was the unknown ahead of him.

CHAPTER EIGHT

It was with a feeling of bleakness that I made my way back towards the tourist street to find a restaurant for some breakfast. I found a suitable place with a view of the spot I had first seen Joe asleep the previous day. I sat down and tried to tell myself that it was more than likely the hangover that had brought on these feelings of anxiety, but for some reason, meeting the man had had a profound effect on me. I ordered a full English and a pot of coffee and sat down to eat and wait. The food was good and had a calming effect on me and I sat for the next hour smoking and drinking coffee while watching tourists arriving for the day. Then, at 10.00 am. I saw him. Still wearing the same grubby tracksuit as the previous day, Joe Fonseca trundled slowly up the cobbled street in his wheelchair, making his way towards his preferred spot in the sun. At that moment I felt a massive wave of relief. Relief that I would at least have the chance to help this man. Even if he was unwilling to accept help. *You can only try, Green. Get to it!* I crushed out my cigarette, nodded at the waitress and stood up to make my way down to where he had parked his wheelchair. It took a couple of minutes to get there but he had seen me approaching and as I did a wide smile formed on his face.

"Morning, Jason," he greeted me. "How are you today?"

"I'm fine, Joe," I said. "I've been thinking about your situation. You mentioned you have a brother in Durban. Are you in contact with him at all?"

"No," he replied sadly. "I haven't spoken to Chris in years. I don't even know if he's alive."

"Well," I said, feeling frustrated already. "Have you tried to make contact with him?"

"I don't have a phone," said Joe, "and I don't have a number for him either."

"Have you ever heard of Facebook, Joe?" I asked.

"I've heard of it," he responded, "but I wouldn't have a clue about how to use it."

Jesus, Green. I thought. *You've got your work cut out for you here.*

"Listen to me, Joe," I said slowly. "I would like to help you if I can. I can get you some new clothes, perhaps a new wheelchair and there is a chance I can find your brother. Would you like that?"

Joe de Fonseca looked at me with a suspicious twinkle in his eye.

"But why would you help me?" he said quietly. " You hardly know me."

"We fought in the same war, Joe," I said. " We grew up in the same country. What have you got to lose? Think about it. A new wheelchair, new clothes. A cell phone for you to use if you need it. I am happy to do this for you if you'll allow me to..."

Joe Fonseca dropped his gaze and looked down at his amputated leg. It was as if he was weighing up this strange offer of assistance from a man he hardly knew. I watched as he took a deep breath and looked up at me once again.

"I've been on these streets for years now, Jason," he said, his eyes welling with tears, "They have become my home. But I am getting old and a new chair would be something I could use. This one causes me a great deal of pain. The clothes will also be great.

This smelly old thing is buggered. As far as finding my brother goes, I don't think I'll ever speak to him again. But I appreciate what you're doing and I'll take you up on your offer of help."

Suddenly I felt a wave of relief come over me. It was as if I finally had a mission I could get my head around. To do some good for this poor, lost soul. I smiled and gave him a friendly pat on his wide shoulder.

"Good man," I said "Now, let's start by getting you some food and coffee..."

CHAPTER NINE

It was three days later. The night was black and the cold was a biting minus 8 degrees Celsius as Maxim Volkov stepped from the black limousine into the yellow lights of the hangar. He had left his house and wife and driven back to the Lubyanka building where he had parked his company vehicle in the giant underground parking lot. From there he had a brief few words with the director one last time before finally getting the go-ahead to start the mission. The driver had met him in the reception of the upper floor and they had ridden down to the parking lot and the waiting limousine to head out to the private airport on the outskirts of Moscow. Volkov had forced the driver to make a stop at the nearest Mcdonald's and had voraciously eaten two Big Mac meals on the way. The boxes and empty Coke cup were still in the footwell of the vehicle as he climbed out. Underfoot, the icy ground crunched as he made his way to the parked jet that stood shining and bathed in the light near the giant hangar doors. Standing near the plane were the two pilots who would fly Maxim and the Wagner men to Dubai. The pilots were drinking coffee and chatting amiably despite the freezing temperatures. As they laughed, great plumes of vapour blew from their mouths like yellow clouds in the lights. As Volkov approached the plane he noticed the two Wagner operatives, Sergei and Yuri approaching from the offices at the far side of the building. Both men were smiling, obviously happy to be leaving on what would be another highly paid assignment. They greeted Volkov with handshakes and attempted to make small talk with him and the pilots. By that time, Volkov's hands were aching terribly from the cold and he quickly put a stop to proceedings in an effort to enter the sleek jet and get warm once again.

"What time are we leaving?" he burst out. "Stop this fucking meaningless conversation! I am freezing. Let us into the plane where it is warm!"

The men, clearly stunned by this violent outburst of temper, immediately stepped aside to allow him to walk over to the stairs that jutted out of the shiny, thin fuselage. Volkov made his way up the stairs while clutching the chrome rail. It was so cold he thought the skin of his palm would stick to it.

CHAPTER TEN

I spent the next four hours pounding the streets while pushing Joe Fonseca around in his wheelchair. During that time we purchased toiletries and seven sets of new clothes including a new tracksuit similar to the one he was wearing when I had first met him. The shop attendants had seemed surprised to see us doing this and many of them recognised Joe and seeing him in their retail outlets was the last thing they expected. Joe was cool and calm during the process taking his time to carefully choose shirts and other clothing. The shoe shopping was a strange experience given he only had one foot but he chose well and I refused to let him wear anything until I had made sure he was cleaned up physically. During the morning and while Joe was shopping, I made enquiries online as to where I might be able to purchase a new wheelchair. It turned out that there was a company in Faro with a mobile representative who would visit to make an appraisal and deliver a new chair custom fitted to the client within 24 hours. I instructed the company to have the rep sent to my hotel room at 4.00 pm that afternoon. This seemed to lift Joe's spirits even more as it had become clear to me that, although he did not show it, the wreck of a chair he was using was causing him considerable pain. With the shopping finally done, I left Joe at a restaurant while I took the bags to my hotel. Whilst there, I arranged a room for him directly next to my own. The hotel was well-fitted for the disabled and wheelchair access was easy. The pleasant receptionist was all too happy to arrange the room and I paid in advance for a week using my credit card. Joe had told me that he was living in an abandoned house with a bunch of gipsy thieves and pickpockets. They extracted rent from him which he paid from his income from begging on the streets. He had told me they were a violent bunch who had assaulted him on many occasions and had even urinated on him while he slept if he was late with his 'rent'. I told him in no uncertain terms that I would not allow him to return there. As I made my way back down the street to the restaurant where I had left him, I wondered if I was making a mistake doing this. Perhaps he would take the gesture as foolish and would simply disappear once again with his new belongings to sell them and return to life on the street. But this was something I was not prepared to entertain. There was no way I would allow him to fall back into that trap. I felt sure there was a certain understanding between us. After all, we were brothers in arms. *Surely that would count for something?* I was acutely aware that many vagrants were quite content with their lives on the streets of major cities.

I had seen documentaries about such things and it puzzled and worried me at the same time. I consoled myself that even if that was to be the eventual case, I would have at least played a small part in trying to help the kindly-faced man. As I approached the street where I had left him, I felt a pang of anxiety that he would have simply disappeared once again. *No way Green. You have his clothes and he is expecting his new wheelchair. He'll be there.* And sure enough, he was. Sitting there under a terracotta-coloured umbrella sipping a Coca-Cola was Joe Fonseca. I was sweating by the time I took my seat and ordered a Sagres before the lunchtime order. Joe seemed as calm and pleasant as ever and we ate freshly grilled sardines with chips and salad over an hour of quiet conversation. Aware that this man knew very little other than his life on the street, I broke the news to him that I had booked a hotel room for him next to my own. He took the news well and I told him he would be free to bathe and then try on his new clothes before the wheelchair salesman arrived at 4.00 pm. We left the restaurant at 1.30 pm. and I pushed him up the cobbled street to the hotel where we took the lift up to his new room. There I left him with strict instructions to get cleaned up and dispose of the smelly old tracksuit he had clearly been wearing for years. He frowned slightly at this instruction and I knew he had become attached to it in some strange way. Standing my ground I told him in no uncertain terms that I would personally burn it if I ever saw it again. Finally, I left him to get on with it and returned to my room to wait for the salesman. Feeling tired but exhilarated, I lay on my bed in the cool air conditioning and stared up at the ceiling as I wondered if what I was doing was simply a waste of time and money. *Who cares, Green? It's fucking happening whether he likes it or not!*

CHAPTER ELEVEN

Maxim Volkov scowled angrily as he sprawled at the back of the sleek Citation private jet awaiting the pilots and the two men from Wagner, Yuri and Sergei. He had checked the toilet and noted with satisfaction that it would suit him should the need arise. The flight was due to take six hours during which he intended to sleep and prepare for the next leg of the journey. There would, of course, be an extended period in Dubai while their cargo was transferred and how long this would take was unknown. It was a great frustration that he would be in limbo for this period and unable to judge how long it would take. Either way, he would get through it and he had told himself he would not lose his temper in the process. The outburst on the apron earlier was mild compared to some he was known for. In fact, Maxim Volkov's violent temper was the stuff of legend within the Wagner ranks and that of the FSB. The pilots, Yuri and Segei had been briefed about this before the trip. But Maxim Volkov was a man whose abilities were tried and trusted by his bosses. For this reason, he had been useful during his long tenure in the ranks. Of course, there had been the occasional murder and multiple rapes, but this sort of behaviour went with the territory for a man like him. The most important thing was he got the job done, and quickly. But the relatively warm air in the interior of the plane did little to lift Maxim's mood. With his retirement looming he saw little chance of any opportunity for his own gain from this mission. It would be, as his hated wife had predicted, simply another errand on behalf of his bosses. Even if the sunken ship did indeed prove to be The Pearl of Alexandria, a salvage operation would take more than six months to arrange. By that time Maxim would be officially retired and on a state pension. At least he had the consolation that by then he would be in the final stages of his exit plan from Russia. The sunshine and the sea on the coast of Croatia would be within reach and he would be free for the first time in his life. Maxim drummed his fingers impatiently on the taut white leather of the armrest. *Why did it always take so long to do these things? Surely everything should have been arranged before his arrival?* The delay was yet another reminder that he was merely a pawn in a much bigger game. It was a further ten minutes later when the pilots and the two Wagner men entered the sleek aircraft and the door was finally closed. Yuri and Sergei took their seats opposite Volkov and exchanged bemused looks with each other as they settled in.

An angry glare from Volkov ensured that no further eye contact was made and both men busied themselves reading the various magazines that were stashed in the racks next to their seats. Finally, the co-pilot came through to announce that they would be departing. Maxim stared out of the small window as the snow and sleet shot sideways across the dimly lit apron. The rumble of the engines grew louder and the small jet trundled forward as it taxied its way towards the runway in the dark, frozen night.

CHAPTER TWELVE

"I'm sorry Jason," said Joe, "That's something I won't do..."

"But why?" I asked, somewhat frustrated "It'll make a big difference, you'll look a whole lot younger."

The time had just gone 3.30 pm. and I had gone in to check on Joe before the arrival of the wheelchair salesman. I had suggested that after the appointment I would take him to a barber for a haircut and beard trim. His wild grey-streaked black hair and beard reminded me of Hagrid from Harry Potter. But it seemed that the limit of my assistance had been reached and this was something he would not do for anyone. Joe simply turned his head and stared at the television which was playing some Portuguese soap opera. I took a deep breath as I stood there in the doorway and felt quietly pleased with the progress I had made. Joe had taken a shower and was wearing his brand-new clothes under the new blue tracksuit. He had even tied the loose leg up neatly as he had done with his old one and a quick glance around the room revealed that he had indeed dumped the smelly old one in the rubbish bin. His skin looked fresh and clean and he had obviously applied liberal amounts of deodorant as the room reeked of it. I took all of this as a small victory and smiled as I walked in and closed the door. At that moment my phone rang, it was the salesman from the wheelchair company. He had arrived early and was asking if he could come up. I told him that was fine and this seemed to lift Joe's spirits immensely and I watched as he trundled around the room on his old chair positioning himself for the imminent arrival of the rep. The man appeared a few minutes later after a quiet knock on the door. In his early twenties with a black beard and nervous eyes, he stepped in and shook both our hands before getting to work. Joe and he spoke at length in Portuguese and multiple measurements were taken over the next hour. At one point I stepped out to the balcony to smoke and let them get on with it. It did strike me that I had no idea how much all of this was going to cost. *It doesn't matter, Green. This is an opportunity to do some good in your life. It will come back to you ten times over.* I had no idea just how fond I had become of the incredibly frustrating but likeable man who was Joe Fonseca. It was as if we had been friends for many, many years and I felt as if I had become his carer in some strange way.

By the time I walked back into the cool of the airconditioned room, Joe was beaming from ear to ear and the salesman was proudly holding up a picture of a wheelchair on an iPad.

"This is the model we have settled on, Mr Green," he said "It is modern and extremely comfortable and easy to use. Mr Fonseca is confident it will suit his needs."

I grunted as I saw the price tag of 2800 Euro tucked into a corner on the bottom left of the screen. But after a minute of further sales talk and Joe's wide, expectant eyes looking up at me, I spoke.

"When can this be delivered?" I asked.

The salesman opened his hands in an open gesture and replied.

"I can have it here by 9.00 am. tomorrow morning, sir."

"Do it..." I said, "And don't be late. We will be here waiting for you."

The salesman nodded graciously and thanked us both before leaving. Finally, I sat down on the bed and looked at Joe who by then was grinning like a Cheshire cat.

"So," I said, "It looks like we're getting somewhere."

"I don't know how to thank you, Jason," said Joe with tears in his eyes. "Why are you doing all this for me?"

I stared at the floor as I asked myself the same question. But it was a question I found difficult to answer. There was no reason other than that we had fought in the same war and grown up in the same country. Finally, I lifted my gaze and looked him in the eyes.

"Why am I doing this?" I said. "I don't really know, Joe. You're a stubborn old prick, but I like you..."

Joe's face was immediately puzzled but within seconds he exploded in a cacophony of mirth. His entire body, which was substantial, wobbled and jiggled as he laughed and I found myself doing the same. It was an unexpected and thoroughly enjoyable moment for both of us and it continued for a good 2 minutes. Finally, I stood up from the bed and walked to the open doors of the balcony. Below, the streets of Faro were darkening and soon the tourist crowds would be making their way to the restaurants and bars for the evening. The breeze was warm and salty and I was feeling good. I turned around to face my new friend and spoke.

"Now," I said "Let's go get some dinner. Those Sagres beers are calling my name..."

CHAPTER THIRTEEN

The twinkling lights of Moscow disappeared quickly as the sleek jet rose into the heavy snow-filled clouds. Suddenly there was only blackness outside the small window and Maxim Volkov sighed deeply as he waited for the stars to appear in the sky above. The journey of six hours would be mind-numbingly boring unless he could find something to occupy his time. Not only was he wide awake, but he was also hungry. Both Yuri and Sergei were still engrossed in paging through the magazines they had lifted from the racks near their seats. Maxim was convinced that neither of them could read and he imagined they were simply staring at pictures and avoiding looking at him, wide awake and hungry again. Of course, there would be food and drink on board. There always was. It was only when the seatbelt light had gone off that Maxim stood and made his way back towards the galley. He could feel the eyes of Yuri and Sergei burning into the back of his head as he did so. He opened the refrigerator and removed a can of Coke and a pack of sandwiches he imagined would be ham and cheese. It was the cheese he craved more than anything. Sure it was not the wonderful yellow stuff from McDonalds but it would do. With his supplies in hand, he turned and made his way back to his seat opposite the Wagner men. He sat and the can hissed as it opened. Both men glanced up briefly, their eyes settling on the food.

"Go on!" said Maxim in a gruff voice, jealously guarding his food. "Soldiers cannot march on empty stomachs. Eat!"

The men exchanged glances and then stood to make their way back to the galley. As they passed him, Maxim was once again reminded of their size. The men were walking towers of pure muscle. Almost Neanderthal in appearance were it not for the close-cropped hair and cleanshaven faces. This gave him a measure of confidence that whatever they faced on this particular mission, there would be no problems. No one in their right mind would tangle with such men. His bosses had chosen well. Yuri and Sergei returned soon after carrying piles of food. They placed it on the tables near their seats and swung them around so that they faced each other as they ate. They also did this to avoid the glare of Volkov who was quietly munching on his sandwiches and sipping Coke.

Maxim stared aghast at the sheer amount of food the men had taken for themselves. It was some ten silent minutes later that he placed the empty can on the table at the side of his chair, brushed the crumbs from his shirt, and reclined the seat backwards. It was time to sleep. That was if his stomach would allow it.

CHAPTER FOURTEEN

The evening was pleasantly warm as I pushed Joe down the cobbled street to choose a restaurant for dinner. The fact that most of the restaurant staff knew him didn't bother me at all and we settled for one with tables outside. There was live music playing in a bar opposite and we took our time with starters of garlic bread followed by a fine dinner of sirloin steak. Joe had his usual Coca-Cola while I drank at least three Sagres beers. By the time we were done, I was pleasantly tired and full. It appeared the efforts of the day had had the same effect on Joe. Around 8.30 pm. we made our way back up the street to the hotel. The old wheelchair was unwieldy and difficult to push and I was pleased that the replacement would be arriving the following morning. I opened Joe's room with his key and took a seat for a moment before heading to my own.

"You mentioned your brother's name is Chris," I said, "is that correct?"

"His real name was Cristóvão," said Joe, a sad look in his eyes, "but we always just called him Chris."

"Why do you say it in the past tense?" I asked. "Do you think he might be dead?"

"I hope not," came the reply, "but I doubt I'll ever see him again..."

"I asked you about Facebook," I said. "You've never tried to use it to find him?"

"Like I said, Jason, I have heard of it but I wouldn't have a clue what it is or how to use it."

The statement frustrated me and I cleared my throat before I spoke again.

"And no one has ever offered to help you find him using Facebook?"

"No," came the simple reply. "Never..."

I stood up and asked Joe to write the correct spelling for 'Cristóvão' on a piece of hotel stationery. He did so while yawning deeply and once again I felt the frustration that had been plaguing me ever since I had met the man. He had clearly given up on ever seeing his brother again. Added to that, he was obviously tired and more than likely unused to the quality and amount of food he had just eaten. I took the piece of paper from him and walked to the door.

You have a good night, Joe" I said, "we must be ready for the new wheelchair at 9.00 am. tomorrow."

Once again I saw the twinkle in his eyes as he looked up at me.

"I'll be ready, Jason," he said, "don't worry about that."

CHAPTER FIFTEEN

Sleep never came for Maxim Volkov. Instead, he spent the entire six hours of the flight to Dubai with stomach cramps and frequent visits to the toilet. Thankfully the extraction fans were strong enough to remove the stench that his bowels produced and he was saved the embarrassment of his colleagues noticing it. This discomfort did his mood no good, however, and by the time the small jet began its descent into Dubai, he was ready to strangle someone. Ahead of him was the operation to remove the equipment they were carrying and the transfer to the second Emirati jet that would take them on to Seychelles. The air conditioning aboard the Citation had dried out his sinuses and he sat there sniffing in misery as he saw the city below. Sergei and Yuri, however, had eaten their fill and had slept like babies for the entire journey. Maxim had stared at them on many occasions, their powerful arms folded in slumber and their almost bald heads leaning to one side. How he envied their youth and fitness. *How could he have wasted the majority of his own life doing the bidding of the powerful men at the FSB? Had it all been for nothing?* Apart from the fatigue and the pain in his stomach, Maxim Volkov's anus was itching. This was a result of his frequent trips to the toilet. He desperately wanted a shower and a clean bed. An idea began to form in his mind as the light for the seatbelts illuminated. He would call the head office in Moscow and tell them that he was feeling unwell. He would then put in a request that he be allowed to take a hotel room for the night. That way, the two Wagner men would take over responsibility for the transfer of their equipment. He would get to rest and recuperate and would even be able to order some takeout food. *Yes*. He thought. *That is what I'll do. The director will have no choice but to agree*. The mission was important enough to them that they would have no choice but to agree. At least then he wouldn't be stuck in transit between the two aircraft and would be exempt from the formalities and hassles of the transfer. Maxim pulled his phone from his pocket as the plane landed in the dazzling sunshine of the desert morning. A half smile formed on his face as he saw he already had a roaming network on his phone. He dialled the number he knew so well and broke the news that there would be a delay. A car was ordered to take him to the nearest 5-star hotel once he had cleared immigration. All of this was done while Yuri and Sergei were peering out of the windows marvelling at the vast expanse of the airport.

When the jet finally taxied to a stop and the co-pilot opened the door, Maxim stood and addressed the two seated soldiers.

"I am leaving you both to complete the transfer of the equipment to the new jet," he said "Don't fuck it up and do not call me unless there is a dire emergency. I have business to attend to and will return when I am done. Goodbye!"

With that, Maxim Volkov stood up, gathered his luggage, and stepped past the two men on his way to the exit door.

CHAPTER SIXTEEN

Feeling tired and lethargic, I opened my laptop and slumped down on the bed. It took a good 2 minutes to find an English channel on the television but eventually, I found the Discovery channel which was showing a car restoration programme. The music in the background bothered me, mindless rock guitars churning out riff after riff but I had to put up with it as there were very few other options. I yawned as I opened Facebook and clicked on the notifications which were mostly news items. I grabbed the piece of paper that Joe had written his brother's name on and typed it into the search bar. 'Cristóvão Fonseca' It came as no surprise that there were many thousands of people with the same name. It would be a mammoth task to trawl through them all in the hope of finding Joe's missing brother. Feeling frustrated, I took a deep breath and stared at the television screen. The mindless drivel continued with bearded men skidding around and burning rubber in their souped-up American cars. Feeling slightly chilled by the air conditioning, I grabbed the remote and set it for a degree warmer than it currently was. My mind was still full of doubts that what I was doing was simply a waste of time. *Will he simply go back to his life on the street after you have spent what may well be many thousands on him? It is possible, if not, quite likely, Green. You do realise this?* I shook my head to rid myself of the negative thoughts and stood up to open the door to smoke on the balcony. In the distance, I could hear the music from the tourist street and there was the sound of laughter and merriment in the air. I lit the smoke and stared out into the darkness over the ocean. My little trip to the Algarve had taken an unusual and very unexpected twist. *You certainly do get yourself into some strange situations, Green!* The steady beat of the distant music was mesmerising and I found myself nodding to it unwittingly as I smoked. Eventually, I crushed out the butt and headed back into the room. After pouring a glass of water, I lay back down on the bed and stared at the television once again. A quick glance at the screen of the laptop served as a reminder that trying to find Joe's brother, Cristóvão Fonseca, would be an arduous and painstaking task. I would need Joe to be present as I did it and I knew it would be frustrating. Still, it was worth a try, and it was something I promised I would do. Feeling sleepy, I took a sip of water and got up to take a quick shower before settling down for the night. By the time I got out of the bathroom, the programme on the television had changed to one about survival in the Rocky Mountains.

I lay there with nothing but the towel around my waist as my eyes drooped repeatedly. It must have been an hour later when I was awoken by a siren on yet another programme on the television. I woke suddenly, feeling confused and disorientated. It was only then that the events of the day came back to me. Feeling annoyed and thirsty, I drank from the glass of water next to the bed and turned the volume down on the television before setting a sleep timer on it. It was only then that I realised that my laptop was still open. The screen had gone black because of the inactivity. I brushed my forefinger across the mousepad to revive it. The screen came to life after a few seconds and once again I saw thousands of results for my Facebook search for Cristóvão Fonseca. But it was as I was about to close the screen that a thought came into my mind. Something Joe had said earlier.

'His real name was Cristóvão. But we always just called him Chris.'

I blinked my stinging eyes as I clicked on the search bar and changed the search to Chris Fonseca. Once again, there were a lot of results but much fewer than my previous search. I propped myself up on my right elbow and scrolled down through the results. It was only when I was two pages down that something caught my eye. The name of the person was Chris Fonseca. He looked roughly the same age as Joe and was pictured standing in front of a lush tropical plant with huge green leaves. But it was something about the man's face, his bone structure, that rang a bell. My finger hovered above the mouse pad for a few seconds before I clicked on his profile. Once done, the screen changed immediately and the man's full profile appeared. A frown formed on my forehead as I stared at the profile picture. The man was young. Certainly younger than Joe. Clean-shaven with neat black hair that was greying around the temples. But it was his face and his nose that bore a striking resemblance to Joe. There was also the smile. The teeth were similar in size. It was the same warm smile that I had come to know in the past two days. With my curiosity now piqued, I sat up and placed the laptop on my legs. I clicked on the profile picture until it filled the screen. I stared incredulously at the picture in front of me. It was as if I was looking at a picture of Joe. A young, clean-looking Joe Fonseca.

"No fucking way..." I whispered to myself under my breath.

Feeling a buzz of excitement, I minimised the picture and clicked on the 'about' section of the profile. The information was all there to see. Chris Fonseca, born in Mozambique, went to school at Umtali Boy's High in Rhodesia and lives in Mahe, Seychelles. I blinked repeatedly as I clicked through the man's profile, studying every picture there was to see. Many were of a boat. Apparently an ocean-going vessel by the name of 'Amelia', it appeared to be a fishing and diving charter boat. But I could not waste any more time looking at pictures of boats and I immediately went back to the pictures of the man who called himself Chris Fonseca. Finding it hard to believe what I was seeing, I stood up and took a seat at the small desk. I placed the laptop in front of me and saved the picture of the man smiling in front of the leafy tropical plant. Having done that, I opened the picture and zoomed in on it. Once again I shook my head at what I was seeing. It was as if I was looking at a carbon copy of old Joe who was more than likely sound asleep and snoring in the room next door. The face was exactly the same, the eyes, the teeth, the smile.

"I don't fucking believe it!" I said out loud.

At that moment I was suddenly craving a cigarette. I stood up and carried the laptop outside where I placed it on the table and sat down to smoke. Still completely incredulous, I gazed at the picture as I put a flame to my cigarette. But by then there was no doubt in my mind. I had found Joe's brother. Suddenly a thought occurred to me. *What if Joe had been lying all along. What if he and his family had fallen out for some reason? Something that happened years ago. Something that would have caused him to break all contact and resulted in him ending up on the streets. What if Joe was actually hiding something from me?* It was astounding that it had been so easy to find the man. Still buzzing with excitement, I turned in the cheap plastic chair and stared at the windows of the next room where Joe lay sleeping. Suddenly I was confronted with the need to make a decision. Should I wait until morning and perhaps after the new wheelchair had been delivered to tell Joe that I thought I might have found his long-lost brother? Or should I simply wake him now and get it over and done with? I stood up in my towel and paced the small balcony as I wrestled with my thoughts. *Jesus Christ, Green, you certainly got yourself into an unusual situation here! Fucking hell!* But my mind was already made up.

Wasting no time, I crushed out the cigarette, picked up the laptop and made my way to the door. I poked my head out to make sure no guests were in the corridor. There weren't. Leaving my own door ajar, I walked the short distance to Joe's room and knocked three times before opening the door. Joe Fonseca was fast asleep in the darkness and my sudden arrival caused him to yell out in fear. Perhaps the years of living with gipsy thieves had caused this panic reaction.

"It's only me, Joe! It's Jason..." I reassured him as I flicked the light switch "Wake up! I've got something I need to show you, now!"

CHAPTER SEVENTEEN

Maxim Volkov stood and gazed through the panoramic windows of his suite on the 17th floor of the luxurious Burj Al Arab Hotel on Jumeira Beach in Dubai. Outside, the view of the Arabian Gulf extended, totally uninterrupted, across to Iran in the unseen distance. Below him, to the right, the beach stretched away lined with the thousands of glittering skyscrapers that made up the Dubai beachfront. Clad in a thick white dressing gown, he scowled as he sipped his Coca-Cola and rocked on the balls of his feet. At least he had been able to take a break from the mission. The 16 hours he had spent in the hotel had been restful and he had been able to wash and take his medication. The room service and Uber Eats had come in handy as well. His superiors had been none too pleased with this interruption to the schedule but they had had little choice in the matter. Up until then, his phone had been silent. This had pleased him. The call from Yuri and Sergei had come an hour later while he was watching hardcore porn on his tablet. This had angered him. The news, however, was good. The transfer of the equipment had been completed with the assistance of the embassy staff and the mission was good to go. The pilots were waiting and there would be no further delays. Volkov took his time packing his freshly laundered clothes and sprucing himself up in the huge bathroom before finally calling the reception to arrange a car to take him to the airport. Surrounded by the trappings of the rich and famous, Volkov felt at home. Although he would never afford such luxury on his own meagre savings, it felt good while it lasted. His own boat was nothing like the massive superyachts that cruised the waters below, but it was a good boat that would serve him well into his retirement. It was a full hour later when he emerged from the elevator into the massive reception area of the seven-star hotel. Waiting in the forecourt were the many Rolls Royce vehicles that belonged to the establishment. Their glittering golden hubcaps sparkled in the blazing sunlight. His own vehicle, a Mercedes, awaited him and he smiled and nodded to the staff as he checked out. The journey to the airport was pleasant and he sat back and relaxed in the air-conditioned rear of the vehicle as it cruised through the gilded streets of the wealthy city. All around were glittering skyscrapers and supercars. It was a place where he felt at home. If only he could have a slice of it all. His anxiety grew as they drew closer to the airport and he began drumming his fingers on his knee as he pictured being trapped in the slim aircraft that would take them to the Seychelles.

The journey would take another five hours. Better than the long haul to Dubai, but still a frustration. *Being stuck with those two meatheads, Yuri and Sergei once again. Their blank stares and smirks. Fuck them!* The traffic built up as the car approached the airport but eventually, they drove into the parking area near the private jet section and up to the drop-off point. As usual in Dubai, he was greeted by the ultra-polite staff and led through the immigration formalities. Once done, it was only a matter of a short buggy ride out to the waiting aircraft. The Canadian Bombardier Global 7500 jet was much larger than the plane they had used to get to Dubai. In fact, it seemed a bit excessive to Maxim as they approached it. Still, it was large enough for him to have his own cabin away from the two meatheads. There would also be 5-star service on board courtesy of the charter company. *No.* thought Maxim. *This will be a whole lot better than the last flight.* With a spring in his step, he left the buggy and took the short walk to the waiting staff by the steps of the sleek aircraft. They welcomed him like the millionaire he was portraying and showed him the interior which was as plush as he imagined it would be. Seated in the front cabin were Yuri and Sergei. Both men stood up and smiled as they saw their boss. Maxim nodded as he passed them and spoke briefly on his way back to his private cabin. Once there, the pretty young hostess smiled as she brought him a glass of champagne. Maxim ogled her as she walked away and he felt the raw animal attraction that had got him into trouble in the past. The uncontrollable sexual urges that had earned him the nickname 'Nasil'nik Rosinki' or 'The rapist of Rosinka' in English, in reference to an affluent Moscow suburb. The woman wore a tight black skirt with silken cream-brown stockings and her white shirt was unbuttoned just enough for him to have a good view of her ample cleavage. Maxim Volkov cleared his throat and stared out of the window to allow the feeling to pass. *Concentrate.* He told himself. *There is a job to do here. The fun part will come later, with any luck.* It was some 15 minutes later when the pilot's voice came over the intercom announcing their imminent departure and Maxim sat back in the luxurious seat and buckled his safety belt. The jet began moving forward and he marvelled at how quiet it was compared to the one he had arrived in, for the previous flight. The dazzling sunlight sparkled off the many other private jets as they trundled off towards the runway.

CHAPTER EIGHTEEN

Joe Fonseca sat up in the bed and wiped his eyes as he stared at me. I closed the door behind me and quickly grabbed a chair which I carried to the right-hand side of the bed. With the open laptop facing me, I sat down and stared at him. The look of confusion on his face was comical and his bushy hair was in disarray. Once again he reminded me of a troll from some fantasy film.

"Now, Joe," I said calmly, "I am going to show you a picture. I want you to look at it and tell me if you recognise the man. Okay?"

"Okay..." he replied, seemingly still confused and disorientated from having been woken suddenly.

With the zoomed-in photograph of Chris Fonseca filling the screen, I turned the laptop so it faced him.

Joe blinked several times as he studied the screen and I wondered if he needed glasses. But a second later, he cleared his throat, blinked once again and looked up at me.

"That's my brother, Chris," he said quietly before looking at the screen once again. "Looks a bit older, but it's definitely him."

Once again I found myself on the edge of exasperation with Joe. *Where is his enthusiasm and surprise? Why is he just sitting there like that with a dumb look on his face? Saying nothing and just quietly acknowledging that I have just found his long-lost brother. The very last family member he has. One he believed to be dead and whom he had thought, up till now, that he would never see again. Fucking unbelievable!* But it was then that I had to check myself. Here was a man who I had lifted from the streets, placed in a hotel and treated like my own brother. These were all things he was unused to. In fact, he probably was quite intimidated by it all. *Baby steps, Green. Take it easy on him.*

"And you're sure about this, Joe," I asked calmly. "That is your brother, Chris?"

Joe took his eyes off the screen and I saw confusion and trepidation in his face.

"Yes," he said quietly, pointing at the screen. "That's my brother. That's my brother, Chris. I'm one hundred per cent sure..."

CHAPTER NINETEEN

Volkov was on his fourth vodka. The alcohol was starting to affect him, as was the sight of the tall, slim air hostess. The smiling lady had delivered a sumptuous meal and now Maxim could barely keep his eyes off her. The way she smiled, the way her hips swung as she walked back and forth from the galley. The sight of her firm, young breasts as she leaned down to serve him. On more than one occasion, he had to force himself to look out of the window and had to reprimand himself for the wild urges that he felt. Still a physically strong man, he could easily follow her into the galley and have his way with her. But no, there was a job to do, and he needed to concentrate. *How was he going to get through this flight with these distractions?* They had only been airborne for two hours and the thought of another three, suffering the temptation that the woman was putting him through was almost torture. It was only then that he realized that he was sexually charged and had been since watching porn on his tablet earlier at the hotel. *Yes*, he thought, *that is what is causing this*. At one stage he considered going into the toilet to masturbate, but he knew that this would be futile. His illness was the reason that would not work. Maxim Volkov needed the real thing. A combination of violence and raw sexual power seemed to be the only thing that worked these days. He took another deep swig of the vodka. Thankfully Sergei and Yuri had kept to themselves during the journey. It was as if they had sensed his mood since leaving Moscow. *Good. They can stay there!* At that moment the air hostess made her way out of the galley towards the front cabin. She was pushing a trolley loaded with food and drink for the two Wagner meatheads. Maxim ogled her shamelessly yet again. The slim shapely legs seemed to go all the way to her shoulders. The sultry, suggestive smile. *She likes me, I know she does. You've still got it, Maxim. You're still an attractive man.* However, Maxim knew that once the flight was done, the aircraft would return to Dubai and there would be no chance of arranging a further meeting with the young lady. This was a part of the elaborate security arrangements for the job. Only when the mission was complete would a new plane be sent to collect them and return them to Moscow. Maxim shook his head woefully as he thought about the debilitating effects of the illness he had been suffering. His sex drive was well and strong, but he had been completely unable to perform normally. There was only one thing that worked for him.

And it was this that had gotten him into a lot of trouble over the years. It had also been the cause of much spite and hatred from his wife who had taunted him and ridiculed his inability to perform. *Fuck her!* he thought. Soon he would never have to lay eyes on her again. *The fucking bitch!* It was two hours later when Volkov was truly drunk, that he found himself feeling slightly unhinged and wildly attracted to the air hostess. He was convinced that she was attracted to him but had no idea that the woman was simply being professional. She had most certainly noticed his leering, but being accustomed to this sort of thing, had kept working as normal. In reality, the air hostess was quite taken with the two hunky men in the front cabin. Their tall, muscular frames, massive appetites and wide smiles. These young men were far more attractive and pleasant on the eye than the leering old drunk in the back. Even though they hardly spoke a word of English. It was then that Volkov realized that the woman was spending more and more time in the front cabin and less attending to him. This angered him deeply and the effects of the drink only served to infuriate him further. But it was in the last hour of the flight, while still drinking, that these feelings of rage began to grow. The primal lust that he felt toward the woman would not go away. But the alcohol consumption had taken a turn for the worse and his judgment was now completely skewed. In the last hour of the flight, he waited for her to return to the galley and then thought about his next move. He watched her as she walked back towards the galley. With his mind made up, he stood to follow her. Padding quietly on the carpeted floor, he made his way into the galley. The woman was standing near the aluminium rack of shelves and drinking from a small plastic bottle of water. Her back was to him and she was unaware of his presence. Once again Maxim cast his eyes over her statuesque figure. Her long legs, wide shoulders, and high heels. The combination of everything she wore set his loins on fire. But he was drunk and in his addled mind, he felt sure - 100% certain that she would welcome his advances. He glanced to the right and saw the door to the toilet nearby. *To hell with it, they could use the bed in his cabin.* Volkov crept up quietly behind the young woman and slipped his right hand around her waist. Roughly, he pulled her midriff towards his crotch and the feeling of power was all-encompassing. *Yes*, he thought, *she will be mine!*

"Hello, baby," he whispered in her ear in a guttural Russian accent. "You know I've been watching you for some time. I think you feel the same way about me, no?"

The young woman gulped and dropped the small plastic bottle to the floor. She spun around with a look of total horror on her face. Before Volkov could do anything, she slapped him across his jowls. The sound was a loud meaty crack. The stinging on his face only excited Maxim more and he was already planning his next move. *Of course, there would be some initial resistance. A quick punch to the temple, just to calm her, and then take her to the bed. Yes! Yes!*

CHAPTER TWENTY

"So what do we do now, Jason?" said Joe, blinking once again. "Can we just phone him? I don't understand."

"No..." I replied "It's not as easy as that, Joe. I would need to send him a friend request or a message and then we would need to wait and see if he replies."

"Oh," he replied, looking confused. "Like I said, I don't know anything about Facebook and I've never used a computer in my life."

"Don't worry about that..." I said "This is good news, make no mistake. I'm sorry for waking you up, I should have waited until tomorrow morning. Now you probably won't be able to sleep."

"I'll have no problem sleeping, Jason," said Joe. "I can't remember the last time I was in such a comfortable bed. This is like heaven."

I chuckled quietly as I stood up to leave.

"Well that's good, Joe," I said quietly. "I'm going back to my room now and I'll send your brother a message. Let's hope he replies. If he does, I'll let you know first thing in the morning. I'll be through to check on you at 7:00 am. I think we should go down, have some breakfast and be back here ready for the wheelchair salesman at 9:00 am. Goodnight."

I took one last look at my new friend before turning off the light. In some way, he looked vulnerable, confused, and elated at the same time. Closing the door quietly behind me, I made my way back into my own room and placed the computer on the desk. I closed the enlarged picture of Chris Fonseca and clicked on the Facebook profile. I sat there thinking for a minute about what to say, then began typing.

'Hello, Chris. My name is Jason Green. I'm sorry for messaging you out of the blue like this, but I have recently made acquaintance with your brother, Joe.

He is currently living in the town of Faro in the Algarve region of Portugal. Over the past few days, I have befriended him and he has told me about you, mentioning that you used to live in Durban, South Africa. I see from your Facebook profile that you are now living in the Seychelles. Joe has told me that he lost touch with you many years ago and I'm sorry to inform you that he has been living rough on the streets for quite a few years. He has lost a leg due to diabetes and is currently in a wheelchair. I have taken him in and given him a room in my hotel. I'm also in the process of trying to help him get a new wheelchair and find him some decent accommodation. I'm not sure of your family history as Joe has told me very little, but I have shown him your profile picture and he has confirmed that you are indeed his brother. All of this has been a bit much for him. He is not computer literate, but I know he is excited that I have found you. If you would like to make contact with him, please do not hesitate to respond to this message or call me on the following number...'

I sat back and read the message I had typed, going through it twice, until I finally pushed the send button. Now there was nothing to do but sit and wait. I had established that this was indeed Chris Fonseca, and if he wanted to contact his brother he need only reply to my message or give me a call. Whether he did or not would be up to him and if there had been some kind of family issue that had caused them to separate in the first place, I would know very soon. *Christ, I hope he does contact us, Green. If he doesn't, it might break poor old Joe's heart.* Still buzzing from the excitement of the discovery, but feeling exhausted, I closed the laptop and walked back to the bedside. I sat down, took a deep breath, and held my face in my hands as I thought through the crazy events of the past few days. It had all happened so fast. The random meeting with Joe, getting him into the hotel, sorting out the wheelchair and new clothes, and then finding his fucking brother. *It's insane, Green. Fucking insane!* Finally, I lay down on the bed once again. The Discovery Channel was playing some mundane programme with awful music in the background. I turned the volume down and stared at the screen until my eyes drooped. It didn't take very long to fall into a deep sleep.

CHAPTER TWENTY-ONE

The sudden assault had come as a complete surprise to the young woman. She immediately tried to back away from her attacker but he had other plans. In a blind, drunken frenzy he lunged forward with his fist raised and attempted to punch her. But the young lady was fit and much too fast. Having been trained in martial arts she knew very well how to defend herself and she responded immediately. As the big man stumbled towards her she brought her knee up into his groin. The move was perfectly timed and she felt the meaty bunch of flesh that was Volkov's genitals. Stunned and in a state of disbelief, he roared in pain as he fell to his knees on the blue vinyl floor of the galley. In the swirling mists of agony, Volkov was suddenly aware of yelling all around him and it was as if his world had descended into one of panic and confusion. The pain was unlike anything he had ever experienced in his entire life. Suddenly he became aware of hands. Strong hands lifting him by his armpits and male voices muttering in his native Russian. In the back of his mind, he knew it was the two Wagner meatheads. Sergei and Yuri had arrived having heard the commotion at the rear of the aircraft. Volkov found himself being carried by the two men and placed back in his seat where he sat curled up with sweat pouring from his body as he writhed. After a minute, he opened his eyes to take a look around. The woman was nowhere to be seen and was obviously holed up in the galley where the assault had taken place. Maxim looked up at the faces of the two men who stood there, hands on hips looking down at him with slightly bemused faces. Suddenly his pain was replaced by embarrassment and pure rage, and he was finally able to speak.

"Get the fuck away from me!" he growled in a strained voice "It was nothing! I am fine, just a little drunk. Go back to your seats now!"

The two men glanced at each other, seemingly undecided, but they had heard his instruction and followed the order.

Maxim Volkov struggled to control his breathing but eventually managed to raise himself to a normal sitting position. The effects of the alcohol had magically worn off by then. Angry, humiliated, and still panting heavily, he wiped his forehead, gritted his teeth and stared out of the small window once again.

CHAPTER TWENTY-TWO

I woke at 6.20 am. and immediately sat up and thought through the events of the previous evening. My immediate worry was for Joe and how he had reacted to seeing the picture of his brother. It had seemed he had been underwhelmed somehow and I wondered again if there had been a family issue that had led to them being separated in the first place. *Perhaps it was because he had been fast asleep when you burst into his room, Green? It could be simply that the events of the past few days have all been a bit much for him? After all, this man has lived on the streets for years now. This will all be a bit alien to him.* Fighting the urge to go and check on him, I took a shower and then boiled the kettle to make some coffee. I stood staring at the laptop and my phone as I waited. With the coffee made, I carried the laptop out to the tiny balcony and sat down to smoke the first cigarette of the day. The morning was cool and bright and the streets below were still quiet. I glanced over at the window of Joe's room and noted with worry that the curtains were still closed. *Leave him be, Green. He's a grown man. Stop worrying and fussing over him.* I stared at the laptop as I lit the cigarette and succumbed to the temptation by opening it. With a gnawing feeling of doubt, I opened Facebook and checked for any new messages. There were none, and I drummed my fingers on the glass tabletop as I stared at the screen. It was as if I was willing the man to reply. But the disappointment was real and I feared it would be for Joe as well. *You don't even know if this guy is alive, Green. It would be a mistake to get anyone's hopes up.* Sipping at the steaming mug, I glanced again at Joe's window to see the curtains were still closed.

CHAPTER TWENTY-THREE

The sleek jet descended through the cloudless sky towards the group of Indian Ocean islands that make up Seychelles. Maxim Volkov had been asleep for the last hour getting over the drinking binge that almost resulted in a mid-air rape. After an announcement by the pilot, Sergei and Yuri had come back to wake Volkov from his drunken slumber. The air hostess had been taking refuge with the pilots ever since he had fallen asleep. This was out of the ordinary but so were the events of that particular flight. She was accustomed to lewd suggestions and the odd grope, but this had been unprecedented and shocking, to say the least. The attempted assault had been reported to the owners of the plane but it had been quickly decided that this unfortunate incident would be best forgotten and put in the past. This was also helped by the huge sum of money offered in compensation by the state for the inconvenience of it all. After a brief radio discussion between the pilots, the air hostess and the head office, it had been decided that no actual harm had been done and life would go on as usual. The passengers and their cargo would be dropped off at the airport in Mahe and the plane would return to Dubai as planned.

Maxim Volkov grunted and moaned as Yuri shook his shoulder to wake him. He stared up with bloodshot eyes and appeared confused at first. As the memory of what had happened returned to him, he groaned once again and snapped at Yuri to fetch some water from the now-empty galley. On his return, Maxim enquired as to the whereabouts of the air hostess. The news that she had spent the last hour of the flight in the cockpit was delivered and accepted by Maxim with a nonchalant shrug.

"Stupid bitch," he grumbled. "She fed me too much booze anyway."

Yuri, speaking in hushed tones, informed him that everything was okay and would go ahead as planned. Maxim drank the water and coughed and spluttered as he heard they were now about to arrive at their destination. He sat up and looked out of the small window to see the glittering azure expanse of the Indian Ocean spread out below him. Up ahead to the left, the beautiful island of Mahe with its high mountainous peaks and thick tropical slopes rose majestically from the water. Feeling better that the whole issue was now behind him, he shooed Yuri back to his front cabin to join Sergei.

Once the man had gone, Maxim stood up somewhat unsteadily and made his way to the tiny but immaculately fitted bathroom near the galley. Once there he studied his face in the mirror. Slightly pale and with greasy hair from the sweating, he decided that he didn't look that bad. *Slightly rugged in fact.* But it was then that the familiar rumblings in his stomach began and he closed his eyes as he waited for them to deepen. The alcohol had taken an expected but unfortunate effect. He would spend the next few hours visiting the nearest toilet and this would only calm down when he had taken his medication. It was only 2 minutes later when he heard the knocking on the door. It was Sergei this time, informing him that they were about to land and that he should take his seat back in the cabin immediately. Maxim Volkov shouted his response and pounded on the door as he rose from the bowl. He quickly washed his hands and face then took one final look in the mirror. *It's fine.* He thought. *You look fine. Now just get through immigration and you can go and relax at the hotel.*

CHAPTER TWENTY-FOUR

I knocked three times before pushing the door open. Half expecting to find Joe still in bed, I was pleasantly surprised to see him up, freshly showered and making himself a cup of coffee.

"Morning, buddy..." I said, as I walked in and took a seat near the table.

"Hi, Jason," he replied, turning in his old wheelchair, "can I make you a cup?"

"No, thanks," I replied, "I just had one. How are you today? Did you sleep well?"

"I'm fine," he replied "Slept like a baby..."

By the look in his wide eyes I could tell his next question would be whether I had heard back from his brother, Chris. I decided to pre-empt it by cutting straight to the chase.

"So," I said firmly. "I sent a message to your brother last night after I left you. I explained our situation and told him you were very keen to get in touch. I left him my number and told him he can contact me on Facebook or on my mobile."

"And..." said Joe with wide eyes, "did you hear back?"

"Not yet," I said. "But we must be patient. There is a 4-hour time difference to take into consideration. It might be that he doesn't check his Facebook often. You have to be prepared to accept that this could take a while."

I watched as Joe's expression dropped and the disappointment was tangible on his old face.

"Oh," he said quietly, "I had kind of hoped..."

"Don't worry," I said with false cheer. "Drink your coffee. We must go downstairs and get some breakfast. Your new wheelchair will be arriving soon."

I sat making small talk with Joe until he had finished his coffee. I did my best to put his mind at rest and assure him that we would get a reply, but I knew that I was giving him false hope. I felt a measure of guilt doing this but somehow I loathed the thought of disappointing him further. Without knowing it, I had become invested in the man's life to an extent that I almost thought of myself as his carer. In the lift on the way down to the restaurant I had to remind myself that this was not the case but I still kept my cheerful outlook to placate him. The breakfast was standard hotel fare, a Mediterranean breakfast of a selection of cold meats, cereals and yoghurts. Joe had no problem eating two helpings and I brought us fresh coffee as we finished. The two of us sat there quietly drinking from the steaming cups as we watched the guests. In my mind, I was proud of my new friend. Here he was, fresh and clean, looking good in new clothes. Okay, he still had his wild, bushy hair and beard, but it was a vast improvement and set to only get better. Of course, there was the niggling ever-present fear that there would be no response from Chris. But that was something I would have to deal with when and if the time came. For now, I had a mission.

"Right," I said as I finished my coffee, "let's get back up to your room. There is a wheelchair salesman on the way."

CHAPTER TWENTY-FIVE

The first thing that struck Maxim Volkov was the heat. It was unlike any he had experienced on his many trips to Africa. This was a soaking humidity that permeated his clothes and soaked his skin almost immediately. He was acutely aware of this as the amount of alcohol he had consumed was now sweating out of him. This, added to the discomfort from his bowels only added to his foul mood and temper. Accompanied by Yuri and Sergei, they made their way to the waiting man from the Russian consulate. He was there to facilitate their smooth arrival and the clearance of their equipment. With contacts in the police and immigration, it was his job to ensure the process was smooth and went ahead without any problems. The four men greeted each other and were quickly hustled off to a low-roofed building normally reserved for visiting dignitaries. Once there they were met by two young immigration officials who welcomed them and quickly stamped their fake passports. Maxim glanced around the plush room and quickly identified the toilets on the left. A quiet whisper to the embassy man excused him and he left the final arrangements to Yuri and Sergei. On his return 15 minutes later he found the three men chatting amiably having cleared all their papers and passports. This news was quickly related to him to which he nodded his approval and immediately asked to be shown to the waiting vehicle. With both Yuri and Sergei instructed to wait for the equipment to be offloaded and cleared, Maxim was led through the building out the back to the waiting vehicle. The embassy man attempted to make small talk as they waited for it to pull up to the loading area but Maxim would have none of it.

"You will remain here with my men to clear our cargo and I will see you later at the hotel," he said brusquely. "Thank you."

Clearly surprised by the unfriendly manner, the embassy man simply bowed slightly and gestured towards the waiting vehicle.

"Of course, sir," he said quietly "It has been a pleasure to assist you today. I trust you will be comfortable in the accommodation we have arranged and I will see you later this evening. Goodbye"

Maxim grunted and slung his bag into the back of the waiting vehicle. In his mind, all he wanted to do was escape the oppressive heat. Thankfully the interior of the vehicle was air-conditioned and he sighed deeply as he closed the door and sat back into the cool leather seat. He closed his eyes as the car drove out of the airport complex and took a right turn eventually coming out on the longest section of straight road in the Seychelles. Only then did Maxim open his eyes to take a look around. The bright afternoon sunlight was dazzling and reflected off the hundreds of expensive-looking boats in the harbour to the right. On his left, the small town of Victoria was nestled beneath the steep green slopes covered in thick tropical foliage that seemed to rise up into the sky. The town of Victoria was quaint and charming having been well-kept and maintained. This was a change from the usual African shitholes he had found himself in, in the past. Maxim nodded in approval as the vehicle veered off the motorway taking a left off-ramp. There were flip-flop-wearing tourists wandering the streets and local markets brimming with brightly coloured tropical fruit and vegetables. Fishmongers' stalls were packed to the rafters with glittering catches and the local Seychellois people looked relaxed, healthy and happy. Hugging the coast, the vehicle wound its way along a dual-lane road surrounded by thick vegetation. Maxim stared out of the window and noticed the trees were laden with fruit and the soil was rich and dark. It was as if every available space was filled with plants of all kinds. There were also a number he didn't recognize at all. It was, by all accounts, a thick tropical jungle. To his left, the precipitous cliffs and steep mountains that made up the interior of Mahe island rose up beyond his vision from the cab of the vehicle. On the right the jungle seemed dark and impenetrable and there were only brief glimpses of bright azure blue of the ocean as the vehicle rounded the bends. Growing increasingly impatient, Maxim leant forward and knocked on the perspex barrier that separated the front of the car from the rear. The driver turned his head briefly and slid the centre of the partition open.

"How long until we reach the hotel?" grunted Maxim in Russian.

"Ten minutes only, sir," the driver replied. "We will be there soon."

"Put your fucking foot down," said Maxim quietly. "I have urgent business to attend to."

CHAPTER TWENTY-SIX

The wheelchair salesman arrived at 9.00 am. sharp as promised. He was carrying a large flat-pack box which he proceeded to unpack as Joe and I looked on. I saw the sparkle in Joe's eyes as he looked at the bright chrome fittings and comfortable seat. The process took a good 20 minutes but finally, the man stood back and announced he was done. It took no time for Joe to extricate himself from his old chair and on to the bed. From there he was assisted by the young man into the new one and I held my breath as I waited for his reaction. This took less than 10 seconds until all of a sudden I was rewarded by the look on Joe's face; he was beaming from ear to ear. Clearly overjoyed, he trundled across the floor back and forth several times as he worked the new wheels and brakes. Many questions were asked in Portuguese to the salesman who was more than happy to answer. Finally, Joe looked up at me once again and spoke.

"It's fantastic, Jason," he said as if in awe. "I never thought I'd ever get out of that piece of shit chair. It's very comfortable."

I nodded then glanced at the salesman.

"I think you can safely take the old one to the dump," I said. "I'm pretty sure we'll have no further use for it."

It was 10.00 am. by the time the young man left. I left Joe wheeling himself around inside, testing the various features as I walked out on the balcony to smoke. Deep down I was very pleased that I had managed to come so far with Joe. I had known all along that his rehabilitation would be no easy task, but he was making great strides with a little help from me. I watched him as I smoked and my fears and worries returned. *What next, Green? What now? You can't simply stop at this and allow him to return to the streets. It only makes sense that you must approach the local social services and make enquiries about finding him some suitable accommodation. Surely there will be a department of social welfare. Someone that'll look after him into his old age. But what if he resists all of that? What if he just says no? Will this all have been for nothing? No, it wouldn't have, Green. You have helped this man. Given him a new lease of life regardless of what happens now.*

Deep down I felt the urge to return to my room and check my Facebook messages once again. *Best not to mention his brother until he does, Green. No need to upset him. Let him enjoy the moment for what it is. He's probably gonna feel a lot less pain and discomfort from now on. It's all good.* I took a final draw from the cigarette and decided that I would spend the rest of the day trying to find suitable accommodation for Joe Fonseca. If needed, I would rent a place and get him set up. I would then approach social services with him once that was done. There was really nothing else to do and I was not prepared to sit around all day. I made my way back into the room and sat down as Joe was busily boiling the kettle for some coffee. Not wanting to wait any longer, I decided to breach the subject of his ongoing living conditions and spoke.

"We need to find you a decent place to live, Joe," I said flatly. "You're almost set up but that will be one of the final things to get done. I suggest we start looking today. Are you up for that?"

Joe Fonseca turned in his chair and looked me in the eye. Once again I saw the fear and trepidation I had seen since I had first met the man. It was as if he was suspicious of any acts of kindness and

I feared that he might object. But it was at that moment that I felt my phone vibrate in my pocket. It had been silent for so long I had almost forgotten it was there. I pulled it from my pocket absent-mindedly and glanced at the screen before I answered it. The screen showed a number and country code I did not recognise.

CHAPTER TWENTY-SEVEN

After what seemed an age, the driver made a right turn and entered the resort. The place was fenced off and there was a boom gate at the entrance. The grand guard house was manned by two uniformed men who were expecting the vehicle. Maxim Volkov sat back as words were exchanged between the driver and the guards. Eventually, the boom was lifted and the vehicle drove further into the lush green jungle that formed the outskirts of the prestigious Banyan Resorts property. Once owned by a famous Hollywood actor, the land had been bought by the hotel group and developed into one of the most luxurious destinations in the world. This seemed fitting for what would be Maxim Volkov's final mission for the FSB. His expectations were high and he was looking forward to some real luxury. The perfectly manicured road wound its way through the dense greenery until it arrived at a large low building made from earthen brick. The driver pulled around and drove into a shaded portico with the reception area to the right. Almost immediately, the door was opened by a slender young Seychellois woman who greeted Maxim with a broad smile. Maxim grunted as he climbed from the vehicle and made his way into the cavernous interior of the reception. The air was crisp and cool from hidden air conditioning ducts and tranquil piped music played from hidden speakers. To the right of the room was a massive waterfall built from local rock and water cascaded down its front causing a bubbling and trickling sound that made Maxim think of a toilet. Instead, he took a seat on some sumptuous couches while the driver went to the reception to check in for him.

Maxim sat there scowling as he looked around but already he was impressed with the choice of accommodation. He knew full well that rooms at this particular resort started at $3,000 per night so there was no doubt he was in for a flawless treat of a stay. The check-in process took less than 5 minutes and Maxim looked up as he saw the driver approaching along with the same young lady who had opened the door. The woman greeted him with the false name on his passport and invited him to follow her to his lodgings. The three of them walked through the front and up a set of heavily polished stone stairs. Only upon reaching the top of these stairs was the true beauty of the place revealed. Spread out in front of them was the flawlessly bright blue of the Indian Ocean. It sparkled and glowed in the afternoon sun and it seemed the colour of it was almost impossible.

Maxim Volkov had never seen anything like it. To the right was the dining area spread out beneath a lattice of thin black poles that afforded just the right amount of shade in the midday sun. Hidden microjets sprayed a fine mist of cool water to keep the wealthy guests comfortable. All around the soothing piped music still played, only disturbed slightly by the lapping of the waves nearby. The horizon was perfectly flat and seemingly endless under a sky that seemed to melt into the ocean. On either side of this main area, the coast stretched around enclosing what was a natural bay of sorts. Tall palm trees leant in towards the ocean surrounding the individual casas, each of which was completely private with their own infinity pools. Linking these was a raised deck road on which guests were transported by golf cart to their private havens. Ready and waiting for them was one of these carts with a smiling driver in a crisp white uniform. The young lady graciously offered Maxim a seat at which point he paused to have a word with the Russian driver.

"Tell Yuri and Sergei to meet me at my room when they get here," he grunted. "I trust there will be no issues with our equipment."

"Of course, sir," said the man. "I will personally supervise everything and will tell them to see you immediately after they arrive. Welcome to Seychelles. I wish you a pleasant stay."

Saying nothing, Volkov sat down on the back of the buggy and watched the young woman who appeared to be his personal hostess as she smiled and took her seat near the driver at the front of the buggy. The tiny vehicle lurched forward and began trundling down the raised wooden roadway that linked the casas. Once again Maxim felt the almost unbelievable heat and humidity even under the shade of the buggy's roof. He closed his eyes as it bumped over the ruts in the wood and cursed the affliction that caused him so much discomfort. Thankfully the journey was not a long one and they arrived at the casa furthest from the main building within minutes. The buggy parked under yet another shaded portico and the slender young woman who had greeted him led him into the plush interior. Maxim was greeted first by his own private chef and butler who smiled and bowed as he entered. Immediately he was offered a tall colourful fruit juice which he guzzled as the tour began.

The upper level of the casa consisted of a kitchenette and hallway that led to a set of polished stone steps which led down to the living area. This comprised a sumptuous open-plan space furnished with exotic Indonesian antiques with low tables and couches. To the right of this huge space was a bar, while on the left was a wide corridor leading to the rooms. Ahead, facing the ocean was a set of tall and wide glass sliding doors. Beyond these were the veranda and outdoor area which formed a shaded sitting area with a jacuzzi and swimming pool. Maxim knew full well that this particular casa cost over $5,000 per night and this was clearly evident by the opulent surroundings. It was unlike anything he had ever seen, let alone stayed in. Not even the world-famous Burj Al Arab, where he had stayed the previous night came close to this level of indulgence. Every room was kept at a pleasant and even 22 degrees with careful humidity controls to maintain optimum comfort for the wealthy guests. Not wanting to seem like a fish out of water and also keen on staying as long as he could with his hostess, Maxim allowed himself to be led through all the many functions and features of the casa. It was a good 10 minutes later when finally the tour was over and the young woman bade him farewell. After getting her name, Maxim said goodbye and ordered the chef to prepare a serving of lobster ceviche and Beluga caviar. Maxim walked over to the bar area and poured himself a liberal tot of Russo-Baltique vodka. *Fuck it*. He thought to himself. *You only live once*. Finally, Maxim Volkov took a casual walk to the sunken lounge and plonked himself down on the spacious cushions of the couch. He took a deep draw of the vodka and stared out at the ocean beyond the windows. *Well*. He thought to himself. *This isn't so bad at all*.

CHAPTER TWENTY-EIGHT

"Jason Green..." I said as I answered the call.

There was a brief moment when the line failed to connect followed by a loud distorted sound. I took the phone from my ear and inspected it to see if it was still connected. It was. I put the phone back to my ear and repeated myself.

"Jason Green. Hello?"

"Hello," said a faint voice. "This is Chris Fonseca. Joe's brother..."

"Hi, Chris!" I said turning to look at Joe who was midway through pouring a cup of coffee.

Joe Fonseca froze where he was and turned to look at me wide-eyed. With the coffee pot held in mid-air, he looked as if he had just seen a ghost. I nodded back at him and spoke.

"I cannot tell what a relief it is to hear from you," I said. "I'm sitting here with Joe as I speak."

"Hi Jason," said the voice on the line. "I couldn't believe it when I got your message this morning. I had given up ever hearing from Joe again and to be honest, I thought he might have died!"

"Nope," I replied, smiling. "He's very much alive and staring at me right now. Would you like to talk to him?"

"Oh my God!" came the shouted reply. "Yes, please! Thank you, thank you!"

I stood up and walked over to where Joe sat in his new wheelchair.

"Joe," I said, holding the phone out to him. "Your brother would very much like to have a word with you..."

Still looking stunned, Joe took the phone from me and held it to his ear.

Hello, Chris," he said with a croaky voice "Is that you?"

There followed a long but tearful conversation between the two long-separated brothers. It came as a huge relief to see the happiness on Joe's face and although the conversation was in Portuguese, there was no disguising the joy on Joe's face. I poured myself a cup of coffee and sat and watched him as he laughed and I saw the tears of joy stream down his face. It was a moment that I had feared would never come but there it was happening right in front of me. *You've done well here, Green. Fucking awesome!* It was some ten minutes later when Joe hurriedly handed the phone back to me and spoke.

"Chris said he would like to make a video call," he said. "Can you do that?"

"Of course I can," I said taking the phone from him.

I hung up after a quick chat with Chris after which I added him to my Whatsapp and made the video call. Chris Fonseca answered immediately and I recognised his face from the pictures on Facebook. It was clear he was sitting in an office of sorts but the man was beaming from ear to ear and clearly overjoyed to be in touch with his long-lost brother.

"There you are," I said with a grin "Hold on while I hand you back to Joe..."

It was clear Joe had never used a smartphone before and I had to show him how to hold the phone away from his face to see his brother. Almost immediately the scene was one of much laughter and animated conversation and I sat back drinking my coffee as it went on. It was after a full fifteen minutes that Joe handed the phone back to me saying Chris would like to speak to me. The man was extremely grateful and thanked me profusely for what I had done for Joe since I had met him. He mentioned the new wheelchair and the fact that I had taken him off the streets as well. It was clear to me that this event was unprecedented in both their lives and was profoundly important. I was personally relieved that my fears that there had been some kind of family breakup had turned out to be unfounded.

Both men were ecstatic to be in contact once again. It was then that Chris began asking what my plans were. Feeling that Joe might feel embarrassed or uncomfortable, I asked him to send me an email to which I would reply immediately. I explained that we were both comfortable in the hotel and would make another video call later in the day. This seemed satisfactory to both men and finally, I hung up after holding the phone out to Joe so he could say goodbye.

"Well," I said looking at the smiling figure of Joe Fonseca "It looks like we have found your brother."

"I know," he replied, looking somewhat shellshocked "I just can't believe it!"

"Believe it, Joe," I said with a half-smile. "It's true..."

CHAPTER TWENTY-NINE

Maxim Volkov spent the afternoon drinking expensive vodka and scheming on how to get the slender young hostess back into his casa. Of course, now that they had arrived in Seychelles, there was a schedule to follow and a series of tasks that had to be completed before the actual mission. But that would only begin in two days and Maxim had already decided that he would spend his downtime relaxing and taking in the sights and smells of the exotic island. The casa was on a level of luxury few people would ever experience in their lives so he was more than happy to spend most of his time there. There would be the annoyance of the two Wagner men, Yuri and Sergei, but he would make sure that they stayed in their own rooms and bothered him as little as possible. The operation they were to undertake there was two days off, enough time for him to acclimatize and relax. *This may well turn out to be one of the better jobs.* He thought as he poured another vodka. By then the events on the plane with the hostess had faded from his memory and his hangover was long gone. *Here I am in the lap of luxury, living life as the rich and famous do. No, Maxim. You must relax and enjoy it. You have worked long and hard for this and soon you will retire. Even if this mission is doomed to failure, you should take in your surroundings and savour the place. Even if the outside temperature is like a fucking Finnish sauna.* This daydream-like state was only disturbed at around 4.00 pm. when there came a knock on the door. *Fuck!* He thought. *Who could this be?* But his frustration was calmed by the thought that it might be the hostess from the hotel once again. Maxim Volkov got to his feet and staggered slightly as he made his way up the stairs past the kitchenette to the main door at the rear of the casa. With a feeling of drunken optimism, he opened the door only to find the driver from the consulate standing there with Yuri and Sergei. Their faces were flushed from the late afternoon heat and their golf buggy transport was parked in the shade of the portico.

"Good afternoon, sir," said the driver. "We have come to inform you that the equipment has been cleared and both Yuri and Sergei have checked into the hotel. They, along with the cargo, are in the adjacent casa."

"I see," grunted Maxim "And there were no problems?" "No, sir," said the man. "Everything went according to plan. Are you free to discuss the next step of the mission?"

"No, I am not!" said Maxim angrily "This will have to wait till tomorrow. It has been a long journey. Goodbye, all of you!"

Maxim slammed the heavy teak door and made his way back down to the lounge area of the casa. As he did this he stumbled slightly on the stairs and called out another instruction to the butler who was waiting in the kitchenette.

"More lobster," he slurred "I want more lobster!"

CHAPTER THIRTY

I left Joe in his room and returned to my own feeling exhilarated and worried at the same time. Now that we've managed to make contact with Chris, what next? Would he support Joe going forward? Would he visit him in Portugal? By the looks of the conversation they had had, I was fairly confident that there would be some kind of assistance offered. It was for these reasons that I was anxious to hear from Chris about Joe's future. I had already committed to finding him a place to stay. Somewhere safe and decent where he could collect state benefits and lead a normal life. Somewhere with facilities for the disabled and some kind of support network. There was no doubt in my mind that such things existed and it was a wonder that Joe had slipped through this net for so long. I sat down at the desk and opened my laptop to check my emails. Just then I felt my phone vibrate in my pocket once again. I pulled it out to see that there was a text message from Chris Fonseca.

'Hi Jason, I was hoping to have a private chat with you. I would like to discuss my thoughts on Joe's situation there in Portugal. Please give me a call when you are alone back in your room. Chris.'

I stood up and closed the sliding doors to the balcony to ensure the conversation would not be heard by anyone. Having done that, I sat down at the desk once again and made the call. Chris answered immediately.

"Hello Jason, thank you very much for calling me," said Chris.

"No problem," I replied, "I'm alone now, please tell me your concerns."

"Well, Jason, I really wanted to thank you from the bottom of my heart once again for finding my brother and helping him, but most importantly for putting him back in contact with me. It's been a worry of mine for many years. This is huge for me. I want you to know how grateful I am."

"Well, I have to tell you Chris, the whole thing was unexpected for me as well. I came out here on holiday and my intention was to hire a motorcycle and ride around the Algarve.

As it turned out, I bumped into your brother and we struck up a friendship. Seeing as we fought in the same war, I couldn't leave him on the streets."

"He speaks very highly of you," said Chris "and I know how much what you have done means to him. Listen, Jason, I have an idea but I'm not sure how Joe will feel about it. Can I tell you my plan?"

"Sure, please go ahead," I said. "I've been wondering the same thing so I'm very keen to hear your thoughts. Right now he is living in some hovel with a bunch of criminals. They treat him badly and are extorting the money he gets from his begging. It's dangerous and unhealthy, and I won't allow him to go back."

"I know, I know," said Chris "I don't want him going back there either. But I have an idea, Jason. My plan is to bring him to Seychelles. I have a big house here and I live alone. I'm not getting any younger and neither is he. It makes total sense to me that he comes and spends the rest of his life here in Seychelles with me, his brother. I have a business here that does fairly well. I'm not short of money and I can support him. In other words, he doesn't have to be on the streets ever again. I will come there and collect him then fly him out here. In fact, I'm already looking at flights to Portugal. As I see it, there's no time to waste. I can be there in the next couple of days. No more roughing it on the streets, no more begging. A decent life for Joe going forward. What do you think?"

I paused for a moment and rubbed my chin as I thought about what Chris had suggested.

"It makes sense to me, Chris," I said. "I was quite happy to set him up here. He has been a bit difficult, but with a little persuasion, he comes around. I have no idea if he has a passport or not but this is something that can be arranged. I suppose you could get an emergency travel document fairly quickly."

"Yes," said Chris, "that is exactly what I was thinking."

"Well, I'll put you on the phone with him again and you can propose this and see what he says. How about that?"

"No," said Chris, "listen, Jason, you have been talking to him for a couple of days now. He likes and trusts you. Would you mind having a word with him? Highlight that I have these plans and see what he says. If he is open to this and is agreeable then we can have another conversation. I'll move on to the next step. My biggest fear is that he will resist and that it might be all too much for him. I really do think it would be better coming from you. What do you think?"

"Well, like I said, I'm happy to have a chat with him over lunch and either way we will call you again this afternoon. The way I see it he has two options. He can stay here in Portugal in a flat or an apartment, or he can get the hell out of here and go live in Seychelles with you. I know what I would do..."

"Oh my God, Jason," said Chris "I hope he sees some sense and listens. If this could be a reality, this would complete my life and finally bring some happiness to both of us. Yes, that's a great idea. Put it to him, tell him you got an email from me and that this is my plan. Ask him what his thoughts are, and if he is agreeable I will fly there immediately and start the preparations to get him out of there."

"I think it's an excellent plan. I'll talk to him and try to stress that this is the best possible outcome for both of you. He can be difficult, but I know him well enough. Leave it with me, we will be going out for lunch shortly and I'll have a word. You can expect a call from us by 4.00 pm. Portugal time."

"Thank you, thank you, Jason," said Chris. "You have no idea how grateful I am..."

We said our goodbyes and I sat there in grim silence for the next 10 minutes. Finally, I stood up and opened the sliding doors to the balcony. I stepped out into the sunshine and smelt the salt in the air.

I took the cigarettes from my pocket and lit one as I stared back at the windows of Joe's room.

At that moment I saw Joe wheel himself towards the window, he slid open the doors and wheeled himself out onto his own balcony. Smiling from ear to ear and looking like the cat that got the cream, he waved at me and spoke.

"Well, hello there, neighbour!" he said with a grin.

I shook my head and chuckled.

"Hey, Joe," I said. "How are you doing?"

"Oh, I'm doing well, Jason" he replied "I'm doing really well..."

CHAPTER THIRTY-ONE

Maxim Volkov dismissed the butler at exactly 4.30 pm. His final instruction was that he was to send one of the golf buggies down to the casa to collect him. He could not quite get the image of the beautiful young Seychellois girl who had welcomed him to the resort out of his mind. It was for this reason that he decided that he would go to the main area of the hotel to find her. As he waited for the golf buggy to arrive, he downed yet another vodka and stared out at the sea. The gentle wind that blew in from the ocean ruffled the fronds of the palm trees on either side of the casa and the scene was one of complete tranquillity. Maxim had ventured out at one stage during the afternoon and sat dangling his feet in the infinity pool with his drink in hand. But the heat had been far too much for him and he had only managed to stay for 5 minutes until he returned to the air-conditioned comfort of the casa. Maxim Volkov was extremely drunk although he had no idea of this. There was one thing, and one thing only on his mind. He would see that woman again and do his best to seduce her one way or another. He staggered up the stairs to the hallway and took a look at himself in the full-length mirror.

"You don't look too bad, Maxim," he said out loud with a chuckle. "In fact, you look pretty good!"

He turned away as there was a knock on the door. He stepped forward and swung it open. Standing there was a young black man in a crisp white uniform.

"Good afternoon, sir," he said with a broad smile "I am your driver. You requested a ride to the main hotel complex. I am ready when you are, sir."

"Wait here a minute, I'll be right out."

Volkov closed the door behind him and walked back to the mirror to take a final look at himself. Satisfied that he was presentable, he made his way back to the door and set off into the humid late afternoon. The buggy ride took less than 5 minutes and fuelled by the alcohol in his blood, Volkov felt the excitement and anticipation rising.

Already, he was planning how he would spend the evening with the young woman seducing her with drink and fine food. Upon arriving, Volkov made a beeline for the bar. He had no idea that he was staggering wildly and getting attention of the wrong kind from the various wealthy guests who had gathered for sundown drinks. The bar staff, being consummate professionals, welcomed him with broad smiles and offered him a seat near the end of the bar to get him as far away from the other guests as possible. He stumbled over, took the seat and immediately shouted an order for a double vodka. The gracious barman nodded his head politely and set about fulfilling the order. He delivered the drink within a minute and Volkov took a deep draw from the heavy crystal glass. Once done, he sat there scowling at the patrons and scanning the area for the young woman who had welcomed him to the resort earlier. But she was nowhere to be seen and this was the cause of much annoyance for him. For the many guests who had been enjoying themselves, the presence of this drunken man was deeply upsetting. They did their best to ignore him and huddled away in groups while trying to avoid eye contact with him. Two minutes later he downed the last of his drink and slammed the crystal glass onto the bar.

"Barman!" he shouted, "bring me another vodka!"

Cringing as he did so, the barman followed his order and poured the drink and as he was delivering it Volkov asked the question.

"That woman from earlier, the one that met us and took me to my casa. Where is she? I wish to see her."

The embarrassed barman bent towards him and replied in a whisper.

"I believe you are talking about our front-of-house manager sir. Her name is Amina. She has knocked off for the day. She will be back tomorrow morning. Is there anything else I can assist you with?"

This information angered Volkov and his mood darkened immediately.

"What bullshit is this?" he shouted, his voice uncomfortably loud, "I thought she was my personal hostess?"

"I'm very sorry sir," said the barman quietly, "I think some of our other guests are getting upset. Would you mind please keeping your voice down, just a little?"

"Why should I do that?" the drunken Volkov roared. "Do you know who I am? I can have you fired at any time. Don't you dare talk to me like that! Fuck you! Get my driver and send another butler to my casa. I will be spending the evening there."

However, as he was making his way back through the bar Volkov stumbled and fell over a small occasional table. He crashed to the polished tiles of the floor breaking one of the legs of the table as he fell. The shocked guests could do nothing except look on in horror at the drunken man who was making such a spectacle of himself.

"Fuck!" shouted Volkov at the top of his voice. "Fuck this place! Where is my driver?"

Moving on all fours at first, he crawled to the nearest couch and pulled himself to his feet. He turned briefly to glare at the audience of horrified guests then laughed out loud as he staggered off to the waiting buggy.

CHAPTER THIRTY-TWO

It was 12:30 when I wheeled Joe out of the hotel to the street. I had left him watching TV during the morning and enjoying the new wheelchair. There was no doubt that it was a good machine, far easier to push and manoeuvre than the previous one. Even the cobbled streets were no challenge and we were at our usual restaurant within 10 minutes. I ordered a beer while Joe had his usual Coca-Cola. I placed the orders for lunch all the while wondering how I was going to make the proposal that Chris had outlined. Once again, I was worried as to whether Joe would accept this offer or not. I was aware that Joe was fiercely independent and difficult to convince to accept new things, although I had found a way around this during our brief but interesting friendship. The atmosphere was pleasant, the temperature was warm and the food was good. Joe and I joked and laughed and I knew that he was in high spirits. I said nothing about it until we were finishing the meal and waiting for dessert before I spoke.

"Listen, Joe," I said. "I had a call from your brother and he has made a suggestion that he wants me to put to you. Now this may come as a surprise, but Chris wants you to go and live with him in Seychelles. He doesn't want you on the streets anymore. I'm sure you understand that?"

Joe looked up at me, his face serious once again, and I saw the watery look in his eyes. Here was a man who had been living rough for years. It was basically all he knew and he was comfortable there. Suddenly along comes this stranger who treats him decently, buys clothes and food and puts him up in a hotel. Then this stranger puts him in contact with his long-lost brother. I could only imagine it was a bit overwhelming. There was a long pause and Joe's eyes dropped to the table before he spoke.

"Did my brother really say that to you, Jason?" he asked quietly "He wants me to go and live with him in Seychelles? My God..."

"That's what he wants, Joe, "I said. "He asked me to speak to you to see how you would feel about it. This is an incredible opportunity. Your brother has a good business there. He has a large house and sufficient income to look after you for the rest of your life. You would never have to be on the street again. It would be a no-brainer for me, that's for certain."

I watched as Joe shifted nervously in his new wheelchair. It was as if he was weighing up his options and I could see the fear and worry in his eyes. It was a good 10 seconds later that he looked me in the eye and spoke.

"Well, Jason," he said "I want you to know that these last couple of days have been amazing. No one has ever treated me as well as you have. I will never forget your kindness. I find the whole thing to be quite unbelievable to be honest. I had resigned myself to the fact that I would be on the streets forever. But thanks to you, all of this has changed and it's all happened so quickly. I'm sorry if I seem ungrateful, but please try to understand."

"I know it has and I can imagine how you're feeling. But I want you to know this is real, this is happening. Your brother wants you to go and live with him. This nightmare can come to an end in the next couple of days. Chris is prepared to fly here immediately. I want you to think about it. Once you have, we'll contact him and let him know your decision."

"I don't think I need to think about it too much, Jason," said Joe "Of course I'll take him up on that. I'd be a fool not to. I love my brother. I thought he was dead. Jason, do you realize this is the best day of my life?"

Suddenly I felt a wave of relief rush over me. It was as if everything I'd been trying to achieve in the last couple of days had finally worked. I had helped an old comrade-in-arms off the streets and put him in contact with his family once again. I smiled as I picked up my glass of beer and held it out towards Joe.

"Cheers," I said, "I'll drink to that. Now, I think we should finish up, head back to the hotel and make that call. This is going to make his day. I have to say, I'm happy for you both. Well done, my friend…"

Joe and I ate our dessert and then took a slow trundle back to the hotel. The afternoon was warm and pleasant and both of us were feeling happy and fulfilled with the events of the day.

I pushed Joe into his room and walked forward to open the sliding doors to allow the sea breeze in. I made sure he was settled and comfortable before taking a seat at the desk and pulling my phone out. Chris Fonseca answered the call within 3 rings. I tapped the button for speakerphone and placed the device on the bed between us.

"Hello, Chris," I said "This is Jason. I'm sitting here with your brother and we have some good news for you. Joe has agreed to your plan and is very much looking forward to coming to live with you in Seychelles."

Suddenly there was a burst of laughter from the handset and this caused Joe to do the same. The scene was one of joy and merriment as Joe and Chris spoke like excited children at the prospect of their new lives together. I let the frivolity carry on for a few minutes before backing into the conversation to get things moving forward.

"Now, gentlemen," I said "I can tell that you're both very happy, but we have serious business to attend to. Chris, you need to get over here to Portugal as soon as possible. I will start arranging for Joe to get a passport or an emergency travel document."

"I'm already on to it, Jason," said Chris "I'm sitting in front of my computer looking at flights as we speak."

But then Joe held his hand up to stop me.

"Hold on, guys," he said "I *have* a passport. It's back at the place I've been staying at. I'm sure it's in the bottom of my bag. I haven't seen it for years, but there's no reason it shouldn't be there."

"Well, that's brilliant news," said Chris.

"Hold on," I said. "Joe, if that passport is there in your bag do you think it's still valid?"

"I have no idea," said Joe with a worried look on his face. "As I said, I haven't seen it for years. I never thought I'd use it again so I guess I just forgot about it. Sorry..."

"Nothing to be sorry about," I said, "this is good news. The first thing we have to do is to get that passport. If it's still valid, this makes our lives a whole lot easier. If it is, there's no reason for Chris to come here. I'll fly with you to Seychelles. My little escape to the Algarve isn't going as planned anyway. I'm free for the next two weeks and I'm happy to take you. If it is valid, we're in luck..."

CHAPTER THIRTY-THREE

Maxim Volkov awoke with a hangover unlike any he had ever known in his life. Still fully clothed and lying on top of the spacious bed, he opened his eyes to see the bright sunlight streaming through the wide windows. He groaned deeply as he turned on his side and blinked in a state of utter confusion. *What had happened? What have you done?* He couldn't remember a single thing since arriving at the resort. Then it all slowly started coming back to him. The expensive vodka, the food, the personal butler, and the slender young woman who had greeted him when he arrived. Maxim groaned again and realized that he was desperately thirsty. Slowly, he pushed himself up into a sitting position, but as he did so his head pounded with unbelievable pain. It was like a giant drum beating constantly in his head and his mouth was dry and bitter. Slowly and carefully, he rose to his feet. The headache was so intense that it caused him to stumble to one side. This only intensified the agony of the pounding headache as he staggered off towards the bathroom. Once there, he took a brief look at himself in the mirror but quickly averted his eyes as the person that stared back at him resembled some kind of alcoholic vagrant. Instead, he turned the tap for the cold water, rested his left arm on the counter and stood there hunched over slowly drinking by hand. It was some minutes later when he closed the tap and turned back towards the door. Shuffling like a cripple, he made his way out of the bathroom through the bedroom and into the corridor that led to the sunken lounge. He wished he was wearing his sunglasses as the bright morning sun pierced his eyeballs like lasers reflecting off the infinity pool and the azure blue of the Indian Ocean beyond. Suddenly there was a voice, an unexpected voice which caused him some mild panic.

"Good morning, sir, how are you today?"

"What? Who the fuck are you?"

"I'm sorry to alarm you, sir, it is just me, your personal butler. I have come to make you breakfast. Can I pour you some juice, sir?"

"Oh, God," said Maxim. "No, no, no. No juice, just coffee. Bring me coffee, please."

"Certainly, sir," said the chirpy young man "Where would you like to take your morning coffee?"

"Wherever you find me, for God's sake. Just bring the fucking coffee!"

Volkov shuffled back to his bedroom and immediately began rummaging around in his bag for antacids and painkillers. He realized then that he had missed his usual medication the previous day so he grabbed them as well. He downed the concoction of tablets with a glass of water and then found his sunglasses. Placing them on his face straight away, he slowly made his way back down the passageway and into the lounge. There he found the butler with a tray in his hands.

"Put it on the table down there," he said, pointing towards the centre of the lounge.

"Certainly sir," said the man. "May I start preparing your breakfast now?"

"No, you may not. What you may do is leave me in peace for the next 10 minutes. I would prefer not to hear you or to see your face until then. When that time is over, come and ask me again. Goodbye!"

The shocked young man backed away.

"Of course, sir," he whispered.

Volkov sat there and poured himself a cup of black coffee. Eventually, the painkillers and antacid began to take effect and he began to start feeling almost human again. His mind went to the mission. He had already delayed it with the stop in Dubai and the news of the event on the jet to Seychelles would surely have gotten to the director. This would have angered him and Volkov felt a pang of anxiety at the thought of the reprimand he would receive back in Moscow. Still, there was plenty of time to rectify things and get the mission back on track. In his mind, he went through the procedures he was to follow upon arrival in Seychelles. *Yes*, he thought. *It's not all bad. We only need to get the equipment onto the boat today. It's not a total disaster.* He sat there forlornly rubbing his temples and sipping the coffee cautiously. *Today we will visit the boat we will use for the dive.*

We will interview the captain and make final preparations for the mission tomorrow. I will have sufficient time to get myself cleaned up and rested and we will go in the afternoon to the harbour. Once that is done there will be time to relax and hopefully not drink as much as yesterday. God knows that was a big mistake and I am feeling it today...

CHAPTER THIRTY-FOUR

"You would do that?" asked Chris.

"Of course," I replied. "My holiday has taken an unusual turn and I don't see that changing anytime soon. I can certainly fly with Joe to Seychelles if the passport is valid."

"Wow," said Chris, "that is very kind of you, Jason. All of this is happening so fast, I feel like I have to pinch myself."

"I know the feeling," said Joe, shaking his head in amazement.

"Well, I don't think we have any time to waste," I said, "we should get down to Joe's old place as soon as possible, retrieve his passport, then get on with booking flights."

"Of course, I will pay for the flights," said Chris. "Once you have the passport give me a call and I'll do so immediately."

I looked up at Joe who sat there with a bewildered look on his face. It was clear to me that as far as he was concerned the speed of developments was unprecedented, unexpected and a little bit disconcerting. Still, he looked happy enough and I saw the excitement of a man who was about to embark on a great adventure.

"Right," I said. "Chris, I will phone you as soon as I have retrieved Joe's passport. If it is valid, you can go ahead and book the flights. There's no time like the present so I think I'll finish this conversation and get on with that right away."

"That's just awesome," said Chris. "Fingers crossed. Can't wait to hear back from you."

I hung up and strode over to the open sliding doors. The afternoon sun was warm on my skin and I lit a cigarette as I stared back at Joe in the room.

For some reason, he had a worried look on his face and I immediately inquired as to why.

"What's wrong, buddy?" I said. "You seem a bit concerned. Either the passport is valid or it isn't. If it isn't, the next step is to get an emergency travel document. It's as simple as that. What's bothering you?

Joe looked up at me and I saw lines of worry on his forehead.

"I'm worried about actually getting it back, Jason," he said. "I told you I was staying with a bunch of really nasty characters and I haven't been back there for a few days now. They're going to be angry and they're going to demand some money from me."

"But it's *your* property, Joe," I said, exasperated. "It's *your* bag. How can they prevent you from getting your own property back?

"Jason," he said "These people are thieves. They are muggers and street criminals. I know for a fact they won't allow me to just simply go there and pick up my bag."

"You think they're going to demand money from you?" I asked.

"Yes," said Joe. "They will. I had to pay them 20 Euros every day just to stay there and if I failed to pay them or had a bad day, they would beat me..."

"Well," I said angrily. "You don't have to come with me, Joe. You give me the address and *I'll* go there and retrieve your bag. And I can assure you, I won't hand over a fucking cent. It'll be a cold day in Hell before I give them *anything*..."

CHAPTER THIRTY-FIVE

Maxim Volkov spent the next couple of hours nursing his hangover. He ate a small breakfast of fruit salad and scrambled eggs and took himself off for a long hot shower. He emerged from his bedroom at 11:45 am. looking and feeling a bit more human. He eased himself down on the expensive sofa and awaited the arrival of the Wagner men. The knock on the door came at 12.03 pm. exactly and Maxim struggled to his feet to go and greet his colleagues. Yuri and Sergei stood there along with the consulate driver from the previous day. All of the men were red-faced and had expectant, but worried looks on their faces. Maxim's immediate thought was that they had heard about the incident at the bar the previous night. Perhaps they had and this, added to the event on the plane on the journey to the Seychelles would have only added to their worries.

"Come in, come in," said Maxim gruffly.

The men followed him through the hallway and down the steps to the sunken lounge. It was clear they were impressed by the opulence of the surroundings and the panoramic views of the ocean beyond the broad sliding doors. Maxim dismissed the butler and told him to wait outside the back door until their business was concluded. The three men sat down nervously and waited for Maxim to speak.

"Well, then," said Maxim. "If I'm correct, we are to take a journey today to view the boat that we will be using tomorrow."

"That's correct sir," said the driver. "The crew are making some last-minute repairs to the vessel but we can go and meet them in the meantime. We are due to leave the port at 9.00 am. tomorrow morning. I would suggest, however, that we only deliver the equipment tomorrow."

"Why is that?" asked Maxim.

"Apart from the diving gear and the weapons, there is not much equipment to move. We can easily do this tomorrow when we arrive at the boat. That way we can be sure that our equipment is safe."

"Are you telling me you're worried about the security of the vessel that we are using?" asked Maxim.

"No sir," said the driver, "we are quite confident, but we would just like to cover all our bases and eliminate any potential for something to go wrong," Maxim grunted in acknowledgement and nodded his head reluctantly.

"Very well," he said. "So, what are we waiting for? Let's get moving right away."

CHAPTER THIRTY-SIX

It turned out that the address where Joe had been staying was very near the tourist street where I had met him. This made sense given the fact that mobility has been a serious problem for him and he had been wheeling himself back and forth. I left Joe in the hotel room and used my phone for maps to make my way to the address. Joe had been extremely worried and had told me to watch out for a man by the name of Marco. Apparently, this was the lead criminal in the group and he would be the one to watch out for. He told me that the criminals who stayed there plied their trade on the streets during the night and not all of them would be awake and at the residence when I arrived. Three times over, he warned me to be careful saying that these men carried knives and would not hesitate to use them. I did my best to put him at ease and told him that I would kill them with kindness. I was not worried about handing over a few Euros but I would not be taken advantage of over what was essentially someone else's property. I made my way down the cobbled street past where I had seen Joe sleeping. As I reached the end, I followed the maps, turning left and heading into the new town. It was some 200 metres up a low hill that I turned right into what appeared to be a distinctly seedy area. There the houses were rough, unpainted and unfinished. Many had crumbling walls and broken windows and it was clear this was a place that few tourists ever got to see. Feeling quite aware of the suspicious looks from the locals, I made my way down the street clutching my phone until I arrived at the address. It was a nondescript house, small and grubby with filthy windows and a brown door with chipped paint. I double-checked my phone to make sure I was in the right place. The curtains were drawn and there was litter on the street. Certain that I'd found the right place, I knocked three times on the door. There was a shuffling noise from the inside and the mumbling of words in Portuguese. Eventually, the door opened with a squeak and I was greeted by the sight of a skinny young man with greasy hair. He wore only faded jeans and his wiry, tanned body rippled with muscles. His skin was pockmarked and his eyes were bloodshot. The man stared at me and looked me up and down with a curious, surprised look on his face.

"Who are you?" he asked.

"My name is Jason," I said, "I am a friend of Joe Fonseca. I would like to have a word with Marco please."

"I am Marco," said the man, "what do you want?"

"Like I said, I am a friend of Joe's," I said. "He is staying with me now. I have come to collect his bag if that is all right with you."

The man's pinched face twisted into a sneer revealing yellow teeth as the corner of his mouth lifted.

"Oh, okay," he said. "I have been wondering where Joe is. He has not been here for quite a few days. We were all worried."

"I can assure you he's fine," I said. "As I mentioned, he's staying with me. Now, can I please collect his bag?"

It was then that I saw the gleam in the man's eye. It was as if he had seen an opportunity to make some money and I knew that I would not get out of there without handing some over. He glanced up and down the street and then spoke.

"Please come in," he said pleasantly, "come in and take a seat."

Knowing that this would be a drawn-out process, I resigned myself to the fact and followed the scrawny figure into the dingy room beyond the door. The space was small, littered and filthy. Three men sat on an ageing lounge suite around a broken coffee table. Immediately upon walking in I could smell marijuana and some other unknown chemical. I glanced down at the table to see a blackened teaspoon, some silver foil and a few extinguished candles. I knew then that the men were using hard drugs, probably injecting heroin. Upon seeing me, the other men's eyes lit up as if they had just found their next meal ticket. It was unnerving and immediately the hair stood up on the back of my neck. I knew there would be no escaping this room without trouble of some sort and instantly I felt the adrenaline pumping through my arms and legs.

"Take a seat, please," said Marco. "I would like to hear about Joe."

Reluctantly I took a seat on a vacant chair. The fabric was damp and smelly. I looked around the filthy room and as I did so, I tried to put on a pleasant face of innocence.

"There's not a lot to tell, really," I said, "he's an old friend and I've come to look after him."

"So why does he need his bag?" asked Marco with a smirk.

By then I was losing my patience. The questions were stupid and I knew they were delaying me for no good reason.

"Because it is his property," I said quietly "and he wants it back."

It was then I noticed Marco's eyes flick to the man on the far right of the room. He gave an almost imperceptible nod as if to warn him that something was about to happen.

"Joe owes us some rent money," said Marco, his face now serious.

"Joe owes you nothing," I said firmly. "Now please, show me to his room. I'm in a hurry."

Sensing the tension rising, the other men shifted in their seats uncomfortably and in a visibly threatening manner. I scanned the room for opportunities, anything that I could use to defend myself if attacked. On the table in front of me were two filthy pint glasses. Both were empty with the dregs of whatever had been drunk in the bottom of them. There was also an ancient wine bottle with a half-burnt candle stuck in the top. I imagined this was used to cook heroin in the blackened teaspoon. All of these things I knew I could use as weapons should the need arise. *This is not looking too good here, Green. Keep your fucking wits about you. This may well kick off in a most unpleasant way.*

"Now look," I said, sitting forward, "I didn't come here for any trouble. I just want his belongings and I will leave you alone. Joe is with me now and you will never see him again. I repeat, *he owes you nothing*. Are we clear on that?"

Marco stood up opposite me. He smiled warmly but there was evil intent in his eyes. I watched as his hand travelled around the back of his jeans. It came back clutching a stubby blade. Still smiling, but with dead eyes, he brandished the blade at me and hissed.

"My friend, you have arrived at a very dangerous point in your life. If you want that bag, you are going to hand over a lot of money, right now..."

It was then that I saw out of the corner of my eye, the man to my right shift in his seat. I knew that he too was retrieving a blade from under the cushion where he sat. The man to my left sat forward and prepared himself for the attack. I knew I had to act immediately and take control of the situation which was rapidly deteriorating. My next move happened in a blur of speed. My right arm reached up and grabbed the greasy black hair at the back of the man's head to my right. With all my strength, I slammed his head down onto the pint glass on the table. It smashed with a dull crunch and the man screamed in horror before passing out. Without pausing, I reached forward with my left hand and grabbed the old wine bottle by its neck. I swung it around to my left, connecting the other man squarely in the face. The blow broke his nose immediately but the bottle failed to smash. There was a dull, gong-like sound and the man crumpled to the floor unconscious. Suddenly the room became a bloody chaos of shouting and screaming. I pulled the bottle back behind my head and slammed it down on the edge of the table. It smashed, leaving the jagged neck in my hand. I leapt to my feet and kicked the table to the left then stepped forward brandishing the jagged bottle neck at the two remaining men.

"It appears you fuckers are slow learners," I growled with gritted teeth."Who wants to try me? Come on, try me, you thieving fucking scum!"

With two of his men crumpled on the floor and bleeding profusely, the stunned Marco stared at me and I could see the shock and fear in his eyes. He knew full well he had picked on the wrong person. It was clear he was a bully and not accustomed to taking any of his own medicine.

"I'm not going to say this again, Marco," I said quietly, "now, let's go and get Joe's bag, shall we?"

CHAPTER THIRTY-SEVEN

Maxim Volkov made his way out of the back door of the casa and sat next to the driver on the front seat of the buggy. The three other men squeezed onto the back bench and they set off towards the main hotel building. Once again, Maxim was aware of the appalling heat and humidity. Having spent so long in the casa, he had forgotten how intense it was. The buggy trundled along the bumpy wooden surface of the rampway as it made its way towards the hotel. Maxim was reminded of this as his stomach rumbled ominously. It was only then that he realized that his symptoms had improved somewhat. *Perhaps it was due to the fact that he had not eaten any McDonald's food for some time?* But this thought was quickly dismissed as the oppressive heat and humidity caused milky beads of sweat to form on his forehead. Eventually, they came to a stop at the main hotel area and Maxim was aware of the eyes of the hotel staff as he alighted from the buggy and stepped inside. He knew he had made a spectacle of himself the previous evening but this did nothing to stop his arrogance and mean streak as he made his way back towards the reception. The ever-polite staff nodded and smiled at the men as they made their way out into the shaded portico at the rear. It took less than a minute for a parking valet to deliver the consulate vehicle and hand over the keys to the Russian driver. The four men climbed into the car with Maxim sitting in the front passenger seat.

"Turn that fucking air conditioning on, now!" grunted Maxim. "It's like living in a fucking sauna. *How do you do it?*"

"You get used to it eventually, sir," said the driver with a forced smile.

The powerful engine revved and the vehicle shot forward as they made their way back through the winding roads of the resort under the thick jungle canopy. Minutes later, they reached the boom gate which was immediately opened. The driver pulled up at the crossroads to ensure there was no traffic, then turned left towards Victoria and the harbour. The drive took less than 30 minutes during which the vehicle roared its way down the narrow road at the foot of the precipitous, vegetation-covered mountains to the right. Every few minutes there was a brief glimpse of the ocean on some deserted beach to the left. The scene was idyllic and peaceful. A tropical paradise of sorts. But this was of no consequence to Maxim Volkov.

He was now a man on a mission and he could think of nothing but getting to the boat and finalizing the arrangements for the following day. Finally, they emerged onto the highway near the town centre and the airport. Up ahead to the left was the port and the heavy traffic slowed them. The driver carried on up the highway and took a left towards the harbour that was crammed with hundreds of vessels. There was a mixture of working fishing boats, pleasure cruisers and superyachts. Maxim was aware that the sports fishing boat they would use to go to the wreck site the following day was owned by the consulate. This was convenient as there was therefore no need to rent from the locals and the operation would remain confidential. The SUV made its way down to the waterline in the glaring sunshine and the ocean sparkled with such ferocity that it stung Maxim's eyes through his sunglasses. They drove down a long concrete pier surrounded by pleasure boats of all shapes and sizes until eventually arriving at the consulate mooring.

The crew was there to welcome them, two young Russians and one middle-aged man who was captain. The four men exited the vehicle and stepped out into the burning sunshine. They made their way across the concrete pier towards the stern of the vessel and the gangway. The crew and captain greeted the men in Russian and hands were shaken as they boarded. After a brief discussion, all formalities and pleasantries were exchanged before the guests were invited to a tour of the boat. A ten-year-old 40 ft cabin cruiser, the vessel was equipped for sport fishing and diving with the latest GPS and other high-tech devices. The tour took them around the bows in the blazing sunshine and it was a relief for Maxim to finally step into the shade of the cabin beneath the wheelhouse. There the men were offered iced bottles of water which they took and drank greedily. But it was only then that Maxim noticed that the engine hatches were open and it appeared that some mechanical work was going on below deck.

"What is this?" said Maxim with visible annoyance "Are you having problems with the engine?"

"No problem, sir," said the captain. "Just general maintenance. We want to be sure that everything is in tip-top condition for tomorrow."

"I see," grunted Maxim, "no, we do not want *any* problems. Everything *must* go smoothly..."

CHAPTER THIRTY-EIGHT

Marco and the remaining man stood there with a look of stunned shock on their faces. With their two compatriots bleeding and unconscious, they realized that they had seriously underestimated their visitor.

"Now," I said through gritted teeth, "the three of us are going to take a walk to Joe's room. When we get there, you are going to show me Joe's bag and I'm going to leave with it. If you try any funny business, I will hurt you, badly. Is that clear?"

The men nodded jerkily and remained silent.

"Good," I said. "Let's go."

The two men shuffled off down the dimly lit corridor to the right-hand side of the room. I followed them through and at the end of the passage, I saw what looked like a grimy kitchen. The space was littered with old takeaway cartons and empty cans. Joe had not been wrong when he had said the place was an absolute tip. It was and it smelt like one too. Halfway down the corridor the two men paused and looked back at me nervously.

"This is his room..." said Marco quietly.

"Open the door and step inside," I said "and remember, you try anything and I'll cut you..."

Marco opened the door and walked in followed by his compatriot. I followed soon after and watched as they turned on the light in the windowless room. The space was a lot tidier than the rest of the house and I could see the many trinkets that Joe had picked up over time.

Worthless as they were, they had meant something to him at one time or another. I could see that Joe had made an effort to keep his tiny room clean in comparison to the filth of the rest of the house. There was a tiny worn-out bed with threadbare blankets and a grimy pillow. A small single globe lamp stood on a rickety table nearby.

In a corner of the room was a large black bag that appeared to be stuffed with clothing. Marco pointed at it and spoke.

"This is the bag you're looking for," he said sullenly.

"Pick it up," I said. "Pick it up and walk out towards the front door. I'll be right behind you both."

Marco did as he was told and the two men filed out the door whilst I stood in the passageway brandishing the broken bottleneck. Slowly, they made their way back into the filthy lounge past their two unconscious friends. Marco paused at the front door.

"What are you waiting for?" I said, "Open the fucking thing!"

Marco did as he was told and the men moved carefully out onto the pavement.

"Put the bag down," I said.

Once again he did as he was told and I followed both men out onto the street, still holding the bottleneck. I walked around where the two men stood and paused on the opposite side of the bag.

"Now," I said, "thank you very much for your help. I think you better go and tend to your friends. I have a feeling they're not going to be too happy when they wake up. I do want to warn you about something though. If *any* of you try to follow me, it will be the last thing you do. Am I understood?"

Both men nodded glumly and stared down at the pavement.

"Go on," I said quietly. "Fuck off back into your filthy hovel…"

CHAPTER THIRTY-NINE

B y the time Maxim made it back to the vehicle from the boat, he was sweating profusely. He climbed into the front seat and immediately demanded that the air conditioning be put on to full blast. He sat there in the cool breeze of the fans as the driver made his way out of the harbour and back to the highway. In his mind, he was preparing for the mission the following day. Everything had been prepared for him. The coordinates had been logged and the equipment cleared. Maxim turned in his seat and stared at the three men behind him.

"I want you to return to the harbour this afternoon with all of the equipment," he said "Make sure it is loaded and secured, and I want Yuri and Sergei to stay on the boat this evening. That way we can be sure that nothing will be tampered with. Is that clear?"

The three men nodded glumly and did their best to avoid his piercing eyes.

"Good," said Maxim. "Now let us go back to the hotel. We have a big day tomorrow. Let's hope everything goes well..."

As the vehicle made its way through the small town of Victoria, Maxim once again began to think of his retirement. His mind wandered as he thought of his gorgeous boat sitting in the harbour in Croatia. How he longed for that peace and tranquillity. To be far away from his nagging wife and to finally be free of the job that he had dedicated his entire life to. Of course, there was the constant worry that the funds he had accumulated would be insufficient to see him to the end of his days. Still, it was better than sitting in Moscow behind a desk for the rest of his life. *Soon, he thought, soon it will all be over and you will be free*. It took 20 minutes of driving down the winding coastal road until finally the driver made the right into the Banyan Resort and drove down to the main hotel building. Maxim wasted no time exiting the vehicle and rushing into the air-conditioned confines of the reception. He quickly surveyed the area in the hope of seeing the young hostess from the previous day but then the memory of his ill-fated trip to the bar the previous night returned and he thought otherwise. After a quick word with the three men, he dismissed them and made his way over to get the golf buggy back to his casa.

The short trip jolted his insides and caused him some mild discomfort, but he arrived feeling pretty good. His butler was waiting for him in the kitchen area as usual. Maxim dismissed him immediately and made his way down into the sunken lounge where he sat and stared out at the ocean beyond. The cool of the air conditioning brought his energy levels back but this did nothing to lift his mood. He quickly slipped once again into a deep state of depression despite the unimaginable beauty that spread out in front of him. It was some 20 minutes later when he could fight the urge no more, he stood up to make his way over to the bar. Once there, he poured a triple shot of neat vodka and downed the lot in one go. The alcohol had a warming, calming effect on him and he savoured the burning feeling of it going down his throat. It took less than three minutes for the alcohol to take effect and restore some feelings of well-being. With his mood slightly lifted, he poured another double tot and made his way back to the sunken lounge. With the heavy crystal glass in hand, he slumped down on the couch, stared out at the ocean and sipped at the drink.

CHAPTER FORTY

I made my way quickly down the street turning intermittently to look behind me to check if I was being followed. I wasn't. It appeared my visit had come as a surprise to the gipsy thieves and after a few minutes, I felt comfortable that none of them would attempt to come after me. Still, I had no intention of running into any of them again and I knew I would have to be careful on the streets in the coming days. The afternoon was warm and balmy and the sun burned pleasantly on my arms as I slowed my pace and began to relax. Eventually, I reached the tourist street where I had met Joe and I turned right to make my way up the cobbles. The holidaymakers were out in force eating and drinking in the restaurants on either side. A couple of them gave me some strange glances. I realized then that I must have looked somewhat strange walking quickly up the street with a bulging, tattered and faded black bag over my shoulder. Still, I was glad I had succeeded in getting it. What remained to be seen was whether Joe's passport was in there or not. It seemed to me that Joe was so far removed from the reality of day-to-day life that it was a miracle that he still had it. I was sweating lightly when I finally arrived at the hotel. I nodded at the receptionist and made my way over to the lifts. Two minutes later I knocked on Joe's door and stepped inside the air-conditioned cool of his room. I saw then that he had made an effort to tidy the space and I knew he was on the right track.

"You got it?" he asked with wide eyes. "Did they give you any trouble?"

"They were a little upset at first, but I got them to come around to my way of thinking," I replied.

Joe looked at me and his eyes narrowed. I could see that he was wondering what exactly had happened at the house. It was as if he knew there had been some violence, but there was no way I was going to tell him. Without pausing, I dumped the bag on the bed and spoke.

"Right," I said. "There's your bag. I'll leave it up to you to open it and find this passport of yours. Let's hope it's there and if it is, let's see if the thing is valid."

Joe wasted no time opening the bag and began tossing all manner of clothing and trinkets all over his bed. The contents of the bag were similar to the contents of his room. Small worthless things he had picked up over the years which for some reason had value to him. There was no way I was going to question him on any of them so I took a seat and watched him quietly as he worked. After what seemed an age he reached what appeared to be the bottom of the bag. By then I had lost hope that he would find the passport but to my surprise, he pulled out the faded document.

"Here it is," he said triumphantly. "I knew it was there somewhere."

"Let me have a look at it," I said quietly.

Joe handed me the passport and it was clear that it had been in the bag for many years. My hopes that it was still valid were rapidly fading as I flicked through it and reached the photograph page. But to my great surprise, the expiry date was a year hence.

"Well, well," I said, "that is quite something..."

"What do you mean, Jason?"

"Your passport," I said, "your passport is valid for another year. Unbelievable!"

Joe raised his eyebrows but appeared somewhat indifferent.

"Okay," he said flatly "That's good news..."

I lifted my eyes from the document, still not quite believing that it was valid and Joe had no idea of it all.

"It *is* good news, Joe," I said, "it's very good news indeed."

"So what do we do now?" asked Joe, once again seeming not to know how to move forward.

"Well," I said, "the first thing we have to do is to call Chris and let him know the good news. This is going to save a whole lot of time and effort. Now nothing is stopping us from leaving. We can pretty much get on a plane immediately and get the hell out of here..."

But as I finished speaking I saw that familiar distant look creeping into Joe's eyes. It was as if he was convinced he was dreaming and that he might wake up suddenly and the events of the past couple of days would never have happened. At that moment, I felt a deep pang of sadness for the man. There was a good person who had fallen down in life. Someone with a genuinely good heart who had simply fallen on hard times. An intelligent and kind soul who did not deserve the hardships he had endured for the past nine years.

"Joe," I said "Do I have to tell you again? This is very good news. You and I can get on a plane and go to Seychelles. Joe, this is fantastic!"

Suddenly I saw his face light up as the realization that this was actually happening dawned on him. I pulled my telephone from my pocket and immediately dialled the number for Chris. Clearly, he had been waiting and answered the call after two rings.

"Hello, Jason, did you get the thing?" he asked nervously.

"I did get it, and you're not going to believe it, the passport is valid."

"No way?" he replied laughing. "That is the best news. How does Joe feel about it?"

"He's sitting right in front of me with a dreamy look on his face," I said, "it's almost as if he doesn't believe it himself."

"Joe, can you hear me?" said Chris.

"I can hear you, brother..."

"Joe, this is happening. This is actually fucking happening! We are going to be together again, and soon!"

I watched as a smile split Joe's face and he looked up with true excitement.

"It's all being a bit much for me," said Joe. "Everything's happened so fast..."

"I know, brother," said Chris, "I know it's a little bit crazy and I'm feeling the same way, but I have to say this is one of the best days of my life. I'm absolutely ecstatic!"

I watched as both men broke into laughter and I sat back in the chair to savour the moment. It was fully a minute later when I finally spoke.

"Right," I said. "So, Chris, now that we have established that Joe is good to travel, I want to let you know that I'm ready to leave at any time. I imagine that all major flights would leave from Lisbon. That is a two-and-a-half-hour drive from here. I think you should start looking for flights right away and call us when you're done. As I said, nothing is holding me back yet and we are ready to go when you are."

"Jason, I've been looking at flights all day. Several flights to Dubai connect from Faro to Lisbon and then onwards. All that's left for me to do now is to book. Let me get on with that right away and as soon as I've got some information and I have made the booking, I will phone you. Is that okay with you?"

I looked at Joe who nodded at me with a half-smile on his face.

"That's perfect," I said. "We will relax here at the hotel and wait for your call. In the meantime, I'll warn the receptionist that we might be checking out early. If you can get us on a flight in the next couple of days that would be perfect. We are both ready to move and are only waiting on word from you."

"That is just awesome! Just amazing. Thank you so much, Jason."

"No worries," I said. "The past few days have been a bit of a roller coaster, but I have to say I've enjoyed them, and I think your brother has too."

I hung up the phone and looked at Joe who sat there with a blank look on his face.

"Don't stress, buddy," I said. "This is in your brother's hands now. We just have to wait until we hear from him..."

"Yes," he replied with a thoughtful look on his face "Everything is happening so fast."

"I know it is," I said. "But *everything that is happening is good.* Think about it, Joe. After so many years of hustling on the streets, you are finally going to have a place to rest. Somewhere where you can be reunited with your family and live out the rest of your years in a decent, healthy environment. How long do you think you could have survived on these streets? It was going to kill you sooner or later."

Joe nodded slowly and spoke.

"You *are* right, Jason," he said. "Everything was on a bit of a downward spiral until I met you. I want you to know that I'll be forever grateful for what you've done."

"Yes, well don't worry about that," I said standing up to walk to the balcony. "Now all we have to do is relax and wait for your brother."

I opened the sliding doors and stepped out into the afternoon sunshine. I lit a cigarette and looked back into the room to see Joe slowly sifting through his meagre possessions. At that moment I felt another pang of pity and sorrow for him. That his life had been reduced to the contents of that tatty old bag. That this man had spent close to a decade wheeling himself around the streets in a rusty old wheelchair. That he had suffered so much at the hands of those thieves that he used to live with. *Bastards!* I smoked in silence and savoured the warmth of the sun on my skin. I was crushing out the cigarette when I felt the phone vibrate in my pocket once again.

Feeling sure it was something work-related, I pulled the device from my pocket and looked at the screen. The call was from Chris in Seychelles. I keyed the button immediately as I stepped into the cool of the room once again.

"Hello, Chris," I said. "What have you managed to organize?"

"Hi, Jason, can you put this on speakerphone?"

I did as Chris asked and placed the phone on the bed. Chris spoke immediately and there was an obvious measure of excitement in his voice.

"Now listen, guys," he said, "I have made a booking for you both to get on a flight at 8:15 tonight. The flight is to Lisbon where you will connect on an Emirates flight to Dubai. There will be a two-hour stopover in Dubai and from there you will fly direct to Mahe Island in Seychelles. All I have to do is click and these tickets are booked. I know it's very short notice, and even I didn't expect this to happen so quickly, but if I go ahead, you guys will be with me in Seychelles by tomorrow lunchtime."

I lifted my eyes from the phone and stared at Joe who sat there, incredulous.

"Well, Chris," I said, "I had expected this to happen in the next couple of days, but I think I speak for Joe and myself when I say you can go ahead and book those tickets. We *will* be ready, and we *will* catch that flight tonight."

CHAPTER FORTY-ONE

The two Wagner men, Yuri and Sergei spent the remainder of the afternoon loading the dive equipment and sundry other items onto the boat in the harbour. All the while they watched the proceedings of the mechanics as they worked on the engine. There was a hushed silence and a nervous energy about them and it seemed as if something was seriously wrong with the vessel's engine. Still, the mechanics worked into the evening and continued to do so while Yuri and Sergei left the harbour to go and find something to eat in the small town of Victoria. The two men returned at around 9.00 pm. to find a string of lights had been erected in and around the engine bay and the same mechanics were still busy at work frantically trying to fix the problem. Questions were asked and assurances were given that all would be well for the mission the following day. At 11.00 pm. the captain knocked on the door of the small cabin where Yuri and Sergei had lain down. The news was not good. Although the mechanics had worked through the day and into the night to try and rectify the problem, it appeared that one of the piston conrods had broken along with some of the valves. They would telephone for the necessary replacement parts but a full repair would take many days if not a week to complete. Yuri and Sergei looked at each other upon hearing this bad news and they knew that their boss Volkov would only respond with rage. It was decided then and there that they would stay on the boat that night. Both men knew that their boss would be drinking and quite possibly completely drunk. It was a risk to disturb him at that time of night and they both decided that it would be far more prudent to break the news in the morning when he had sobered up. Either way, it would not be pretty. The mission had already been delayed and this news would only enrage him more. Already it seemed he was deeply unhappy at being there and he was a man with very little patience. Deeply worried, the two men dismissed the mechanics and settled down for the night. The warm waters of the Indian Ocean lapped against the fibreglass hull as they drifted off into a troubled sleep.

They awoke the following morning at 6.00 am. and immediately called the driver from the consulate. He was horrified at the news, knowing that the screw-up would only add to the tension and discomfort of the mission. There was no doubt that their superiors in Moscow would be informed of this and there would be trouble and consequences for all involved.

It was decided that the men would spend the next two hours on the boat before travelling to the Banyan Resort to break the bad news to their boss, Volkov. The time was spent in an uncomfortable silence and the men fidgeted nervously as they ate a breakfast of fruit salad and bread rolls. The now useless boat had been due to leave the harbour at 10.00 am. that morning. For the mission to go ahead, there would have to be other plans made. This would mean further delays and disruption to the mission. But there was simply nothing that could be done. Their vessel was beyond repair for the time being and a pragmatic approach was necessary to complete the mission. The three men came off the boat at 8.00 am. in the morning and climbed into the vehicle to make their way to the Banyan Resort. The drive was spent in solemn silence and no one spoke for the 20 minutes that it took to reach the gates. Once they had arrived at the main hotel building, they parked the vehicle and made their way into the reception and out to the front where they would board the golf buggy to take them up to Volkov in his luxury casa. Not knowing what to expect or how they would be received, the three men made their way to the door and stood in silence as the driver knocked on the heavy wood.

CHAPTER FORTY-TWO

The hotel receptionist had been kind enough to print out our boarding cards and tickets. I called and booked a wheelchair-friendly taxi to arrive at the hotel at 5 pm. The flurry of activity since the news that we would leave for Seychelles that night had been non-stop. Joe appeared to be slightly nervous and unsure of himself and I made regular trips to his room to check on him. His meagre worldly possessions including his new clothes would fit easily into my luggage but he insisted on using the tattered old black bag that I had retrieved from his former home. We sat for the rest of the afternoon drinking coffee and talking. Joe was concerned about wheelchair access in the aircraft. I explained to him that times had changed since he had arrived in Portugal all those years ago. That the airlines were well-equipped to deal with the disabled and that he should not worry about that at all. Chris had been kind enough to book business class seats all the way to Seychelles. This was an unexpected bonus and would certainly make Joe more comfortable on the long journey. I found myself marvelling at the strange and rapid events of the past few days. It was certainly true that everything had happened very fast and the last thing I expected was to find myself on a flight to Seychelles. Still, I was happy that things had worked out and deep down I knew I was doing something good for the life of my new friend, Joe. I had no idea how long I would spend in Seychelles, probably just a few days to make sure he had settled properly and then I would return to Portugal to continue with my holiday. But that was all secondary and I decided to roll with the punches and take it one day at a time. Although I had spent many years in various countries in Africa and the Indian Ocean, I had never been to the Seychelles. A picture postcard group of islands stuck in the middle of nowhere. A place of dreams and of expensive honeymoons and one I had never pictured myself ever visiting. At 4:40 pm. I told Joe I thought it would be time for us to go down to the reception to wait for the taxi. Once again as he looked up at me, I saw the apprehension and fear in his eyes.

"Don't worry, buddy," I said, "you and I are going on a great adventure. One with a very happy ending..."

As Joe regarded me I saw the trust in his eyes when he spoke.

"Thank you, Jason," he said. "I know you're right. I just can't stop thinking this is all some kind of dream. A dream from which I will waken and I'll still be stuck in my old life."

"Your old life is exactly that, Joe," I said. "It's time to put that behind you and move on to a bright new future. Now, are we ready to go?"

"Yeah," he said. "Let's do it..."

The taxi arrived at 5.00 pm. on the dot and, as promised, it had full wheelchair access with a ramp on the sliding door. The driver appeared to be very well used to driving disabled people and pushed Joe into the cab with ease. My luggage and Joe's tatty old bag were put in the back and I climbed in and sat next to Joe. The short trip to the airport took only 15 minutes and I watched Joe as the vehicle left the old town and progressed smoothly along the motorway. He stared out the window at the hazy, yellow evening with a slightly melancholy look on his face. To keep his mind off the events of the day, I made an effort to keep talking to him. This was a distraction for him but I knew deep down he was worried. When we arrived at the airport soon afterwards, I noticed a change in Joe. It was as if it all suddenly became real at that moment. I paid for the taxi with cash and stood outside to have a final cigarette. Finishing it, I crushed it out in the ashtray and walked back to where Joe sat in his wheelchair near the doorway.

"Well, buddy." I said, "Let's go to Seychelles."

The airport staff were helpful with the wheelchair and we were quickly whisked through security into the departure lounges. The flight to Lisbon was on time and the short hop lasted only 50 minutes. Once we arrived at Lisbon International Airport we wasted no time heading to the gate for our next flight, to Dubai. By then I could see the excitement building in Joe. Once again the staff were very helpful and we were taken to our business-class seats before the rest of the passengers had even boarded.

Joe was amazed by all the trinkets and facilities that came with the business-class seats. He was like a kid in a candy store and fiddled with the remote for the TV while he drank the fresh orange juice served by the staff. After what seemed an age, the plane took off and flew up into the night, en route to Dubai. We ate a fine meal and I drank a few beers to pass the time before settling down to watch a movie. All the while I kept my eye on Joe but I was pleased to note that he had fully embraced this new adventure and seemed to be on board with everything. I was in a deep sleep by the time the plane began descending into Dubai. The flight had been 7 hours and I rubbed my eyes as I turned to look at Joe who seemed to be wide awake.

"Have you slept at all?" I asked groggily.

"No, I haven't," he said. "I watched three movies..."

I reached for the bottle of water in the holder next to me and drank from it as I returned my seat to the upright position.

"You have to try and sleep on the next flight, Joe," I said. "You don't want to arrive exhausted. I'm sure your brother will have something special planned for you."

"Yes, you're right, Jason," he said. "I'll make sure I get some shut-eye on the next leg."

The giant aircraft descended to Terminal 3 and being in business class, we were the first to disembark. Waiting for us was a buggy with a driver who would take us to the next gate. There was barely time to stop and look at the shops while we were whisked through the massive building. Feeling the desperate urge for a cigarette, I insisted the driver stop at the Winston lounge for me to have a quick smoke. No sooner had I finished, than we were whisked off to the gate for the next flight. The aircraft was smaller than the giant A380 we had flown from Lisbon but the business-class seats were just as luxurious. By then I could see that Joe was indeed very tired and I told him, in no uncertain terms, he was not to attempt to watch any more movies. He agreed to this and promptly fell asleep soon after the first in-flight meal was served.

I too was dog-tired and slipped into a deep slumber soon afterwards. The flight was smooth and uneventful and it was only the announcement from the flight deck that we were beginning our descent that woke me. I cranked my seat into the upright position and watched as Joe did the same thing. But it was only then that I saw the astonishing sight through the window at my left elbow. The Indian Ocean spread out in all directions in the bright sunshine. Above the clouds, the sky was a deep blue and the sea far below seemed to blend with the sky on the horizon. It was beautiful and daunting at the same time. Having had very little time to do any research on the Seychelles, I felt as if I was heading into the unknown. It was then that the pilot announced that there was a heavy tropical downpour happening on the main island. In the distance, I could see the storm clouds below. The seatbelt sign was illuminated and in my heart, I knew we were in for a bumpy ride. This fear came true as we approached and descended through heavy clouds with rain streaming past the window and as the giant aircraft came in to land I could tell that it was crabbing to the left. This was an effect caused by strong side winds and I glanced at Joe to see if he was feeling nervous as well. Thankfully, the plane landed without incident and once again we were the first to disembark.

As usual, the Emirates staff were helpful and made sure that Joe and I were quickly whisked off to immigration. The tiny airport building was white in colour and stood out against the backdrop of the dark green mountains in the distance. All around us, the tropical storm raged and it was as if the rain was coming down sideways. It was only then that we were told that the pilot had been considering abandoning the landing and heading for Reunion Island instead. Thankfully, he had made the decision to land in the storm and we had arrived safely. The immigration procedure was fairly standard but they did require an address at which we would be staying. Chris had given this to us in advance so the pain of filling in a short form for each of our passports was short and we were free to leave. It was with a great sense of anticipation that I pushed Joe's wheelchair through the tiny duty-free store and on through the arrivals gate. Standing there, as promised was Chris Fonseca. Upon seeing his brother he rushed forward and both men embraced and sobbed uncontrollably for a good few minutes. I stood back to allow them their time together after so long and I was filled with a warm feeling of accomplishment. It was indeed a beautiful sight and I felt privileged to have been a part of this grand reunion between two long-lost siblings. Eventually, Chris stood up and wiped the tears from his eyes.

"Jason," he said as we shook hands. "It's a *real* pleasure to meet you. I feel like I've known you for years but it's only been a matter of hours."

"I know, it's all been a bit crazy, Chris, but we're both happy to be here. This is a great day!"

CHAPTER FORTY-THREE

Maxim Volkov stood at the heavy door. His face was a pale grey colour and the whites of his eyes looked sickly and yellow. There was a pervasive aroma of vodka around him and he was a very angry man.

"What are you talking about you fucking idiots?" he screamed "You assured me yesterday that everything was fine, that we would be completing our mission today and there were no problems. What the fuck has gone wrong now?"

"I'm sorry sir," said the driver. "We worked into the night and the mechanics did their very best, but there is a serious problem with the engine. I have to tell you there is no way we are going to make the mission today. I'm very sorry, sir. I know this is the last thing you need to hear."

"You're fucking right it's the last thing I need!" said Volkov. "What the fuck am I going to tell the director? Already this mission has been full of problems and setbacks and now you come to me to give me the news that you have fucked up once again. It is like I'm working with fucking children! If I could, I would kill you with my bare hands right now!"

"Please, sir," said the driver. "Let us sit down and think about how to salvage things. There are plenty of fishing and diving charters available on the island. We can pick and choose and find one this morning. With the correct preparation, we could complete the mission tomorrow morning. I know it is a setback not being able to use the consulate boat, but these things happen sir. We did our best."

"Your best was not fucking good enough!" shouted Maxim. "I think you better come inside and we will have to think of a way to rescue this mission before it all goes to fucking hell. God knows it already has!"

The four men made their way into the hallway and down into the sunken lounge.

"Get the fuck out of here!" shouted Volkov at the butler. "I will call you when I need you again. We have important business to take care of ."

Volkov wasted no time pouring himself a double vodka as the three men sat down. His right hand shook slightly as he downed the powerful spirit. It seemed to have a calming effect on him and it was a full two minutes later that he poured another and turned to face the three men who sat expectantly waiting for him.

"Now," he said, "What are we going to do to get ourselves out of this fucking mess?"

CHAPTER FORTY-FOUR

The mood was jovial and there was much laughter as I pushed the wheelchair out of the arrivals hall into the shaded area outside. Joe and his brother could not stop talking and there was much backslapping and laughter. The rain was pelting down, falling in great sheets and the nearby palm trees whipped in the wind. I took the opportunity to light a cigarette and enjoy the moment. It was a great pleasure seeing the two brothers reunited and I knew I had done the right thing. It seemed Joe was a brand new person, his face was happy and animated and the lines of worry gone from his forehead. The conversation continued as I smoked until eventually Chris turned to me and spoke.

"Well," he said with a grin, "I think I better go and get the vehicle. It's over there in the parking area. You guys wait here. I'm going to get soaked!"

But the air was warm and humid and it seemed the prospect of getting wet was not a bother for Joe.

"Not at all," said Joe "I don't mind getting wet. Let's all go through the rain. We can change later..."

Once again there was more laughter from the brothers and I shrugged as we all decided there would be no harm in walking through the warm rain.

I pushed Joe's wheelchair across the pedestrian crossing and on into the parking lot. Chris led the way and we sloshed across the tarmac which was partially submerged in water. Eventually, we arrived at his vehicle which turned out to be a minibus. This was convenient given the fact that Joe was in a wheelchair. The bags were quickly loaded into the back and Chris and I made quick work of getting Joe into the vehicle. Once done, I climbed into the front seat while Chris jumped in at the driver's side and started the engine.

"Now, gentlemen," said Chris "I have to make a quick stop at the office to drop something off. I'll be two minutes, and then we'll make our way down the South Coast road back home."

The fact that we were all completely drenched did nothing to dampen our spirits and the feisty conversation continued as we drove out of Seychelles International Airport and made a right towards the small town of Victoria. I sat and stared out of the window, gazing up at the steep mountains that made up the centre of Mahe Island. The vegetation was thick and a dark emerald green and as I opened the side window I felt the warm rain pounding on my arm. The air was sweet and fragrant with tropical blossoms and fruit and the smell of the sea was everywhere. It didn't take long for us to reach a small industrial hub near the harbour. Chris made a right turn and drove to a set of factory units close to the water. He pulled up in front of a shop by the name of CF Charters. I immediately assumed the name stood for Chris Fonseca. The logo had a picture of a sunset with a silhouette of a boat to the front.

"Well, guys," said Chris "This is my office. I have to run in and give something to Jimmy. but I'll be right out and we can head home."

I watched as Chris made his way into the building. True to his word, he reappeared less than a minute later with a young mixed-race man following him. Handsome and with long curly black hair, the young man appeared to have a fixed grin on his face as he raced up to my window. Still smiling he glanced in at us and spoke.

"Welcome to a very rainy Seychelles!" he said. "My name is Jimmy, I work for Chris. I'll see you all later after work."

The young man raced back into the building as Chris climbed into the driver's seat. We did a U-turn and headed back to the entrance of the complex.

"So, you met young Jimmy," said Chris. "I guess you could say he's my right-hand man. He lives in the cottage at the bottom of my garden. Since my divorce, it's pretty much been him and me running the show. He's a nice lad from a good family, always willing, always smiling. A good bloke and I'm not sure what I would do without him, to be honest. You'll get to know him later, I know you'll like him."

Chris made a left turn and headed back down towards the airport.

Soon enough we left the outskirts of Victoria and entered the twilight of the jungle. Still, the rain poured down all around us thrashing against the trees but as before, nothing could dampen our spirits. The mood was buoyant and everyone was laughing and enjoying the moment. Eventually, we took a right turn up a narrow road with a steep incline. Chris explained that his house was in a residential area high up in the mountains. He went on to say that it was a few degrees cooler up there and that his house offered panoramic views of the Indian Ocean and the islands beyond. I looked at the jungle around me and glimpsed pleasant colonial-style houses amongst the thick foliage and fruit trees. It seemed the very island was alive and the rich soil was littered with fallen fruit of all descriptions. The road continued winding its way up, negotiating tight hairpin bends with perilous drops to the left. All the while we were gaining altitude and the views of the ocean to my left grew more and more expansive. After some 10 minutes, we levelled off and made a left turn down yet another mountain road. There were several houses there, obviously for the wealthier residents, as they were larger and better appointed than the others I had seen nearer the coast. We drove along for another 3 km until Chris made a left turn up a dirt road. The tarmac ended and ahead of us was a single house. Wide and modern, it appeared to have been recently built and had been completed to the finest specifications. Chris pulled up into a covered parking area near the back door and eased the handbrake on.

"Well, gentleman," he said, "Here we are..."

Chris and I wasted no time climbing out and removing the bags from the back of the vehicle. We placed them in a dry area near the back door and walked back through the rain to retrieve Joe from the vehicle. With his long hair still wet and his beard glistening with moisture, Joe resembled a drowned rat. But he was a happy drowned rat and the fact that he was soaking wet did not seem to bother him at all. After getting him into his wheelchair we pushed him to the back door which Chris unlocked. It was only when we got into the hallway that I saw how truly beautiful the house actually was. In front of us was a huge open-plan lounge and kitchen with giant bay windows at the far side. The views down to the Indian Ocean below were unparalleled from that height and in the distance I could see La Digue and Praslin Island. Slowly the clouds and rain started to clear and rays of warm sunshine began poking through the grey.

Feeling slightly in awe, I pushed Joe's wheelchair through the lounge and up to the wide windows. Knowing we were keen to see the view, Chris stepped up and slid the windows open so I could push Joe out onto the wide veranda beyond. The view was one of gobsmacking beauty, unique and unlike anything I'd ever seen. It appeared Joe was equally in awe of the sight that lay before him. We paused, speechless for a few moments until Chris stepped up and stood beside us.

"Well, Joe," he said "I can't believe I'm actually saying this, but here goes. Welcome home, my brother. Welcome home..."

The three of us paused in stunned silence for a good while until Chris spoke again.

"If you look down there towards the end of the garden you will see Jimmy's cottage. That marks the boundary of the property. The gardens to the left and the right are all maintained by him. As you can see there's an abundance of fruit trees and to the back of the property we have a vegetable garden. Jimmy takes care of that too. Being a handsome young man, he has his fair share of girlfriends. He seems to enjoy his life and I couldn't hope for a more loyal worker. He'll be along later after work and we were planning to have a fish barbecue. I hope that's okay with you?"

Joe and I were in full agreement even though we were still mesmerised by the view.

"Now," said Chris, "I think it's a good time to show you to your rooms and you guys can wash up and get changed into some dry clothes. We can meet back here on the veranda afterwards. How does that sound?"

Joe and I agreed and we were led back into the main house and down a long corridor to the right. I followed Joe into his new room which turned out to be a hugely spacious setup with wide bay windows looking out to the ocean below. He even had his own balcony where he could wheel himself out for his morning coffee. I watched his face as Chris showed him around the room and demonstrated the various gadgets and devices. It seemed once again that he thought he might be in some kind of dream from which he would wake up. It was as if it had all been too much for him and he was once again overwhelmed.

Chris proceeded to unpack his bag and place his new clothes in the cupboards to the left of the television. The giant double bed was covered with a white Egyptian cotton duvet and the room was well-appointed. Had it been a hotel, it would almost certainly be a five-star resort. It appeared that Chris Fonseca had done well in his business. This was a comfort to me knowing that Joe would never again have to worry about money. Finally, Chris stood back after packing the clothes, put his hands on his hips and stared at us.

"Well, Joe," he said. "I hope you like your room. If you don't, we can change it or I can put you somewhere else."

"No, Chris," said Joe. "It's wonderful, I love it..."

The two brothers exchanged knowing glances and I saw the tears well up in both men's eyes. This was a moment that none of them expected would ever happen. Something that had been missing from their very souls had been returned to them and I stood silently watching them savour the moment. After what seemed an age, Chris cleared his throat and turned to me.

"Well, Jason," he said with a smile. "Allow me to show you to your room. It's right next door. Then I'll go off and we can all get out of these wet clothes and meet back on the veranda. How does that sound?"

"Perfect," I said. "Let's do it."

My room was a carbon copy of Joe's room albeit a little smaller. It was at least three times bigger than the one I had just come from in Portugal and the view outside the wide windows was nothing short of spectacular. Chris left after showing me around and I immediately peeled off my soaking clothes and took a shower in the ensuite bathroom. Ablutions complete, I dressed and stepped outside to smoke a cigarette. Above me, the clouds had parted and the vivid blue sky was uncluttered and deep in colour. Ahead in the distance, a giant rainbow had formed over La Digue Island.

The left-hand end of it plummeted down into the island as if there was indeed a pot of gold there right enough. *Joe has found his pot of gold,* I thought. *Oh yes, he most certainly has landed with his ass in the butter. You've done well here, Green. You've done very, very well.* Feeling warm and satisfied, I left the room and made my way back along the corridor to the lounge and kitchen area where Chris was busy preparing a mountain of ingredients. He looked up at me and smiled.

"I hope you like seafood!" he said.

"I most certainly do," I replied. "So does Joe..."

The man in question, Joe Fonseca appeared soon after. He had changed into his new clothes and had made an effort to tidy up his mop of unruly hair and beard. Freshly bathed, he seemed happy and his face was animated as he wheeled his way into the lounge.

"What can I get you gentlemen to drink?" asked Chris "I've got everything..."

I settled for a local beer while Joe ordered his usual Coca-Cola. Chris delivered our drinks and we made our way back out to the veranda to witness the spectacle of the late afternoon sun heading for the horizon. The air was warm and there was a steady breeze coming in off the ocean. I looked around and marvelled at the spectacle of sheer paradise I had found myself in. The three of us sat around a wide table and soaked in the atmosphere, revelling in the wonder of the events of the past few days. It was as if it was impossible to wipe the smiles from both men's faces, such was their happiness. The afternoon progressed at a lazy pace and at roughly 4:30 pm. young Jimmy arrived. He immediately shook both of our hands vigorously again and welcomed us once more to Seychelles. Moving away, he busied himself preparing the barbecue which was lit as the sun went down. The evening was one of quiet happiness and sumptuous food and there was much laughter and frivolity for all. Yawning, I glanced at my watch to see that it was 9.00pm.

"Well, gentlemen," I said, "I'm sure you two have got plenty to catch up on so I think I'm going to leave you here to do that and take myself off to bed."

But the two men would have none of it and insisted I stayed for one more drink before retiring. It was 10.00 pm. when finally I made my way back along to my room. I lay on the comfortable bed and stared up at the ceiling as I went through the events of the past few days in my mind. I had never experienced anything like it in my life and I was sure that I never would again. One thing was certain however, I knew I had made friends for life with Joe and Chris. And not to forget young Jimmy as well. It was as if their family was complete again. Happy and ready for what lay ahead in the future. *There would be no more dangerous street life for Joe Fonseca. No gipsy thieves robbing and threatening his life and beating him. No, here he would be safe and well looked after for the rest of his days. There would be no more worries, no more begging, no more filth and violence.* I smiled as I closed my eyes and exhaled. I was tired. A little tipsy but a lot tired. Quickly I drifted off into a deep peaceful sleep and didn't open my eyes again until morning.

CHAPTER FORTY-FIVE

"I cannot believe that this has happened!" growled Volkov. "The director is going to be very, very upset. Already this mission has had several setbacks and he is not pleased at all. I cannot speak for him, but I can guarantee there will be consequences."

"Sir," pleaded the driver. "Please try to understand we did everything we could to fix the boat so the mission could go as planned. But there was catastrophic engine failure which will take many weeks to repair."

"This should have been sorted out before we arrived," grunted Volkov. "We are prepared, you are not..."

"My apologies, sir," said the driver rubbing his hands together in desperation. "My sincere apologies..."

Volkov scowled at the three men who sat in front of him but the vodka was starting to calm his nerves and he saw an opportunity for another lazy day ahead.

"Very well," he said. "I will call the director shortly. We must keep in mind the time difference between here and Moscow. I will wait until he is in his office and make the call. Only then will I know how we should go forward. For now, I would appreciate it if you all got out of my sight and waited next door. I would like to eat my breakfast alone. I will summon you once I have made the call. Pray for a good result, gentlemen, pray hard..."

The three dejectedly left the building and made their way back to Yuri and Sergei's casa. Maxim summoned the butler and ordered him to make a breakfast of eggs benedict with an ice-cold bloody mary to wash it down. By then the butler was truly in fear of his guest who seemed to be constantly drunk or angry or both. The disdain with which he treated the staff was disconcerting and frightening at the same time. Still, being the professional he was, he went about his duties clinically and politely and prepared and served breakfast to the Russian in lightning time. He was relieved to be dismissed after delivering a further pot of coffee and he quickly made his escape.

Maxim inspected his Vostok watch. The time had just gone 11.00 am. and he knew it was time to call the director. Mentally, he prepared himself for the difficult conversation that would follow. There would be questions, questions and more questions. The director had a keen mind and an uncanny ability to picture the situations that Maxim found himself in. It was as if he was alongside him on his various missions and would constantly point out his shortcomings and mistakes.

The conversation lasted ten minutes during which Volkov was grilled on every event since they had left Moscow. Eventually, it was decided that they were to make enquiries and find a private charter vessel to complete the mission. Their equipment was safely on the island and all that was really needed was a ride out to the GPS location where the underwater anomaly had been detected. It was with a sense of relief that Maxim ended the call. The bosses in Moscow had reluctantly agreed to his plan. Feeling smugly satisfied, he ambled up to the bar and poured himself another vodka. He carried the heavy tumbler over to the bay windows and stared out at the astonishing vista of the Indian Ocean beyond. The brief was simple. Find a vessel. Find a suitable charter vessel and get the mission done as soon as possible. All that was needed was confirmation that the anomaly was either the wreck they were looking for or not. Once that had been established, they would return to Moscow and be done with it. Maxim pulled the phone from his pocket and dialled the number for Yuri. The call was answered on the first ring.

"Get back here, now," said Maxim. "I have spoken to the director. We have a new plan..."

CHAPTER FORTY-SIX

"How did you guys sleep?" asked Chris.

"Very well indeed, thanks," I replied.

"Like a log," said Joe. "Very comfortable."

We had met on the veranda of the house at 8:30 am. I had been awake for two hours and had sat drinking coffee on the balcony of my room. At first, when I had awoken, I had no idea where I was. Then it all came back to me slowly. The unexpected events of the past few days and the journey from Portugal to Dubai and on to Seychelles. It had all been very much a roller coaster ride but one with a happy ending. I walked out to the veranda to find Joe and Chris drinking coffee and happily chatting away as if they had never been parted in the first place. I made inquiries as to where Jimmy was but had been told he had left to go to work as was the usual procedure. Chris had told us about his love and passion for his work. He waxed lyrical about his beautiful offshore fishing and diving boat that he had bought years previously and lovingly maintained. It turned out that Chris had made a fair amount of money in Durban in business and had decided to move to Seychelles in search of a more peaceful life away from corporate greed and stress. Here he had found his peace, built a steady business and fashioned a beautiful home for himself in the high mountains of the island. His life was now one of easy pace and very little stress and he would do no more than four charters per week taking tourists out to the surrounding reefs and islands for deep-sea fishing and scuba diving excursions. We ate a breakfast of fresh fruit salad with yoghurt followed by scrambled eggs on toast. When we had finished and were sipping on coffee Chris announced that he had to go to work that morning.

"I'm sorry to have to leave you guys, but duty calls," he said. "You're more than welcome to come with me. I am the boss after all..."

"Sure, I'll come with you," said Joe. "What do you say, Jason?"

"Why not?" I replied. "I'd be interested to take a look at this boat of yours."

"Well, that's settled," said Chris with a smile. "You guys sit here and finish your coffee. I'll go and change and we'll leave in say, 15 minutes. How does that sound?"

"Perfect," I said. "See you then."

The drive took us back down the mountain on the winding road through the jungle-like terrain until we reached the southern coastal road once again. From there we made a left and headed back towards Victoria past the airport. The drive took 20 minutes and we arrived in the harbour and stepped out into the blazing sunlight of the morning. The heat was extreme and added to the humidity it made for a steamy atmosphere. We wasted no time getting Joe out of the minibus and made our way into the air-conditioned comfort of Chris's office. Sitting there, beaming from ear to ear was Jimmy. He stood up and welcomed us like we were old family and immediately offered us coffee. It was a simple office decorated with artwork and posters of the islands and the surrounding reefs. To the rear was a door that led to the workshops where repairs and maintenance were done. Chris gave us a tour of the entire operation and explained that it was a simple, scaled-down version of some of the larger charter operations on the island. He had no intention of expanding his business and was quite happy operating with his one single luxury vessel. Joe sat with Chris at the main desk while he attended to emails while I wandered around the front office drinking coffee and gazing at the various pictures of diving and fishing expeditions. It was half an hour later when Chris stood up and spoke.

"Well, guys, would you like to see the boat?" he asked.

"Sure," I replied. "Can Joe come along with us?"

"Of course," said Chris. "We can take a walk down the pier, it's not far from here."

We stepped out into the mid-morning heat and crossed the tarmac road that led to the pier. Jimmy stayed behind to man the phone and to receive any clients that might arrive out of the blue. As we walked, Chris explained that the website he operated was the main source of business and most of his clients would discover him and make their bookings there.

He mentioned that he had several wealthy clients on his books who were repeat customers who would come back year after year. They were both scuba divers and fishermen and it was clear that Chris was happy to cater for either. It seemed to me that he had carved out a perfect lifestyle in Seychelles. A beautiful house, a lucrative little business that ticked over nicely and the fact that he was doing something that he loved was a bonus. The arrival of Joe was seemingly the cherry on the cake. We passed several expensive-looking pleasure vessels and eventually arrived at Chris's. It was moored in deep water which was as clear as glass. Joe sat in his wheelchair on the pier while Chris and I climbed aboard and he gave me a quick tour. It was obvious that the boat was a source of great pride for both Chris and Jimmy as all of the fittings gleamed in the sunlight and the entire boat was immaculate. Not wanting to leave Joe out of proceedings, Chris snapped a few photographs of the interior which we showed to Joe as we disembarked. Chris promised Joe that he would take him out to sea as soon as he could arrange wheelchair access. With the boat tour done, we made our way back to the office and the luxury of the air-conditioning. Chris had been right when he had mentioned his house up on the mountain was a lot cooler than down there in the harbour. We drank another cup of coffee in the office then Chris suggested we head into Victoria for some lunch. Jimmy had arranged his own packed lunch and stayed back at the office while we drove into the quaint island capital. We passed a statue of Mahatma Gandhi and drove past an old cemetery before arriving at the world-famous clock tower. Chris parked near a restaurant on the main street and we made our way into the open-fronted establishment to sample some Creole cuisine. Much to Joe's horror, Chris ordered the bat curry while we ordered cheeseburgers and chips. The three of us sat there and enjoyed a leisurely lunch under the old fans that spun lazily above our heads and I gazed out at the town from the balcony of the restaurant. Here the pace was slow and very much on island time. This was far from the hustle and bustle of Europe and the people appeared to be more friendly and gracious in their exchanges with others. They would greet each other and smile and take time to stop and chat for a while before moving on with their business. The food was excellent and it was just after 2.00 pm. when we climbed into the vehicle to make our way back to the office. I was feeling pleasantly full as we took the slow drive through Victoria back to the harbour. Once there, I browsed magazines as Joe sat with his brother at the desk and chatted away. It was clear both men were comfortable and happy in each other's company.

This was a good thing considering they would spend the rest of their lives together. Chris was busy showing Joe how to operate the computer while Jimmy busied himself in the back attending to some engine parts. At about 2:30 pm. the quiet murmur of their voices was shattered by the phone ringing. Chris answered and it sounded like he was talking to some prospective clients. After a brief conversation, he hung up and smiled at me before speaking.

"Looks like a couple of clients coming in this afternoon," he said. "Russians by the sound of them."

I nodded at him and went back to browsing the magazine which was full of pictures of expensive boats and yachts.

We spent the next hour in comfortable silence with the television in the background. I was feeling replete, satisfied and pleasantly sleepy but decided to go out for a smoke Being around 3.30 pm the sun had made its way over the mountain behind me and I stood in the shade of the building and lit up. I felt my body relaxing as I slipped into island time while I stood there smoking and watching the boats bob about at their moorings. As I was crushing out the cigarette I saw a vehicle come to a halt in the parking area near us. There were four men in it and for some reason, they appeared stressed and had strained looks on their faces. This was in contrast to the general laid-back ambience and happiness of the surrounding population who appeared content to go about their daily business at a slow pace. Thinking nothing of this, I stepped back into the cool of the air-conditioned office, took my seat once again and browsed another magazine. Seconds later I saw the door of the office open and three of the men from the vehicle stepped inside. The very sight of them sent a cold shiver down my spine. The front man, clearly the boss, was heavily built and had greasy blonde hair and a slightly sickly pallor on his face. Behind him were two walking mountains of men. They must have stood six foot six each and were powerfully built and rippling with muscle. All the men had deadly serious looks on their faces, completely devoid of humour. It was an eerie and unsettling sight, to say the least. Staying silent, I watched the men as they gazed around the office. It was then that Chris stood up and walked forward to greet them. Smiling and pleasant as usual, he offered his hand to each of the men which they reluctantly shook.

Joe, seeing that there was business at hand, wheeled his chair away to the right and busied himself studying pictures and maps on the wall. Chris invited the men over to his desk and offered them seats. The men grudgingly followed him and took their seats as offered. But there was something about the men, something was wrong with them, these were not happy-go-lucky holidaymakers booking a fishing trip. *No*, I thought, *something's up here, that's for sure, Green*. From where I sat I was within clear earshot of the conversation that followed and whilst I pretended to be studying the magazine, I listened attentively to the conversation as it began.

"Now, gentlemen," said Chris. "I believe you're looking for a charter. What can I do for you?"

"That is correct." said the older of the three men "We would like to book a diving charter for tomorrow, if possible..."

"Certainly, we can do that," said Chris. "We have a superb boat and I can take you to some of the best reefs in Seychelles..."

"That will not be necessary," said the older man as he drummed his fingers on the arm of the chair.

"I see," said Chris, looking somewhat confused "So you have a location of your own, I presume?"

"That is correct," said the man.

"Can you tell me where this is?" said Chris. "I need to know so that I can give you a reasonable quotation for the trip."

"It is 60 km to the east of Praslin Island," said the man "We have a precise GPS location."

Chris checked his computer screen as if checking a map.

"Just a moment," he said as he studied the screen "I'm looking at the general area you mentioned and there are no reefs out there. It's not going to be very interesting for sport diving, are you sure about the location?"

The older man cleared his throat and I saw the veins in his neck bulge with frustration.

"The location of the dive site and the purpose of the charter is no business of yours!" he said angrily in a guttural Russian accent "We are simply looking for a boat to hire. That is all. Are you able to provide one for us or not?"

The man's voice was chilling and straightaway I felt the hairs stand up on the back of my neck. *These fuckers are up to no good, Green. You can be sure of that.* Chris cleared his throat and smiled before he spoke.

"Certainly," he said handing over a brochure. "Our boat is fully equipped for diving. We can also offer catering for the day."

"We have our own equipment!" snapped the man. "Everything we need we have already. We will have no need for your catering either."

I could see by the expression on Chris's face that this was indeed a very unusual encounter and I took my time to study the men out of the corner of my eye. The man who was speaking, who appeared to be the boss, was fairly elderly. His two companions were clearly the muscle. Bouncers or bodyguards of some sort. *Perhaps he's simply some bad-mooded Russian oligarch? Maybe he's just having a bad day?* But deep down, I knew these men were up to no good. Still, I kept quiet and watched and listened to the proceedings.

"Very well," said Chris. "I apologize. It's unusual for clients to come on board with their own equipment but there is absolutely no problem. I can give you a quote right now. All you need to do is sign a few papers, make payment and your charter is booked. How does that sound?"

"Good!" said the man. "That is why we are here..."

"One moment," said Chris as he reached over to his printer. "I just need to print an indemnity form and a receipt. Now a one-day charter will be two thousand US dollars. How will you be paying sir?"

"We pay with cash," said the man impatiently. "Yes, go ahead, give us your forms."

I could see that Joe was out of earshot and was engrossed in studying some maritime book he'd found on a shelf. I watched as Chris printed the forms and handed them to the man sitting opposite. He took them and glanced over them quickly then pulled the pen from his top pocket and signed both. Having done that, he handed the papers back to Chris and pulled out a wallet which was stuffed with $100 bills. He proceeded to count them out in a disdainful manner then tossed the notes on the table so that they spread out in front of Chris. The gesture was both rude and disrespectful and I felt the tension building in my arms as I watched. Chris, being a gentleman, gathered up the notes and counted them one by one. All the while the two huge men sat either side of their boss impassively, their eyes staring at Chris, cold and humourless. Having counted the money and confirmed it was the correct amount, Chris opened a drawer and placed the notes inside.

"Well, gentlemen, thank you very much," he said. "Your charter is booked for tomorrow morning for a full day. We are at your disposal anytime from 6.00 am. onwards and we have plenty of fuel to take you to wherever you need to go. Our GPS system is live and functioning well and we look forward to welcoming you on board then."

"My people will be here at 7.00 am. sharp to load our equipment onto your boat. Make sure everything is in good working order. We have already had problems with another boat and we do not wish to have any more with yours. Is that clear?"

"Yes indeed, sir," said Chris "Our vessel is in tip-top condition. We will be here at 7.00 am. waiting for you. Don't worry, we'll get you to your location without any hassle."

The older man grunted and stood up followed by his two goons. He nodded at Chris as if he was appraising him one final time, then turned to walk back to the door. As they passed me, one of the large men looked me in the eye. It was then that I realized they were no normal tourists. This was a military man. His eyes were those of a killer, cold and emotionless. The whole episode had happened so fast that I found myself puzzled and slightly anxious as they made their way out the door into the afternoon heat. Seeing the men had left, Joe wheeled himself back to the desk completely oblivious to the strange and unsettling encounter. With the glossy magazine still clutched in my hand, I stood up and walked over to take a seat in front of Chris's desk.

"That was pretty strange," I said. "Are they typical of your usual clients?"

Chris chuckled and raised his hands as if to dismiss the incident. Perhaps he was trying to minimize it in front of his brother and simply pass it off as a difficult client.

"They were different," he said, shaking his head. "But hey, a charter is a charter. Who am I to argue? We need to keep the wheels of industry turning, don't we?"

"I guess so," I said, feeling puzzled. "Is it normal for clients to arrive with their own equipment?"

"Some people do arrive with their own fins and masks, but certainly not their own scuba bottles and regulators. Anyway," he said, pushing the computer screen away from himself "As I said, a client is a client. Some are easygoing, some not so. Being in the service industry we have to cater for all sorts. Normally they're happy to visit our best fishing and diving spots and they would leave the choice of those locations up to me. But like I told them, we're here to serve and if a client wants to go to a location of their own, who am I to argue?"

I frowned and nodded as I thought about the men's demeanour. There was no doubt in my mind there was something extremely sinister about them. These were not your average holidaymakers. *Don't interfere in his business, Green. You'll be spoiling what is a very joyous couple of days. Just keep quiet and enjoy the two brothers getting back together. Chris's business is none of yours...*

CHAPTER FORTY-SEVEN

Maxim Volkov sat in grim silence on the journey back from Victoria to the resort. His mind raced through the events of the day, trying to anticipate any potential problems that could arise the following day. The fact that Yuri and Sergei were both unaware of the actual purpose of the mission added to his worries. All they knew was that they were going to dive at a specific location and take underwater photographs. Only Maxim himself had full knowledge of the mission's true objective.

Based on the information he had gathered from the website and the brochure, the charter vessel seemed suitable for their needs. However, he couldn't shake off the concern about the charter boat staff. They were the weakest link in the chain, and depending on the mission's outcome, it remained to be seen whether they would need to be eliminated or not. Vital intelligence was missing, and the potential for further complications weighed heavily on his mind.

It was at that moment that Maxim made up his mind and turned in his seat to speak to Yuri and Sergei.

"Listen to me," he said. "Once you drop me back at the resort, I want you to return to the charter company and discreetly investigate the owners. I need all the information you can gather— names, addresses, their background, anything relevant. I don't care how long it takes, but we need this information to ensure our safety. Make sure no one suspects a thing. Understood?"

"Yes, sir," Yuri and Sergei replied in unison.

Volkov then addressed the driver.

"You will accompany them. The three of you will carry out this important task. Only when we have this vital information will the head office be satisfied that the mission can proceed as planned. You possess valuable knowledge of the island and are a familiar face. You can move around unnoticed and are acquainted with the territory and its people. Assist Yuri and Sergei until everything is clear, and then report back to me. This must be done tonight before the charter begins at 7 a.m. tomorrow. Is that understood?"

"Yes, sir," said the driver. "No problem at all. We will do as you wish and return with the required information."

"Good," Volkov replied. "There can be no more mistakes. God knows there have been enough already."

CHAPTER FORTY-EIGHT

W e spent another pleasant hour at the office, chatting away among the four of us. Eventually, we decided that Chris, Joe and I would head back home, leaving Jimmy to complete the preparations for the charter the following day. It seemed to be standard procedure for Chris and Jimmy would return with his own vehicle once the working day had ended. As we made our way back to the minibus, loading Joe in the back, everyone seemed cheerful. We took a slow drive past the airport and down the coastal road before turning right and winding our way up the steep hills. It was a relief to reach the cooler climes of the mountain. The air was clearer and sweeter, not to mention a few degrees cooler than the oppressive heat and humidity down on the coast.

We decided to freshen up, and the three of us planned to meet on the veranda for evening drinks before dinner. Joe and Chris seemed as if they had never been apart, enchanted by each other's company. While I was pleased to see their happiness, the memory of the three men earlier in the office lingered in my mind. I had been trained to spot danger and dealt with dangerous individuals throughout my life. There was no doubt in my mind that those men were indeed dangerous. It struck me as strange that Chris had dismissed them simply as more clients. *How had he not picked up on their demeanour or their rude way of talking? Perhaps he was simply content to be with Joe, and such details didn't cross his mind.* With this worry, I retreated to my room for a shower.

Afterwards, I brought my laptop out to the balcony and checked my emails while enjoying a cigarette. As expected, there was nothing important, so I closed the laptop and sat back, gazing out at the magnificent vista of the Indian Ocean below.

"Jesus, Green, you find yourself in some strange situations," I muttered to myself. "Some good, some bad, and some downright strange."

I smiled, thinking about the interaction between Joe and Chris.

"Enjoy the moment, Green. You've done well here. Enjoy the moment."

Half an hour later, the three of us reconvened on the veranda, and we were soon joined by Jimmy, who had returned from work. Jimmy skilfully cooked a delicious steak dinner, which we enjoyed under the stars. It was nearing 9 p.m. as I sipped on a fine whisky, and I decided to bring up the topic of the unusual clients who had visited the office that afternoon.

"So," I began, "is everything prepared for your clients tomorrow, this mystery charter?"

"Yep," said Jimmy. "Everything is set, and we'll be ready from 7 am."

"You should come with us on one of these trips, Jason," suggested Chris. "You can stay up with us on the wheel deck while I drive, and Jimmy tends to the clients. It'll give you an idea of how the operation works."

I glanced at Joe, who looked at me with an open expression on his face.

"You should go, Jason," he said. "I'm more than happy to sit here and enjoy the view. It's been a long time since I was able to relax, and I'm quite happy to do that."

The offer to accompany Chris on the charter was unexpected but certainly piqued my interest. I had been unable to think of much else the entire afternoon and evening and the thought of joining Chris on his dive charter the next day really intrigued me.

"I wouldn't mind doing that," I replied. "Are you sure it'll be okay?"

"Sure," said Chris. "I'll just tell them you're a member of the crew. You and I can stay up on the wheel deck, it'll be good company for me and you can see what I do for a living here in Seychelles."

"Fine," I agreed. "I'm more than happy to go with you. I was thinking about those clients earlier. They seemed a bit strange, and when you told them there would be no fishing or diving at the location, they were quite insistent on going there anyway. What did you think of them?"

"You know, Jason," Chris responded, "The client is always right. If a client wants to go somewhere, I'll take them. Who am I to argue?"

"I guess you're right," I conceded. "You've got to do what you've got to do."

"So it's settled then," said Chris. "The three of us will leave tomorrow around 5:30 am. and prepare the boat for the clients for 7 a.m. Are you sure you'll be okay here by yourself, Joe?"

"I'll be perfectly fine," assured Joe. "I could sit up here on this veranda all day, every day, and just stare out at the sea. I love it here."

Chris paused, and a smile formed on his face.

"I can't tell you how glad I am that you love it here, Joe," he said.

The evening continued with us chatting and laughing for the next two hours. It turned out that Joe had a stockpile of terrible jokes and was a bit of an amateur comedian. We sat there, berating him for his jokes, but he kept coming up with one after another. Overall, it was a thoroughly enjoyable evening, and by the time I headed off to bed, I felt content and satisfied. However, as I lay down on the bed and stared up at the ceiling, my thoughts once again returned to the three strange men who had visited Chris's workplace that afternoon. *Something was not right, Green. Something was very off about them. Those people were up to no good, make no mistake. Tomorrow will be interesting indeed. Keep your eyes open, keep your distance, and maybe you can find out what they're all about.*

CHAPTER FORTY-NINE

I woke at 5:00 am. and slid open the wide bay windows to step out on my balcony. Away to my right the sun was just rising over the horizon and the sky was an incredible salmon pink. The waters of the Indian Ocean looked like glass and were perfectly flat right out to the horizon. The air was cool, a soft breeze touched my face and everything was silent. While I stood there smoking a cigarette the birds first began to chirp heralding the dawn of a new day. The staggering beauty in which I'd found myself was almost overwhelming and for a moment I forgot about the three strange men who would be chartering Chris's boat that morning. I crushed out the cigarette and walked back into the room to put the kettle on for coffee. I stepped into the shower and stood there for 5 minutes all the while pondering the strange mannerisms of the oldest of the three who appeared to be the boss the previous day. He had a strange sickly look about him and what appeared to be a terrible temper. Then there were the two heavyweights who were accompanying him. Literal mountains of muscle, devoid of any emotion and if it wasn't for the strange circumstances, I would have put them down as stone-cold killers. *You're speculating here, Green,* I thought. *You can't see the forest for the trees. They might just be exactly what they are supposed to be. A group of holidaymakers going out scuba diving. Why is it you have to see the worst in people? Why don't you just relax and enjoy yourself, for Christ's sake?* I stepped out of the shower after berating myself and poured a cup of coffee. I took it back out to the balcony to watch the sunrise as I drank it. Draining the cup, I dressed, grabbed my phone and left the room heading to the lounge. As if on cue I found Jimmy and Chris there waiting for me. Both of them greeted me with smiles.

"Morning, Jason," said Chris cheerfully. "You ready to go out on the boat?"

"I certainly am," I replied. "Looking forward to it. Have you seen Joe this morning?"

"Yeah, I popped my head into his room earlier. He was chilling out watching TV. He said he might go back to sleep before coming out and making himself some breakfast."

"Excellent," I said. "He's settling in well."

"Seems like it," said Chris. "I couldn't be happier. Now if everyone's ready, I think we'll head out and make our way down to the harbour."

The three of us walked out the back door and jumped into the minibus. The drive down the mountain was quiet at that time in the morning and there was very little traffic to deal with. We made the left turn at the South Coast Road and headed up towards Victoria. We arrived at Chris's office at 6:00 am. on the dot and Jimmy made off to ready the boat for the clients. Chris and I went into the office and I made coffee for the three of us as Chris checked his emails. Jimmy returned a few minutes later and informed us that all was well and the boat was fuelled up and ready to go. We spent the next half hour chatting and keeping an eye on the door for the imminent arrival of the Russian clients. As promised, they arrived at 7:00 a.m. this time in a black minibus. The older one walked towards the office as Chris and I came out.

"Good morning," said Chris cheerfully. "The boat is ready to go and we're looking forward to a fantastic day out on the ocean."

But the older man simply scowled at us and grunted.

"Good," he said. "Let's hope there are no problems."

Without waiting for a reply, he turned and spoke to the two muscle men who had climbed out of the van. He issued a series of instructions in Russian and I watched as the two huge men retrieved a series of large black canvas bags from the rear of the vehicle. It was then that I recalled that they had said that they would be bringing all their own equipment and would have no use for any of Chris's. The two men shouldered two bags each and were led down the pier to the waiting boat by the ever-smiling Jimmy. It took two trips for them to complete loading the boat and when it was finally done, they came back and spoke to their boss in Russian. The older man nodded in approval and turned to speak to Chris.

"We are ready now," he said. "Let us go..."

We all made our way down the jetty and Chris and I stood back as Jimmy climbed aboard first followed by the Russians. Chris followed them with me in tow but it was then that the older man turned and snapped at Chris.

"All three of you aboard," he asked, "is this normal?"

"Yes," said Chris. "Young Jimmy is our deckhand and Jason and I will be upstairs at the wheelhouse navigating and driving the boat."

The older man glared at me with suspicion in his eyes and I immediately felt uneasy. Still, the cheerful nature of Chris and Jimmy seemed to calm the situation and the man simply nodded and grunted as he made his way into the cabin of the luxury vessel. Feeling the need to make myself scarce, I climbed the ladder up to the wheel deck and began polishing fittings while listening intently to the conversation between the client and Chris below.

"Here are the coordinates," said the man. "We wish to go to this exact spot and anchor. Once we arrive, my men will dive. That is all we require from you. Is that clear?"

Chris took the paper from the man and studied it briefly before speaking.

"No problem at all," he replied. "We're ready when you are."

"Good," said the Russian. "Let's get moving then. We have no time to waste.

With the driver standing on the jetty and Jimmy dealing with the fenders and mooring lines, Chris climbed up and started the powerful engines which gurgled and spluttered behind us. The Russian driver stood with a serious look on his face and I watched him give a solemn wave as the boat left its mooring and headed across the limpid morning waters of the harbour. The three clients kept to themselves in the cabin below while Chris navigated the boat out of the harbour and into open water. The sun was rising in the perfectly blue sky and the sea was calm as the seagulls swooped overhead. Behind us, the grand green vista of Mahe Island rose up into the sky with its dramatic peaks and heights whilst, before us, the splendour of the Indian Ocean spread out to the horizon on all sides. Chris advanced the throttle and the boat began to pick up speed, its powerful engines churning the water, the bow carving a wake like a hot knife through butter. The sparkling water was creamy on the sides and turbulent behind us as we gradually and steadily gained speed until the bows settled and we were on the plane. It was exhilarating and for a while I forgot about the strange men in the cabin below, such was the beauty of our surroundings. Chris activated the GPS system and punched in the coordinates which had been scribbled on a piece of paper.

"How long to get there?" I asked over the drone of the engine.

"At this speed, about an hour and fifteen minutes," said Chris "Once we get out of the archipelago, if the water is flat, we might be able to do it quicker. We'll see what it looks like once we get out there. It's not an area I've ever been to before as there's no fishing or commercial diving there. Still, gotta do what the client wants, hey?"

"Sure," I said. "The customer is king."

Chris smiled as he opened the throttle further and the powerful engines sent the beautiful boat racing over the swells. The repetitive motion of the boat and the droning of the engines had the effect of putting me into a slightly hypnotic state and I found my mind wandering as we travelled. It was some 40 minutes later that I saw the island of La Digue in the distance and Chris called out to me over the wind.

"Going to make a right turn here and head out into the open sea," he shouted, pointing at the GPS screen.

I nodded as I pulled sunglasses from my pocket. The blazing sun was glaring off the perfectly blue water and I realized then that we were heading into the unknown. Although there was a steady blast of wind from the speed of the boat, I could feel the day was becoming hotter by the minute and I was grateful for the overhead canopy above the wheel deck. Still, the clients kept to themselves in the cabin below and never once ventured out on the deck. I turned around and looked back at the island of La Digue as it slowly disappeared into the distance, while ahead the slightly intimidating open sea stretched away to the horizon with no land in sight. Chris seemed relaxed and at ease at the helm of his beloved boat and I could see that this was a man who was content with his lot in life. It was some 40 minutes later when Chris began easing off on the throttle and turned to me to speak.

"We're getting close to the GPS spot they want," he said pointing at the screen.

"Hell of a distance from land," I replied. "Seems like we're in the middle of nowhere."

"Yeah," he said "and the depth gauge is showing 60 metres to the sea bed."

"What do you think they're doing here?" I asked as he eased the engines down.

"No idea," said Chris "I don't know and I don't care. All I know is they're paying good cash. Who am I to question that?"

I nodded and gave a half-smile in agreement, but in the back of my mind, I knew that something was up. A minute later Chris called out and shouted at Jimmy to drop anchor. We had arrived at the spot. Once happy that the anchor had caught and we were secured and stationary, Chris shut the motor off and climbed down the chrome ladder to inform the clients that we had arrived. Feeling the need to stay out of the way, I remained where I was and watched proceedings from the upper deck.

The three men stepped out of the cabin and it was immediately clear to me that the boss was unwell. His face had taken on a greenish complexion and it looked like he had vomited several times. The client was suffering from seasickness. The two big men busied themselves and began pulling their aqualungs and other equipment from the bags. It was then that the old man spoke with a warning.

"There will be no photographs," he said. "It is strictly prohibited. Is that clear?"

"Sure, no problem," said Chris.

The man looked up at me and then on to Jimmy as if to drum this point in and I nodded enthusiastically in agreement.

The man appeared tense and quiet at the same time and this struck me as curious. This was no pleasure cruise. This was not sport diving. These men were here for a reason and a very serious one at that. From behind my sunglasses, I pretended to busy myself while all the time watching the men below. It was then that the boss man spoke once again to Chris.

"We have no need for your help," he said. "You may return to the wheel deck."

Chris raised his hands in a gesture of surrender.

"No problem," he said. "Please carry on..."

I watched as the two muscle men placed the aqualungs at the deck side along with their buoyancy regulators, masks, fins and wetsuits. Next, the two men began stripping down to their shorts. It was only then that I saw the tattoos. One of the men had it on the left of his chest while the other one had it on his right shoulder. Both tattoos were identical and I immediately knew I had seen the symbol somewhere before. The image was one of a menacing-looking skull set against a black background. The skull itself was white with grinning teeth and was surrounded by the silhouette of gun sights. The sight of these tattoos indicated to me that these men were part of an organization. And it was an organization that I was vaguely familiar with. Immediately I reached for my phone in my pocket and carefully withdrew it. Keeping my movements out of sight of the men, I activated the camera and held the phone low while taking a few snapshots. I took 15 photographs in total capturing images of both the tattoos and the three men. I knew that if I was caught there would be trouble, so I kept my motions and movements clandestine. The two younger men quickly donned their wetsuits and helped each other with their equipment.

I replaced the phone in my pocket as they began mounting the bottles on each other's backs. Jimmy busied himself throwing in a diving buoy to mark the spot where the boat had stopped. All the while Chris seemed uninterested and got on with maintenance work on the wheel deck. But I could not get the images of the tattoos out of my mind and I was itching to take another look at the photographs and study them. *Where had I seen this image before? What significance did it have and why did the two men have the same tattoo?* I knew a simple Google search would find the answer but for the moment I had no idea. *Still, at least you have images, Green. You can check it out later, no problem. For now, just keep going and act like the happy-go-lucky crew member you're supposed to be.* I watched as the boss sat down on a bench seat, seemingly unwell. He shouted to Jimmy to get him a bottle of water which he clumsily fumbled open. All the while the two heavyweights readied themselves for their dive. One of the men unpacked a series of underwater cameras. They were top-of-the-range models which I knew would not be cheap by any measure. It appeared that whoever was funding them was not short of money and I knew whatever they were doing was significant.

This was definitely not a sport diving excursion. This was something very serious indeed. The cameras were attached to the men's weight belts and finally, they turned to speak to their boss. A couple of words were muttered in Russian to which the older man nodded and dismissed them with a casual wave of his hand. With that, the two men sat down on the side of the boat, gave each other the 'okay' sign and flipped over backwards into the water. They bobbed about on the surface for a while as they adjusted their equipment then slowly sank below the surface. I watched as their figures grew smaller and smaller as they descended into the transparent waters of the deep blue depths below. With the two men gone, the boss man stood up unsteadily and made his way back into the cabin. I was sure that he was about to be sick again as he appeared desperate and his face had turned a ghostly white.

Beads of sweat had formed all over his face and arms and it was clear the man was deeply uncomfortable. Obviously, the intense heat and glare had affected him badly and I for one was glad to be in the breeze up on the wheel deck. Suddenly we were left alone and everything fell silent around us apart from the soft lapping of the water against the hull. The heat came down like the exhalation of a blast furnace and the humidity was deep and oppressive.

Normally I would have jumped in the water to cool off but I had to keep up the image of the helpful crew member and would continue to do so. It was then that I heard the retching and hurling from the cabin below. My suspicions had been correct and the Russian was being violently sick. I glanced at Chris who looked back at me with a smile and wink.

"Looks like life on the water doesn't agree with this chap," I said quietly.

"You can say that again..." replied Chris.

The stillness and heat built steadily as we waited bobbing around on the slow swell. In my mind, I pictured what the two men might be doing underwater. At a depth of 60 metres, there was no telling what was going on in the blue depths below. There was cheerful conversation between Chris and Jimmy and I took this as the usual banter aboard ship on a normal working day. I kept myself busy helping Chris with whatever tasks he gave me on the upper deck but all the while my mind was preoccupied. The minutes dragged on and it was a full half an hour before I saw bubbles in the water nearby indicating that the men were surfacing.

"Divers coming up!" shouted Jimmy.

At this call, the boss man appeared from the cabin to investigate what all the fuss was about. He stood there steadying himself against a handhold at the side of the deck and I studied his complexion once again. The man appeared no better than he had been previously. Having applied sun cream, his face was pale and covered with beads of milky sweat. A few moments later the divers surfaced and ripped off their masks. As they removed their mouthpieces, I could see both were smiling.

It was clear that they had found whatever it was that they had been looking for. They shouted a few words in Russian to their boss on the deck who quickly admonished them and motioned for them to be quiet. Slowly, the two men made their way around the stern of the boat and climbed the ladder to the lower deck. Once aboard they carefully removed the camera equipment from their weight belts and then helped each other with their diving equipment. All the while there seemed to be a heated conversation between the three but I could tell from their demeanour that there was a sense of elation and accomplishment. These were not disappointed men. *No, definitely not, Green. They have found something, that is for certain.* Once the men had removed their wetsuits they quickly made their way back into the cabin and closed the door behind them. There was no way for me to tell what they were discussing, but it was clear that the conversation was directly related to what they had seen underwater. Chris seemed happy cleaning the top of the deck of the boat and Jimmy continued with his tasks as usual below. It was 20 minutes later when the boss man stepped out of the cabin and looked up to speak to Chris.

"It seems our work here is done," he said. "We would now like to return to the harbour. Let us go immediately."

"Yes, sir," said Chris while giving a cheerful salute.

With those instructions, Jimmy deftly retrieved the diving buoy and the anchor while Chris started the engines. Chris opened the throttle and we sped off in a wide arc heading back towards La

Digue Island and civilization once again. It was a great relief to be moving and the wind cooled the sweat that covered every part of my body. It was reassuring to see the outline of land in the distance on the horizon. We had been completely isolated with the clients and there had been something deeply unsettling about that. The boat sped on over the calm ocean and eventually, the tropical paradise of La Digue island appeared on the horizon.

Nearing the island, Chris made a left turn and headed south. Soon enough the high granite peaks and lush tropical jungles of the mountains of Mahe appeared in front of us. I turned to look at Chris who grinned as the wind blew through his hair. Over the drone of the engines and the thumping of the hull on the swells, I ventured

"Looks like it was an easy day's work."

"Yep," he replied. "I can't complain. We can head back home, relax and have a cocktail. What do you think?"

"Sounds good to me,"

Some fifteen minutes later Chris skilfully steered the boat back into the harbour at Mahe. Jimmy jumped off and attended to the fenders to secure it safely at its mooring. Only then did the three men emerge once again from the cabin. It seemed that the old boss had forgotten his sickness and a measure of colour had returned to his face. He seemed very pleased with himself. Waiting on the jetty was the driver who had brought them in the morning. He appeared anxious and several words were spoken in Russian between the men. It took the heavyweights no more than 10 minutes to unload the diving and camera equipment back on the jetty. The men proceeded to carry the equipment back to the waiting minibus parked near the front of the office. It was only then that the older man returned wishing to speak to Chris.

"Thank you," he said, grudgingly. "We will let you know if we need your services again."

"No problem," said Chris cheerfully. "We're at your service."

So it was almost over as soon as it had begun. The men made their way back to their vehicle and drove off. After completing a final check of the boat, Chris and I left Jimmy cleaning the cabin and made our way back to the office. The time had just gone 1:30 pm. and it was a relief to step inside the air-conditioned space. In my mind, I could think of nothing except the tattoos I had seen on the two men. They were emblems I had seen somewhere before although I just couldn't put my finger on it. However, I decided to keep quiet and go along with the events of the day. Chris busied himself on his computer while I browsed a magazine. Jimmy returned some 20 minutes later and it was decided that the shop would shut early and we would all return home to join Joe. With the charter satisfactorily completed and the office locked up, we made our way back to the vehicle for the short drive south and up the mountain. The winding road was busier at that time of day but the steadily cooling temperatures were a relief and eventually, we pulled up into Chris's driveway and made our way into the house through the back door. It came as a surprise to find Joe in the kitchen busy preparing and marinating a chicken for a barbecue.

"Oh, hey guys," he said. "You're back earlier than I thought you would be."

"Yep," said Chris. "Strange clients. Booked a trip 60 km. into the middle of nowhere, dived for half an hour and came back. I can't complain, it's all good. I see you're preparing a culinary treat for us?"

"Oh yes, tonight we eat like kings!"

But I was too preoccupied with the memory of the tattoos to join the chat. I excused myself and told Joe and Chris that I was heading for a shower. I quickly made my way back to my room and opened my laptop as I checked my phone. Thankfully the light out on the water had been perfect and I had captured several good-quality images of both the men and the tattoos. I was able to zoom in on the pictures and email them to myself.

Once done, I did a reverse Google search on the image of the tattoos and the result was immediate and disturbing at the same time. The tattoos were the unofficial logo of the Russian mercenary group, Wagner. I knew I had seen it somewhere before and remembered then that it had been on a documentary about the activities of the group in central Africa. It was now clear that the clients were on a very serious mission indeed. These men were trained killers. Paid soldiers of fortune. Vladimir Putin's private army who operated with brutality and impunity throughout the world. *What was it they had come to look at so deep under the waters of the Indian Ocean? Why would they risk hiring a charter vessel instead of using one of their own?* I found myself staring at the logo as my mind raced through a multitude of possibilities. I decided then that I would keep quiet about what I had found. There was no point in upsetting either Chris or Joe on what was probably the happiest occasion of their lives. *No point in doing that, Green. You keep this to yourself. Let them enjoy their reunion.* But deep down inside I knew I would have to return to that same place in the middle of the Indian Ocean. I knew I would have to go down to see for myself what was there. I stood up, walked out on the balcony and lit a cigarette as I digested it all. *What on earth were they doing?* As I smoked I glanced over towards the veranda some 20 metres away. Chris and Joe were busy preparing the barbecue and plumes of smoke wafted up in the breeze. Both men smiled and waved at me.

"Got a cold beer here waiting for you, Jason," shouted Chris.

"Keep it for me," I replied. "I'll be right there."

I stepped back into the room and closed my computer before taking a quick shower and grabbing a change of clothes. By the time I made it back to the veranda, young Jimmy had arrived and was beaming from ear to ear. He was carrying four large lobsters that he had picked up from some fishermen near the harbour. Chris handed me an ice-cold beer as promised and I took a seat next to Joe.

The balmy breeze and pleasant atmosphere of the late afternoon continued as the sunset came and night encroached. Above, the canopy of stars, unsullied by light pollution was clear and distinct. Joe and Jimmy prepared a fantastic meal and all of us were silent as we ate. By unspoken consent, we moved to the edge of the veranda to watch as the moon rose over the Indian Ocean below. I chose my moment and queried, "Do you have any work tomorrow, Chris? Any charters booked?"

"Nope," he replied. "Looks like tomorrow we have a day off. I can live with that..."

"Well, that's what I wanted to talk to you about," I said. "I would like to be a paying customer. I would like to charter your boat tomorrow."

Chris looked across at me with a puzzled expression on his face.

"You don't have to pay me for anything, Jason," he said "I'll take you anywhere you want to go, free of charge. You want to do some fishing?"

"No," I replied seriously. "I want to return to the same spot we were at this morning. I want to dive there and find out what those men were looking for."

A frown formed on Chris's face as he spoke.

"Why would you want to do that?"

I had decided I would play my cards close to my chest and use the fact that I worked as an insurance fraud investigator as an excuse.

"Call it curiosity," I replied. "It's part of my job. I figure those men were there to look for, or at something and I can't stop thinking about it. Could be absolutely nothing, but I'd like to check it out."

My explanation seems to make sense to Chris and he nodded in agreement.

"Well, sure thing, Jason," he said. "Jimmy and I can run you out to the spot tomorrow morning. It's the least I can do considering what you've been through to get Joe here."

"No," I said. "I insist. This is an unusual request. It's only fair that I pay my way."

"Well, okay. We will deal with that, but certainly, we can head out there tomorrow and young Jimmy will dive with you while I stay on board."

"Great," I said "Thanks very much. Now, let's have another beer."

CHAPTER FIFTY

Maxim Volkov felt as if his insides had been turned inside out. He had never expected to experience such extreme seasickness aboard the boat and as a result, he felt weak and drained. Nonetheless, the fact that Yuri and Sergei had made a discovery on the ocean floor was enough to further whet his interest, and he knew he would have to continue once they returned to his luxury accommodation. Yuri and Sergei had been instructed not to say a word to the driver about what they had seen, and there would be a meeting once they all returned to his casa.

During the intense heat of the afternoon, the driver dropped them at the portico of Volkov's upmarket resort and the three men made their way through the reception towards the buggy station, where they could get a lift to their rooms. Volkov wearily made his way into his lounge and slumped down on the comfortable sofa as he awaited the arrival of Yuri and Sergei after they had stashed the equipment in their own rooms. The two men arrived soon after and their boss instructed them to connect the cameras to the computer equipment on the main desk. This exercise took 10 minutes, but eventually, the two men stood to attention and summoned him to come and view the footage they had taken underwater. Maxim had given explicit instructions to take photographs of the name of the vessel, should it be there and then carry on with further photographs and videos of the superstructure of the wreck. Yuri and Sergei had no idea what they were looking for and were simply following instructions to document what they had found.

Feeling slightly better thanks to the air conditioning, Volkov stood up and walked over to the desk, taking a seat while Sergei began flicking through the various photographs, images, and videos they had recorded underwater. It was in the first five photographs that Maxim saw the nameplate on the bows of the rusted old ship. There was no mistaking it; this was the Pearl of Alexandria. The very fact that they had found the vessel caused him to sit up in his seat and study the images with renewed interest. All along, he had doubted the existence of this wreck, but now he was confronted with digital proof that they had indeed found the vessel in question. This changed everything, and suddenly the discomfort and pain of the day were instantly forgotten.

Volkov spent the next hour perusing the photographs, studying and copying them to the hard drive of his computer. All the while, Yuri and Sergei stood on either side of him calmly as he worked. Finally, when he had studied all of the files, he saved them to his hard drive and told Yuri and Sergei to take a seat in the lounge.

"You men have done good work today," he said. "It is of the utmost importance that you do not say a word to anyone about what you have seen. That includes the driver. He must not know what you saw underwater. Is that clear?"

Both men nodded firmly in agreement.

"I have to say that I doubted the existence of this wreck, but what you have done today has helped to prove that it does indeed exist. This has now become a mission of the utmost importance to the Russian state. I cannot tell you how crucial this is, and I want you to understand this. Now we have a small problem. The men who took us out to the dive site today must be eliminated. As you know, the original plan was to use a boat belonging to the consulate. Sadly, that was not to be, and now we find ourselves in the unfortunate situation of having witnesses to today's operation.

Now, I know you have done your homework, but tonight I want you to make sure that the three men who accompanied us today are eliminated. You have the equipment to make this happen, and I want it done by the end of the day tomorrow. Is that clear?"

"No problem," said Yuri. "We will start work on that immediately and come back to report to you our plan once we have one."

"Good, very good. Now, I am tired, and I have to send this information back to Moscow. Leave me alone now and come back to me when you are ready. None of those men must be alive by this time tomorrow. That is all."

Maxim Volkov watched as the two men left the apartment. Once they were gone, he made his way back to the desk and began compiling an email to the director.

But as he worked, he began to think about the implications of the discovery they had made that morning. No one had seen that boat in over 85 years. No one knew it existed anymore. It had been consigned to the dustbin of history. Yet, there it was in the Seychelles, and he had just found it. It had come back from the dead, and sitting in its holds was a fortune in gold. Five metric tons of it, to be precise. More than enough to set him up for the rest of his life, and comfortably at that.

As he worked, a plan began to form in his mind. *Why couldn't he simply squirrel away a tiny bit of that gold for himself? A retirement fund, so to speak.* It was a very tempting possibility and one that he could not get out of his mind. But his retirement date was soon, and there would be no possibility of retrieving any of the gold for himself. *No,* he thought, *there must be a way.* The state would take at least six months to arrange a salvage operation. There would be much to organize and piles of red tape to cut through. *No, Maxim, you know the truth. You know the settings, and you know the prize that lies at the end of the rainbow. You must secure a piece of this fortune for yourself. You deserve it after all these years of hard work and dedication. Oh yes, you deserve it.*

CHAPTER FIFTY-ONE

Yuri and Sergei worked diligently throughout the afternoon and into the early evening, utilizing the salvage equipment they had brought into the country to fashion a bomb. The device consisted of a simple yet effective Semtex plastic explosive attached to a digital timer. Their plan was to connect this device to the ignition system of the charter boat they had used that morning. Once the boat's engines were started, the timer would activate, and after two hours, there would be a powerful explosion. In one fell swoop, all three men from the boat crew would be eliminated, and their disappearance would be attributed to an accident at sea. However, they still needed to deal with the fourth man, the one in the wheelchair. They planned to take care of him personally after witnessing the other men leave on the boat. The plan was simple, elegant, and effective, ensuring that all witnesses would be deceased by the following evening.

At 7 p.m., they phoned Maxim to inform him that they were ready to present their plan. Maxim sounded drunk and angry, but this was not out of the ordinary. He instructed them to come over immediately and present their plan of action. Upon arrival, they found Maxim sprawled out on the couch with a crystal tumbler of vodka in his hand.

"Sit down, sit down," he said gruffly. "I trust you have come up with something workable."

Yuri and Sergei went through their vision of eliminating the men while Maxim sat there nodding and drinking vodka. There were a few questions, as there always would be, but finally, Maxim sat forward, leaning in.

"Yes," he said. "It all sounds good to me. When will you go to place the explosives?"

"We will go this evening," said Yuri. "We will leave at 10:00 p.m."

"Very well," said Maxim. "Be careful. We don't want any trouble on this island."

The driver from the consulate arrived at 10 p.m. sharp. Yuri and Sergei climbed into the vehicle after loading their black bags into the back. The instructions were simple: they would be dropped off at a location 2 km from the harbour and would only be collected once a phone call was made. This way, they would be free to move through the darkness to enter the harbour, locate the boat, and plant the bomb. Aware of the importance of the mission, the driver remained silent as he drove through the dark jungle towards the small town of Victoria. Yuri and Sergei disembarked at a predetermined spot and stealthily made their way through the darkened streets.

The security at the harbour was flimsy, almost non-existent, and it took them only two minutes with a pair of wire cutters to gain entry and move through the shadows towards the waterfront. They crouched in the darkness, scanning the area for security guards, but it seemed that if there were any, they were either occupied or asleep, as there was not a soul in sight. The men watched and waited for another hour before making their move. The beautiful boat was within their reach, and they swiftly gained entry, discreetly stashing their equipment in the cabin doorway. As trained soldiers, they began their work almost immediately.

Accessing the engine bay of the modern vessel was relatively simple, as was locating the electrical system. Within a minute, they opened the seals and found a suitable location for the makeshift bomb. Connecting the device to the ignition cables and wires was straightforward, and within an hour, the bomb was live and ready. Yuri and Sergei spent another hour double-checking their work and concealing any evidence of their presence. Unless there was a major engine problem, there would be no reason for anyone to enter the engine bay or inspect the electrical system, ensuring that their actions would remain undiscovered. Once the ignition switch was activated, the timer would begin its countdown, and after two hours, the boat would be obliterated by a tremendous explosion.

With their task accomplished, Yuri and Sergei carefully made their way back to the jetty, blending into the darkness and the shadows of the nearby buildings. They retraced their path, passing through the hole in the fence and exiting the harbour without leaving a trace behind. It was 2 am. when they made the phone call to alert their driver, who promptly picked them up at the same spot he had dropped them off earlier. To any onlookers, they would merely appear to be a pair of intoxicated tourists enjoying their night out in the town. They entered the vehicle and drove through the night back to the resort, their mission completed.

CHAPTER FIFTY-TWO

I awoke at 6.00 am. and took a cup of coffee out to the balcony. Once again, the staggering beauty of the archipelago of the Seychelles was laid out in front of me. The lush tropical garden was dripping with fruit and blooming with flowers, and dew on the recently mown grass glistened like diamonds in the morning sun. But that morning, I felt the anticipation and excitement of the unknown. *What had those Russians been looking for? What had caused them to travel out into the middle of nowhere to an undisclosed GPS location and dive 60 metres down? You're going to find out today, Green. Oh yes, you're going to find out.*

After another cup of coffee and a shower, I made my way up the corridor and into the lounge to find Joe busy wheeling himself around the kitchen, making pancakes for everyone. It was a pleasure to see him happy in his newfound home environment, and it was clear that everyone else was enjoying seeing him settle in. I could not have expected the bizarre events that had led to my being there, but I would not have had it any other way. I was feeling excited and exhilarated, ready for the adventures of the day. Chris and Jimmy were cheerful and sat talking animatedly at the breakfast table as we ate and drank more coffee. At 8:30 am. we bade farewell to Joe and made our way back to the vehicle to head down to the harbour. The sky was perfectly blue above us, and the people of the island went about their business in their own inimitable laid-back fashion. We cruised into the harbour just after 9:00 am. and Chris spent 10 minutes dealing with emails in the office while Jimmy readied the boat and the diving equipment.

It was half an hour later, and the morning was already unbearably hot when we started the engines and chugged off through the harbour into the open water beyond. Using the same GPS coordinates as the previous day, we set a course for La Digue Island and Chris opened the throttle. The breeze from the speeding boat was welcome and once again, I felt the exhilaration and excitement tingling through my body. The open water was smooth that day, and we arrived at the dive location 15 minutes earlier than the previous day.

"Right," said Chris as he studied the GPS. "We are now at the exact spot we were yesterday."

Jimmy dropped the anchor while I climbed down to the lower deck to change into my wetsuit. Chris came down to assist us, and it was only then that I noticed Jimmy intended to dive without a wetsuit.

"You don't think it'll be cold down there?" I asked.

"Jimmy never uses a wetsuit," said Chris. "He prefers the authentic skin diving experience."

"Suit yourself," I said. "I, for one, don't intend to get cold."

"What is the exact depth at this place?" I asked.

"You're looking at about 60 metres, so you're going to have to make a stop on the way back up to decompress. Are you sure you're confident enough to do this, Jason?"

"Yes, I'm 100% positive," I replied. "And plus, I've got young Jimmy here to assist me."

"Well, that's fine. I wish you guys a pleasant dive, and I'll be waiting for you when you're done. Enjoy."

Chris helped us to attach the last of our equipment, and I attached my phone to my belt where it was housed in a waterproof plastic case Chris had provided. Finally, Jimmy and I sat on the side of the boat and gave each other the 'okay' sign before tumbling backwards into the warm water. With a final wave to Chris, we descended beneath the surface. I gazed down into the seemingly endless deep blue expanse, devoid of any visible fish. The blue grew darker and darker as we went deeper, captivating me. Keeping a watchful eye on the anchor rope, Jimmy and I continued our descent. Jimmy, a skilled diver, displayed his expertise as his muscles rippled under his coffee-coloured skin. The water temperature dropped noticeably within the first 10 metres. I scanned the depths beneath me, but nothing came into view amidst the deep blue.

At the 20-metre mark, I paused and looked at Jimmy once again. He seemed completely at ease and at home underwater, as if it was his natural habitat. We exchanged the 'okay' sign and continued our dive into the mysterious depths. It was at this depth that I spotted it—a massive dark structure stretching over 100 metres into the blue. As we descended further, it became clear that we were observing a sunken ship. I turned to Jimmy to gauge his reaction, and his widened eyes behind the mask indicated his astonishment. *What the hell is going on here, Green? This is what the Russians came for. No doubt about that.*

Reaching a depth of 40 metres, I paused to take in the breathtaking sight before us. The weathered steel ship appeared ancient, its superstructure partially broken as if it had fractured upon sinking, neatly split into two sections. Intrigued, we swam down toward the bow, searching for a nameplate, a common feature on vessels. Despite the ship resting on its side, I could clearly make out the wheelhouse and the railings encircling it. Several moments later, we arrived at the bow. The sand beneath us was pristine white, interspersed only with rocks and ship debris. The triangular bow loomed above us as we looked up towards the surface, which at that depth resembled a giant celestial silver mirror. The visibility was exceptional, with multitudes of tropical fish gracefully swimming around us. Aware of the potential presence of moray eels and other marine predators, our fascination outweighed any fear.

And then I saw it—the nameplate, clearly riveted into the steel hull. Someone had meticulously cleared the sediment, revealing the words "Pearl of Alexandria." Without hesitation, I unclipped my phone from my weight belt and snapped several photographs. Satisfied, Jimmy and I swam away from the ship's vicinity, capturing a few more shots of the hull and the wheelhouse from different angles. The ship had been submerged for a significant period, evident from the pervasive rust and sediment and the absence of human remains.

Carefully, we approached the wheelhouse door, which had rusted open, its glass shattered long ago. I signalled Jimmy to stay put as I cautiously made my way inside, mindful of sharp edges and loose metal shards. My eyes gradually adjusted to the dim light, allowing the scene inside to reveal itself. Amongst the desolation, three skeletons remained, their clothing and flesh long since deteriorated. One of them appeared to be resting on a sofa in the sediment, its eye sockets chillingly vacant. A tiny crab scuttled out of an eye socket and disappeared into the silt. One of the crewman's skeletal hands gripped a rusted steel railing, mirroring my own position. Searching for any additional clues or information, I found nothing but the presence of these lifeless sailors. Once again, I retrieved my phone and captured several photographs of the eerie scene inside the wheelhouse.

It was then that my gaze fell upon a necklace adorning one of the skeletons below me. Made of silver, it glimmered in the gloom. Curiously, the pendant bore the shape of a swastika. Frowning inside my mask, I reached forward to retrieve it. As I tugged gently, the vertebrae of the neck gave way, and the skull tumbled into the silt. I glanced towards the door and noticed Jimmy hovering there, observing me. Sensing the darkness and spookiness of the place, I decided to take a few more photographs and make my exit.

Jimmy and I ascended another 5 metres, swimming along the hull until we reached the break in the superstructure. The ship had come down at a steep angle, with the bow striking the sand and the cargo's weight splitting the structure.

Jagged, rusted metal marked the point of rupture as if a colossal force had torn it apart like a Christmas cracker. With great caution, we descended between the sharp edges of the severed hull, entering the dark and foreboding interior of the cargo hold. It was clear that whatever had been stored there had long since decayed. I regretted not bringing additional lighting equipment to explore further. As we descended towards the debris-covered sand, I noticed steel crates—eight of them in total. Seven remained lodged within the hold, while one had spilled out during the hull breach, and was partially buried in the sand. Jimmy followed closely behind as I approached the crate. The area surrounding it showed signs of disturbance by the Russian divers the day before. Two sturdy steel handles flanked the trunk. I grasped one handle with my right hand and wedged my fins into the sand for leverage. Despite my efforts, the trunk refused to budge, suggesting an extraordinarily heavy load. I wondered if this had been the primary focus of the Wagner men. The mystery intrigued and completely fascinated me, causing time to slip away as I gazed at the trunk and the interior of the cargo hold, my mind whirling.

Suddenly, a powerful explosion ripped through the water, felt as a physical blow rather than heard. It seemed as if a colossal weight had been dropped on the water's surface above us. The sound reverberated, foreign and out of place in an environment filled with only the sound of bubbles from our regulators and our own steady breathing. Confusion etched across my face as I looked at Jimmy, who mirrored my bewildered expression with wide, fearful eyes. Sensing imminent danger, I signalled for us to ascend back to the boat. However, as I glanced upward, I saw debris slowly descending through the blue water, hinting at the chaos unfolding above. By then, I had no doubt that something was seriously wrong. I glanced at Jimmy, only to find him staring back at me in alarm. Wasting no time, I gave him a thumbs-up sign, indicating that we should both ascend immediately. We began swimming upward, leaving the giant steel hull beneath us. However, as we ascended, it became clear what had transpired on the surface. There had been a massive explosion, and fragments of the boat were falling all around us. Shattered pieces of fibreglass, twisted metal, fabric, and engine parts rained down like a scene from a horror movie.

Despite the chaos, I stayed focused and continued swimming upward passing the first signs of tragedy—a severed leg slowly sinking through the crystal-clear water, leaving behind a trail of red mist. Soon after, a hand, severed at the wrist, followed suit. I glanced at Jimmy and saw that he was now in a state of panic. *What the fuck is going on?*

Knowing I needed to keep a cool head, I gripped Jimmy by the arm and shook him, locking eyes with him. I flashed him the 'okay' sign, though I was well aware that everything was far from okay. Just then, I saw Chris's torso slowly descending through the water, barely five metres away from us. A red mist of blood clouded the water around it. I knew this would attract ocean predators, but I never expected them to arrive so quickly.

Out of the blue, the first of them appeared—a vision from hell. It was a hammerhead shark, at least 15 feet long, gliding lazily towards us. I stared into its cold, dead black eye as it passed within 10 metres of us. Feeling panic rising within me, I forced myself to remain still, but suddenly, the hammerhead twisted its body and raced towards the torn, white flesh of Chris's bleeding torso. It seized the rib cage in its razor-sharp teeth, violently shook its head, and disappeared into the depths, leaving behind a cloud of blood. *What the fuck? Jesus Christ!* I thought, realizing the magnitude of the situation I had found myself in. It was then that I heard Jimmy's muted screams beside me. I turned to see what had caught his attention and was horrified to witness three more sharks emerging from the deep blue. The first one circled around us, steadily and cautiously. The bolder creatures dashed forward, engaging in a feeding frenzy on the intestines and other body parts raining around us.

At that moment, I realized I was trapped in what seemed to be a nightmarish horror movie. Everything began to move in slow motion, and I felt vomit and bile rise in my throat, burning its way back up. Jimmy, now in a state of pure panic, wriggled his torso away from my grip, slipping through my fingers. He swam frantically, trying to escape from the sharks.

The disturbance in the water immediately caught their attention, and more of the vile creatures seemed to appear out of nowhere. It was as if I had been plunged into a surreal nightmare, with massive creatures materializing all around us in the crystal-clear water. But then, my worst fear materialized. One of the larger white sharks broke ranks with the others and darted towards Jimmy. I watched in horror as its cavernous mouth opened, revealing hundreds of diamond-shaped, razor-sharp teeth. The giant mouth engulfed Jimmy around his bare waist, and I could only watch helplessly as the teeth sank into his flesh while the creature thrashed from side to side. Bile and vomit filled my regulator as I witnessed at least six other sharks racing towards the feeding frenzy, tearing Jimmy's flailing body to pieces amid a cloud of red mist and blubbery white flesh.

CHAPTER FIFTY-THREE

Carrying a heavy crystal tumbler of vodka, Maxim Volkov stumbled as he approached the large sliding glass doors. He slid them open, allowing the warm, humid air of the night to rush into the air-conditioned lounge around him. He could smell the salt in the air and hear the wind rustling through the palm trees on either side of the casa. Being close to midnight, the air was slightly cooler, and he stepped out on the wooden decking, making his way towards the jacuzzi. Once there, he carefully climbed down and lowered his naked body into the warm water. As he settled into his seat, he let out a deep sigh and gazed out into the darkness of the night over the Indian Ocean.

In his alcohol-addled mind, he could think of nothing except the gold that had lain at the bottom of the ocean for almost a hundred years. Five metric tons of precious metal, undisturbed and untouched, forgotten by the world, and waiting for someone to find it. And that someone had been him. *Yes, Maxim*, he thought, *you are the one who has found this treasure. It is you who must benefit from it. Make no mistake, this is part of your destiny. Yes, you will own a portion of that gold. The question is how, not when or if.* Maxim brought the glass to his mouth and swallowed a mouthful of the expensive vodka. The alcohol had a pleasant burn in his throat, further steeling his resolve.

He remained in the jacuzzi for another half an hour as his mind continued to turn over the idea of the five tons of gold at the bottom of the ocean. It was 1:00 am. in the morning when he began laughing hysterically, his voice echoing through the night like that of a madman. He laughed until he eventually passed out, his rotund belly bobbing in the frothing water of the jacuzzi.

CHAPTER FIFTY-FOUR

It all happened so quickly, and I found myself in a scene of unimaginable horror: alone in the ocean, surrounded by sharks, 60 km away from the nearest land. My dive buddy, whom I had just witnessed being ripped to shreds by a school of hungry sharks. The boatmaster had been blown to pieces above me, and the debris of the shattered boat rained around me, falling to the ocean floor below. On numerous occasions, I told myself that this must be some kind of bizarre nightmare, that it couldn't actually be happening to me. Unfortunately, it was all too real, and I hovered there in the water, frozen with terror. I realized then that remaining still would be my best chance of survival, and that flapping around in a panic would only serve to attract the apex predators that surrounded me.

Swallowing the bile that filled my mouth, I steeled my nerves and slowly adjusted my buoyancy device to help me rise slowly to the surface. The unimaginable horror of witnessing young Jimmy ripped to pieces by the merciless predators had burned a vision into my mind, and I struggled to hold on to my sanity in that moment. It took a huge effort to tear my eyes away from the circling sharks and look upwards, but finally, when I did, I saw the shimmering white mirror of the surface not far above me. *But what the hell would I do when I got there?* There was no boat, no life raft, nothing—nothing but open water for miles and miles around. I had no choice but to continue rising, and I looked around me once again, cautiously watching the hideous creatures that had multiplied exponentially, drawn in by the scent of blood. Two humans had lost their lives that day, and the feeding frenzy was in full swing below me. My greatest fear was that I would be next on the menu.

Stay calm, Green. For Christ's sake, stay calm. If you want to get through the next few minutes, you better stay calm. But all I could think about was those smiling, gaping jaws tearing into my flesh. The terror would not subside, no matter what I did or told myself. I had no idea how long it was, but eventually, I broke the surface, instantly blinded by the intense sunlight and the reflection from the water. But in my mind, all I could think of was the circling monsters beneath me. One nick on my skin, one drop of blood, and I knew they would tear into me mercilessly.

With great effort, I brought my vision from underwater to the surface and looked around for anything I could grab for more buoyancy. But there was nothing, not a trace of the boat in sight. I slowly turned around, desperately hoping for something to cling to, acutely aware that flapping around on the surface would make me an appetizing target for the sharks. I forced myself to calm down and breathe. Then, I saw it—a 5ft length of fibreglass hull attached to some thick yellow insulation, floating just 10 m away from me. Instantly, I knew this was my only hope of getting out of the water and away from the sharks. The current was pushing me further away from it, and I knew that if I didn't act immediately, it would soon disappear from sight and be gone forever.

I lowered my mask into the water again and saw the horrors beneath me still circling, slowly getting closer. It wouldn't be long before they realized the feeding frenzy was over, and if they wanted to continue, I would be next. With the faintest of movements, I began finning towards the chunk of floating fibreglass, all the while keeping a watchful eye on the nightmare beneath me. After what felt like an eternity, my head bumped into the jagged edge of the hull. *For fuck's sake, Green, you've just gone and drawn blood in the worst possible place*, I thought to myself. But I kept calm and slowly pulled myself up and onto the fibreglass chunk. Thankfully, the thickness of the insulation lifted my body, and I lay there on my stomach with my legs still dangling in the water.

Removing my aqualung was difficult and dangerous as it required a lot of movement and splashing around, which could attract the creatures below. But I had no choice, so I persevered until I had removed it and placed it in front of me on the fibreglass. It was then that I realized there was only one person in the world who knew we were out there that day—Joe. But he had no idea where we were, and nobody expected him to. For the first time in my life, I felt absolutely alone.

Determined not to become part of the food chain, I cautiously moved my body forward on the unstable slab of fibreglass. The extra weight of my upper body, combined with the aqualung, caused the front of the slab to partially submerge, and I accidentally breathed in a mouthful of water. I spent the next 5 minutes coughing and spluttering, with the taste of bile burning in the back of my throat. Not wanting to risk any part of my body being in the water, I brought my feet up and held them in that position. Finally, I was out of the water, although most of my body was still partially submerged to a depth of about 4 inches.

Once the coughing fit subsided, I began to assess my situation. It was bleak, to say the least. I was 60 km. away from the nearest land, with no one aware of my location or what had transpired. I was at the mercy of the ocean and the currents. Already feeling thirsty, I cautiously looked around for any floating water bottles or anything I could drink, but there was nothing. Just an endless expanse of water as far as the eye could see. The terror of what I had witnessed wouldn't leave me, and my mind played tricks on me, seeing shark fins in each pointed wave I spotted. Again and again, I told myself it wasn't real. *You need to concentrate, Green.*

If you want any chance of getting out of this situation alive, you better fucking concentrate!

Then I really became aware of the power of the sun generating the blazing heat surrounding me. Thankfully, I had chosen to wear a wetsuit, but the black neoprene rubber attracted heat, and the sun beat down on me mercilessly. It was far from an ideal situation, but at least I was out of the water, safe for now from the hungry predators circling below.

CHAPTER FIFTY-FIVE

"Has the job been done?" Volkov asked.

"Yes, sir. Everything has been done according to your instructions," Yuri replied.

"And are you sure there are no loose ends left to be tied up?"

"No, sir. Everything has been taken care of. One hundred per cent."

"Very good," Volkov said with satisfaction. "I have been in touch with Moscow, and they are very pleased with what we have discovered here. I will contact them again, and I believe we can expect to leave within 24 hours. Well done on your work, and I will message you as soon as I know our time of departure. You may go now."

Yuri and Sergei nodded curtly, then made their way to the door and out of the luxurious casa. Volkov groaned and rubbed his eyes. He was suffering from an almighty hangover, unlike any he had ever experienced. However, one positive thing was that his irritable bowel syndrome seemed to have cleared up. The terrible symptoms had subsided, and he attributed it to the healthier food he had been eating since arriving on the island. It was an unexpected bonus, but his mind was preoccupied with what had consumed him since the discovery in the ocean.

The two muscleheads from Wagner had no idea why they were there, but Volkov realized they would both be key to his plans moving forward. His problem now was how to execute the plan that had been formulating in his mind. He stood up shakily and walked over to the bar to get himself a bottle of mineral water. As he reached the bar, he noticed the nearly empty bottle of vodka from the previous evening, causing him to visibly wince.

He carried the glass of water over to the large sliding doors and gazed out at the bright blue waters of the Indian Ocean. He had already made up his mind to take some of the discovered gold. The question was how to do it, which presented a difficult proposition since he was still employed by the Russian state. However, an idea had been developing in his mind for some time now—a feasible idea, especially given his current health condition. The director was well aware that he was not a healthy man, and this could be used to his advantage if he could carefully plan everything. If he could do that, he could put his idea into action, and Maxim Volkov would be set for the rest of his life. *Yes*, he thought to himself, *of course you deserve it, Maxim. A lifetime of hard work and dedication. You deserve it, and you shall have it. As God is my witness, you will have it...*

CHAPTER FIFTY-SIX

The awful panic and horror of the situation began to subside at around 3:00 pm. that afternoon. My ankles, hands, and the back of my neck were already terribly sunburned from lying uncomfortably on the slab of fibreglass. My body itched uncontrollably under the neoprene rubber of the wetsuit, but at least I was safe from the sharks. Finally, I was able to calmly assess my situation, think things through, and put the horrific memory of Jimmy's death out of my mind, at least for a while.

I looked at my watch and saw that I'd been stranded in the middle of the ocean for a good six hours now and in that time I had not seen a single sign of life. Not even a seagull had flown above me, let alone any sight of land. I became acutely aware that I had no idea of the direction I was drifting. And certainly, I was drifting - of that I was sure. It became apparent to me that I could well be drifting further and further out to sea, a prospect which was just too awful to contemplate.

I had donned my goggles on a few occasions and cautiously looked underwater to check for sharks. Thankfully, they seemed to have disappeared for now, and this was a brief but very welcome respite from the terror of the morning. Up until that point, I had taken no time to think of the circumstances that had led to this situation. But one thing I was sure of: the explosion had been no accident, and foul play was indeed part of what had happened. The Russians were almost certainly to blame, and there was no doubt in my mind that they had intended to kill us all.

However, it was at that moment that I saw a shadow in the water below me. My heart sank once again as I relived the terror of seeing the sharks eating Jimmy alive. Just to be sure, I donned my goggles and briefly poked my head into the water. But what I saw was not a shark; it was a giant barracuda. The ugly creature seemed to have come up from the depths directly towards me, and I was aware of the double rows of teeth that could inflict terrible injuries. Feeling the urge to protect myself, I gripped the aqualung and held it by its valve, ready to bash it into the nose of the creature should it approach too close. The fish must have been at least five feet long, and it circled around me with its slender silver body glittering in the sunlight, baring its grotesque two sets of razor-sharp teeth. I was aware that barracudas were aggressive fish and had been known to attack humans. My worry was that if I was bitten on any part of my body, I would bleed, posing another serious problem for me - more sharks.

Feeling completely helpless, I screamed out loud and shoved the aqualung towards it. Clearly spooked, the fish darted off into the blue, and I never saw it again. And so, in that uncomfortable position, on my stomach with my feet raised up, I lay there, half-soaked in the water, for the next two and a half hours. In that time, I began to try to ascertain the direction in which I was drifting, but there was simply no telling. To cut a long story short, there I was, trapped and alone, completely isolated in the middle of the Indian Ocean with little or no hope of rescue.

It was in this dire situation that I lay there, with the water lapping against the jagged edges of the fibreglass slab, as the sun began to set. Strangely enough, it was one of the most beautiful sunsets I'd ever seen. To the west, a series of low-lying clouds had formed, and the entire sky turned golden yellow, with rays of sun beaming down with celestial beauty. But the coming darkness brought its own fears. Many creatures of the sea would rise to the surface to feed at night.

By that stage, I was extremely thirsty, and I could feel my tongue swelling up in my mouth. This was as dangerous as being stuck in the middle of the ocean, and the only consolation would be that death would be a lot slower. To mitigate the absolute terror I was feeling, I closed my eyes and began to picture happier times. Repeatedly, I told myself to stay calm, as panicking would do me no favours at all. I lay like that, half submerged in the salty water, for a good few hours and when I opened my eyes, it was night. Overhead, a canopy of stars pricked the sky with such beauty that it was unfathomable that I was beneath them all, suffering such fear. The water had calmed down to a gentle swell and all was quiet.

Feeling helpless and strangely bored, I reached out over the fibreglass slab and pulled my arm through the water. Almost immediately, there was a green glow of microscopic plankton, illuminating behind the path of my hand. The colour was similar to emerald, and it appeared dreamy and psychedelic. I found myself doing it several times with both hands. It was then that I had the idea of swimming towards where I knew land would be. I had seen the direction of the setting sun, and I knew that we were 60 kilometres east of La Digue Island when we had anchored.

Cautiously, I lowered my legs and began finning towards the west. As I did so, I glanced behind me to see the swirling mass of glowing green plankton in the water. But then it struck me that I was creating a beacon of sorts on the surface of the ocean, which would attract any sea creatures that may be lurking in the depths below.

I was making myself a target unnecessarily, and I immediately changed my mind and stopped doing it. The fact that I was unable to swim brought on yet more feelings of hopelessness, and I painfully raised my feet again and lay there silently.

However, coming from the heat of the day, the act of stopping swimming caused my body temperature to drop suddenly, and I began to feel cold. Within half an hour of lying there, my teeth began to chatter uncontrollably, and I could do nothing except tense my body, screw my eyes shut, and do my best to get through the night alive. Although I was dog-tired, extremely thirsty, and hungry, sleep was completely impossible. In fact, I did not dare sleep because I knew that if I were to fall asleep, I would risk falling off the precarious slab of fibreglass and into the water. In the darkness, I might lose the slab, and I would then surely drown.

In this semi-comatose and dreamlike state, I lay there, half-soaked, for six hours. Suddenly, in the dead of night, I felt a thump on the bottom of the fibreglass slab. I awoke with a start and realized my mouth was stuck closed. Something had hit the fibreglass slab from underneath, and I had no idea what it was. I opened my eyes in a panic and fought the urge to scream as I saw that I was surrounded by great swirls of luminous microscopic plankton. But it was not me that was making the swirls, and I had no idea which creatures were causing them.

All around me were vivid explosions of light in the water. I propped myself up to watch them, and I could see that they appeared randomly within a 10-metre radius of where I was. The fear I felt was unbelievable, and I expected to be hit by some giant creature at any moment. At that moment in my life, I knew I was at my lowest point ever. I truly did not expect to survive the night, let alone make it to land.

CHAPTER FIFTY-SEVEN

The three Russian men walked across the concrete apron towards the aircraft waiting in the blazing sun. They made their way up a short set of steps and entered the sleek jet, the pilot closing the door behind them. It took approximately 30 minutes for the aircraft to take off into a perfectly blue and cloudless sky. Maxim Volkov sat brooding, staring out of the window at the endless ocean below. In his mind, he had formulated a plan but needed the help of the two Wagner men to put it into action. For over 24 hours, he had ruminated and worried about this plan, but finally, he knew the time was right to make his proposal.

Yuri and Sergei were both completely oblivious to the reason for their trip to Seychelles and the subsequent dives to the wreck. Volkov's plan was to call a meeting with the men and explain what the trip had really been about. He would then pitch the idea to them, offering a vast amount of money to join him in his mission to recover at least one of the steel crates. A hostess emerged from the galley and served the men drinks and food, which Volkov quietly consumed. It was an hour into the flight when Maxim poked his head into the front cabin and spoke to the two mercenaries sitting there.

"Both of you," he said, "come back to my cabin. I need to talk to you."

The two men stood up, wearing surprised expressions, and followed him back into his private cabin. Once there, Volkov, usually gruff, offered them seats and asked if they were comfortable. Feeling somewhat confused, Yuri and Sergei nodded, indicating that they were perfectly happy. Sensing that the time was right, Volkov decided to make his case to the two men. With a quick glance towards the front cabin, he leaned forward in his seat, resting his elbows on his knees before speaking.

"Now, Yuri and Sergei," he said, "I want you to listen to me very carefully. You don't know the purpose of our visit to Seychelles, and you have no idea why you were instructed to dive down to that ship. Well, I'd like to inform you that the ship is of great importance. So much importance that the state decided to send us here to check if it was real or not."

Intrigued, Yuri and Sergei leaned forward, listening intently to their boss.

"Now, listen here," he continued. "That ship, the Pearl of Alexandria, went missing soon after the Second World War. It has been lost since then and almost completely forgotten. That was until one of our Russian ships picked up an anomaly on the ocean floor, matching the size and shape of the said ship. Now, gentlemen, I have to tell you that the ship was carrying 8 tons of pure gold. In fact, the crate that you photographed, the one that you tried to lift, is one of them. I'm sure I don't have to tell you how much this gold is worth but let me just say it's around 360 million United States dollars. Now, gentlemen, as I'm sure you can tell, my health is not so good these days, and I am considering retiring from the FSB. But what I want to talk to you about, in private, is that gold. No one in the world knows it's there, except the three of us and the director at the FSB. What I am suggesting is that nothing is stopping us from returning there and removing one of those crates. If we were to do so, it would never be known, and we would all become very, very rich men. Of course, the state will launch a salvage operation at some stage, but it will take at least 6 months, perhaps even longer, to arrange and commence. What I am proposing is that the three of us form an alliance, a business venture of sorts. I will apply for early retirement on the grounds of my ill health. The two of you will simply leave the Wagner group and disappear. Now, gentlemen, I have the money and the resources to fund a salvage operation. I'm not suggesting we attempt to remove all the crates, of which there are 8 in total. No, that would be greedy you see? What I am suggesting is that we return before the state can get here and remove just one crate. I have done the calculations, and I estimate that the gold in one crate alone will be worth close to 60 million US dollars. Gentlemen, I'm sure I don't have to tell you, but that is a fortune, unlike anything you will ever hope to see in your lives. This is within our reach. We can be back here within a month, 6 weeks at the most. It will be a simple salvage operation to remove one of those crates. Think about it. No one will be the wiser. We will simply disappear with our money and never be seen again."

Yuri and Sergei's faces were transfixed with concentration. It was abundantly clear that the figures Volkov had mentioned had sparked their curiosity.

Their boss had been right; it was a mind-boggling amount of money, a figure unlike anything they would ever see. Enough to set each of them up for life anywhere in the world. The two men sat there, fully absorbed in their thoughts, but it was Yuri who spoke first.

"And there would be no risk of us being discovered?" he asked.

"None at all," said Maxim. "As I mentioned, the state will take at least 6 months to arrange a salvage operation of that scale. It might even take a year before they arrive. You two have no ties and are free to walk away at any time. As for myself, I have a 'get out of jail' card at my disposal. My health has not been good for some time now, and with a simple letter from my doctor, I am confident I will be granted the early retirement that I need and deserve. Once that is done, there is nothing stopping us from returning here. As I said, I have the money and the resources to fund an operation to retrieve just one of those crates. We would not be competed against by the state or anything that I know of. They will arrive in due course and simply retrieve the crates, completely oblivious to the fact that we have beaten them to it. Are you seeing this picture clearly, gentlemen? This is too good to be true!"

Yuri turned in his seat and briefly stared at Sergei before speaking.

"Well, sir," he said, "I cannot speak for Sergei, but I will tell you now that you can count me in. There will never be another chance like this, and it seems almost too easy. Yes, boss, I am 100% in with this plan."

Less than 10 seconds of contemplation passed before Sergei spoke.

"Both of us are due some leave when we return to Moscow," he said. "Give us the instructions on where to go, and we will be there. I will join you on this mission, and I'm very happy to do so."

CHAPTER FIFTY-EIGHT

I regained consciousness sometime before dawn and in the darkness, I accepted that I was going to die out there. I contemplated simply letting my body fall off the slab of fibreglass and drift away, thinking that at least my death would be quicker. These thoughts ran through my mind for a good hour until something deep inside me told me not to give up. I allowed myself to slip back into a state of semi-consciousness where my fears bothered me less, and my burning thirst was forgotten. I have no idea how long it was after that when I was wakened by the rising sun.

After hours in darkness, the simple sight of the horizon turning pink behind me was one of the greatest blessings I had ever experienced. The sight gave me hope, even though my body was close to shutting down. The hope inside me grew and I began to plan a possible way out. The boat explosion had occurred 60 km east of the island. I had no idea in which direction I had drifted during the night, but I knew I had to try and swim for it. As long as I kept the rising sun behind me, I would be swimming towards the west, and there would be a chance, however small, that I would see land.

Before the sun had even broken the horizon, I dropped my fins into the water behind me and began kicking. Despite my completely exhausted body and fear of sharks, I kept the motion going, slowly kicking with my eyes closed, only opening them to check if I was still moving in the right direction. A few hours later, the heat of the day began, and it felt as if my entire body was lying in the coals of a blast furnace. The exposed skin on my ankles, hands, and the back of my neck burned fiercely in the sun.

But in my mind, there was nothing for it but to persevere and keep going. I have no idea how long it was, but several hours later, I opened my eyes to see the sun directly above me. By then, it felt like my body was being eaten alive by the saltwater, and the pain I felt was excruciating. Still, I kicked and kicked, gritting my teeth as I lay there roasting in the midday sun.

At that moment, I looked ahead of me in the direction I was swimming, and to my surprise, I saw a small green clump on the horizon. *Could it be the island? Could it really be La Digue, or was I seeing things?* It took several minutes to convince myself that this was no dream and that what I was seeing in the distance was indeed La Digue Island. The sight of it was a tonic for my soul, and instantly I knew there was hope. However, I had no idea how far away I was from the island. All I knew was that I had to make it, no matter what. But the fact was, I had been going for well over 24 hours by that stage, and I was exhausted and dangerously dehydrated.

It was then that I began to feel my sanity slipping, and my brain filled with erratic thoughts. As much as I tried to fight them, I found myself slipping into some strange kind of daydream again and again. At one stage, I almost fell off the slab of fibreglass but quickly righted myself, splashed my face with water, and continued. With my tongue twice its usual size and my lips sore and blistered, I pressed on in the blazing heat of the day.

By then, every inch of my skin was wrinkly and flaking, and once again, I felt like I was being eaten alive by the saltwater. My vision became blurred, and even the sound of the lapping water around me began to echo in my ears. I have no idea how long it was after that, but I heard a sound that I recognized behind me. There was no mistaking the whirring sound of a helicopter. Instantly, I turned my body to look up and was blinded by the sun but approaching me from the east was a helicopter. There was no mistaking it, and I knew I was not hallucinating.

However, the altitude of the aircraft was such that I doubted whether it would see me in the middle of the vast blue expanse of the Indian Ocean. But I knew I had to try and signal it using something reflective. I pulled my scuba tank towards me and frantically attempted to use the dial of my watch and my regulator to flash sunlight at the pilot. Suddenly, a spring of hope welled up deep inside me as I thought that I might just escape with my life. But the helicopter continued flying along its path and never slowed down once. I watched it pass overhead and continue onwards towards the island as a terrible sense of gloom and hopelessness descended over me once again. *They're not looking for you, Green. They have no idea you are here. They don't know there was an explosion. If that was a search party, they wouldn't have been travelling in one direction and so quickly. That was a standard commercial flight and nothing to do with a search and rescue mission.*

Feeling completely defeated, I turned back onto my stomach and resumed the dreadful drudgery of kicking towards the distant island. I have no idea how long it was after that when I lifted my head once again and stared towards the island. To my surprise, the land had doubled in size, and I realized that I was making real progress.

I assumed that the current must have been helping me, and this spurred me on further to continue. I began pushing harder and harder, kicking the fins in an effort to reduce the space between myself and the island.

Unbeknownst to me, my fins were chafing my ankles, and they were now bleeding profusely into the water. I was aware that sharks can smell one drop of blood in one million drops of seawater, but as I had no idea that I was bleeding, I continued kicking. It was about 20 minutes later that I saw the ugly triangular fin to my left. At first, I thought it was some kind of toy, perhaps a piece of plastic that had been floating in the water. But I soon realized it was a shark, and a large one at that. My heart sank at the sight of the hideous creature. How could I be tormented two days in a row by these vile beasts?

It was only then that I glanced behind me and saw the blood running down my wetsuit. Once again, I was unable to kick, unable to swim, and I was now at the mercy of the currents. The sharks that surrounded me disappeared thankfully, and I lay there in a state of complete exhaustion and desperation, clinging to the side of the board. The hardest part of it all was knowing that the sharks were nearby and any attempt I made to swim would bring them back in numbers. I lay there once again and slipped into a semi-comatose state.

Sometime later in the late afternoon, I heard the crashing of waves. By that stage, I had been adrift in the ocean for 29 hours solid, and there was very little strength left in me. I lifted my head and slowly opened my eyes, only to see yet another horror in front of me. There was no sandy beach for me to gently float up to. The current had pulled me towards the north side of the island, where the waves crashed into massive jagged rocks. Razor-sharp, black, and glistening, they rose out of the water like the teeth of some giant beast. The water slammed repeatedly into these rocks, and the spray rose up into the air like rooster tails.

At that moment, I could do nothing but laugh as I resigned myself to my fate. Fighting the current would only attract the sharks, and going with the flow would only result in a very painful and certain death.

CHAPTER FIFTY-NINE

Maxim Volkov wore a sly half smile as he shovelled pig feed into the heated pen in the barn of his small farmyard, located at the rear of his modest residence in Moscow. Outside, the temperatures remained dangerously cold, prompting him to transfer his livestock of pigs, chickens, and goats into the barn for the long, dark winter months. The farmyard served as a source of solace and escape from the pressures of work and the outside world. Maxim cherished this space, where he could tend to his beloved animals and find respite from his wife, Ulyanka's constant teasing and prodding.

Five days ago, Maxim had submitted his resignation letter to the FSB, citing serious health issues. This marked the end of his lifelong career with the agency. The news of the missing ship, The Pearl of Alexandria, being found had softened the blow to some extent. While there were condolences and promises of bonuses, Maxim knew they would be insignificant in the grand scheme of things. With a letter from his personal doctor excusing him from all duties, he had spent the following day packing up his luxurious office and moving its contents back home.

However, his resignation had not pleased Ulyanka at all. Her immediate reaction was one of disappointment, ridicule, and scorn. She repeatedly accused him of weakness and berated him every day from the time he told her of his resignation. Yet, the thought of returning to Seychelles with the two men from Wagner to retrieve one of the steel crates consumed Maxim's mind. The prospect of a massive sum of money awaited him—an elusive windfall he believed he deserved as a reward for his years of hard work and dedication. The fact that no one would discover their secret made it all the sweeter.

During the past week, he had made a point of staying out of Ulyanka's way. He often drove out in the early morning, working on his mobile and laptop to make the necessary arrangements with Yuri and Sergei. While he would return home most afternoons, he sought solitude in the farmyard, far away from his nagging wife. He envisioned a future where Ulyanka would find herself alone, living in a one-bedroom flat in Moscow's south side. *The fucking bitch!* he thought. *She deserves every minute of loneliness she will have from then on. And she can cook as much of her disgusting borscht as she pleases. Fat bitch!*

Maxim had also frequented his favourite fast-food joints, which triggered his irritable bowel syndrome (IBS) symptoms once again.

Yet, nothing could dampen his excitement for the future—a stash of money so immense that he would never have to worry about it again. He even contemplated purchasing a new motor yacht, a big and expensive one at that. While he already had his beloved cruiser moored in the port of Zadar, Croatia, the substantial amount of cash he was soon to acquire would allow him to broaden his horizons. *Yes, life is good right now*, he thought as he shovelled another load of feed into the pen. He closed the inner section of the stable doors, satisfied with his work in the barn and made his way back to the main doors. As he walked into the bitterly cold air, he braced himself, knowing that soon the cold would be a thing of the past and he would spend his golden years in warmer climes. However, just as he was about to hang the shovel on the rack with the other tools, he heard the icy crunch of footsteps from outside. He paused, and to his surprise, saw his wife, Ulyanka, enter the barn.

Ulyanka, dressed in her heavy winter coat, thick leggings, and boots, approached with her gloved hands on her hips, staring at him with a mixture of contempt and anger. Her rosy, chubby cheeks and button-like nose seemed lost amidst the expanse of her face. She unleashed her shrill voice upon him.

"Always in here with these filthy animals! Either at work or in here, hiding away from the world. Is that what you intend to do for the rest of your miserable life, Maxim?"

He, maintaining his composure, responded quietly. "The animals must be fed, my dear, especially in winter."

Unyielding, Ulyanka interrupted him. "Shut up, Maxim!"

Her face grew increasingly red with each passing second.

"While all of your colleagues rose through the ranks and actually achieved something, this will be you! Poor Maxim, feeding his chickens and waiting to die! You always were a useless husband. How on earth did I end up like this? My mother was right about you!"

With a shake of her head, Ulyanka's cheeks wobbled, displaying her deep-seated contempt. Without another word, she turned and began walking back up the frosted path toward the house. Maxim's grip on the shovel tightened as he watched her progress up the path. Years of torment and suffering at her hands bubbled up within him like a boiling cauldron. His peripheral vision blurred with a red mist as he lifted the heavy implement, holding it behind his back. Without uttering a single word, he swung it down with all his might, the blade striking the back of Ulyanka's head. The force of the blow sent painful shudders up Maxim's arms, the sound echoing like a sombre church bell.

Silently, Ulyanka collapsed, her face hitting the icy dirt of the pathway. Maxim stood there, staring down at his wife's lifeless body. Slowly and calmly, he circled the rotund figure until he stood parallel to her fallen head. With a focused determination, he lifted the shovel high above his own head, repeatedly striking Ulyanka's skull. The repeated jarring impacts sent no discomfort through his arms as he continued his merciless assault. It was a full minute later when Volkov dropped to his knees, panting, his face flushed and glistening with sweat.

The back of Ulyanka's head had become a gruesome mess of brain matter, blood, and shattered bone. Yet, Maxim gazed at his work with a sly half-smile. *The bitch is dead*, he thought. *The bitch is finally dead!*

CHAPTER SIXTY

I lay there, laughing while staring at the mass of jagged rocks that lined the coast. The waves crashed into them, leaving creamy foam-topped swirls all around. By then, my skin was so soft from the constant exposure to seawater that it would take very little to rip through. I knew then that my only option would be to try to turn around and swim in search of a better landing spot. *Perhaps there's a beach or stretch of sand nearby*. But I knew that in searching for this, I would be exposing my bloodied ankles to the water and the sharks that prowled these waters. However, I was weaker than ever, and it was an effort to simply lift my head, let alone swim away and risk it all once again. In a state of complete exhaustion, I dropped my head and closed my eyes. *Just a few moments to rest, Green. Then you get going. You have to get out of this fucking nightmare!* But it was only then that I heard the noise. There was no mistaking the sound of a small outboard engine. Its revs rose and fell as it powered through the crashing waves. With a smidgen of hope, I lifted my head and looked to my left. What I saw then lifted my spirits, and I knew there was a good chance I would survive. Bobbing up and down and fighting the incoming waves was a tatty old wooden fishing boat. There were two figures on board, an old man and a younger teenager. Both were dressed in tattered, grubby shirts and were obviously making their way out for a day's fishing. I raised my left arm and shouted at the top of my voice. But by then, all that came out was a feeble croak. My tongue was stuck to the roof of my mouth and swollen to twice its usual size. Again and again, I waved and yelled until I saw the older man turn, and his eyes met my own. *He's seen me! They've fucking seen me! Thank God!* I slumped back on the fibreglass slab and watched as they turned the boat and raced towards me in the surf. The next thing I knew was the feeling of hands. Strong hands that gripped me from under each arm and pulled me from the water and over the gunwale of the tiny boat. I slumped in the ribbed bottom of the boat and was immediately aware of the pungent stench of fish. With my open eyes staring into the blazing sun, the younger man hauled my aqualung and buoyancy regulator into the boat and placed it beside me. I could hear the men talking; it sounded like French, but I knew then that these were simple Seychellois fishermen, and they were speaking Creole. Clearly aware that I was in bad shape, the older man made his way back to the motor while the younger man handed me a large plastic bottle of water. It took some effort to bring it to my mouth, but it was deliciously wet, and it will forever be the best-tasting water I have ever drunk. I remember taking six mouthfuls of the stuff, and it was as if I could feel it penetrating my dried cells and giving life immediately. Then, all of a sudden, I was surrounded by a wave of darkness and I lapsed into unconsciousness where I lay.

CHAPTER SIXTY-ONE

Maxim Volkov stood frozen, panting heavily as he gazed down at the lifeless body of his wife. Reality set in slowly, and his eyes widened as he blinked repeatedly, surveying the scene around him. Fortunately, his smallholding provided enough seclusion to ensure there were no witnesses to the savage attack that had just occurred. Gradually, Maxim began to piece together the events that had led him to this point. There had been no control whatsoever, and the entire incident had unfolded purely on impulse. He felt no pity or remorse for the brutal murder, but rather a profound sense of relief and the belief that justice had finally been served. No longer would he be ridiculed and mocked by the wretched Ulyanka. *No, she had found her place in a far better realm. And so have I.* However, a new problem emerged—what to do with the body?

At that moment, an idea formed in his mind, and he set about executing it immediately. Abandoning the shovel smeared with blood and brains, he walked slowly around until he reached Ulyanka's feet. Wasting no time, he grasped her boots and lifted her feet, surprised by the sheer dead weight of her lifeless body as he dragged her into the barn. It had been a long time since he had any physical contact with his wife, but the weight reminded him of their past encounters. After a few arduous minutes, he finally managed to pull her up and onto the sloped concrete floor near the pig pen.

At the centre of this sloping floor lay a drain hole running to a septic tank and soakaway. This mechanism was used when clearing out the pig pen, ensuring efficient removal of swill and excrement with a concentrated jet of water from a nearby hosepipe. Ulyanka's face, with the back of her head smashed in, was now visible, still adorned with the contemptuous expression she wore when she left the barn. This only intensified Maxim's determination to complete the task at hand.

Slowly and methodically, he began to undress his deceased wife. He started with her boots and continued with her heavy woollen leggings. Next, he removed her underwear, disturbed to find that in death she had involuntarily emptied her bowels. Nevertheless, it did not deter him, and he proceeded to remove each piece of clothing until her body lay completely naked on the cold concrete floor.

Maxim retraced his steps to the tool rack near the entrance, retrieving a set of keys from his pocket. Approaching a steel cupboard to the left of the tool rack, he unlocked it to reveal an array of power tools, including a Ryobi chainsaw. This particular tool had only been used for cutting firewood once a year before winter. He had never anticipated employing it for the purpose of dismembering his wife's body. Placing the chainsaw on a nearby wooden bench, he refuelled it from a red plastic container. Satisfied with its functionality after priming and a couple of pulls on the cord, Maxim, wearing a half-smile, turned around and walked back to his wife's lifeless form.

Within a mere ten minutes, he had completed the gruesome task, reducing Ulyanka Volkov's body to seventeen separate pieces, now covered in blood and splattered with bone fragments. He began lifting each severed body part and throwing them into the nearby pig pen. These Northern Siberian pigs, a crossbreed of short-eared Siberian pigs and large White Boars, were bred for their dense bristle covering and undercoat, designed to withstand the extreme climate of northern Siberia. These animals would consume anything, and he knew well that by morning, there would be no trace left of his detested wife.

As the sky darkened outside the barn, the work continued under the eerie yellow light of exposed bulbs hanging from the roof of the dilapidated structure. The cacophony of grunts, snuffles, squeals, and screams emanating from the pig pen indicated the animals' strange enjoyment of this new, unusual meal. When the last body part had been hurled into the pen, Maxim calmly crossed over to the coiled-up hosepipe and pulled a length of it from the spool. He released the valve and a concentrated jet of pressurized water blasted from the nozzle. Standing there calmly, he sprayed the concrete floor, watching as the pools of blood, bone, and fat were washed away, disappearing forever down the drain hole. With the task complete, he rolled up the hosepipe and returned to the pig pen, closing the upper half of the stable door once more.

Finally, Maxim Volkov gathered his wife's clothing and walked over to the wood-fired boiler at the far end of the barn. The old steel door emitted a loud clank as he opened it, revealing red-hot embers and burning coals brightly glowing inside. Before tossing the gathered clothes into the fire, he brought them to his nose, inhaling one last scent of the woman he had once called his wife. He discarded the clothes into the coal chamber, ending with the boots. Standing upright, he calmly made his way back to the barn door, closed it behind him, and embarked on the short walk back to the house.

CHAPTER SIXTY-TWO

I heard the sand crunching under the wooden hull of the small boat, and I was aware of the sun shining directly on to my closed eyes, along with the sound of male and female voices around me, all speaking Creole. I opened my eyes as I felt strong hands lift me from the boat and stand me up in ankle-deep water. It appeared that I had arrived at a small fishing village on the north coast of the sparsely populated island. Nestled under the palm trees beyond the beach were a group of rudimentary dwellings made from mud bricks under thatch. The two men on either side of me helped me as I stumbled towards them. The thought of getting into the shade was something I had not imagined would happen to me again, so it was a blessed relief to feel the green grass under my bare feet as I was led into the darkness of one of the small buildings. Once there, I was laid down on a bed of reeds and allowed to be still for a while.

By then, the water I had consumed had taken its miraculous effect, and I could feel the strength coming back into my body. The soft voices of the islanders cooed and purred all around, and I opened my eyes to see a woman handing me yet another bottle of water. This time it was chilled, and I cannot explain how wonderful it was to drink from that bottle. In my mind, I saw the swirling nightmare of the sharks and the luminous plankton, but I had made it to land in one piece and would live to see another day. It was around 10 minutes later when I stood up and began removing my wetsuit, which was still damp and clinging to my skin. It took some effort, and there was a fair amount of pain on the sunburnt areas of my skin, but eventually, I was free of the clinging neoprene and I lay back down on the reed bed, exhausted.

Soon after, a young man arrived who spoke fluent English. He introduced himself as Edward, the son of the old man who had pulled me from the surf. He spoke calmly and softly, mostly curious about how I had ended up where I was. I told him there had been a boating accident and nothing more. He pressed me further, asking how long I had been out at sea and if there was anyone else missing. I knew that telling him the truth would involve the police, so I lied and told him I had been the only person aboard the boat.

"You are very lucky, sir," said Edward.

"I know," I replied, "I know..."

My strength returned incrementally over the next hour and eventually, one of the ladies came through with a plate of sliced fruit. Now sitting upright, I proceeded to munch my way through the pile of mangoes, pineapple, papaya, and starfruit. The food only served to strengthen me further, and with my skin dry, Edward handed me a tattered cotton shirt to wear along with my shorts. It was an hour later when I finally felt strong enough to stand up, and I was led to a common area near the hut where I sat in the shade and drank yet more water. It appeared I had become somewhat of a novelty, as there were by then several children from nearby villages who had arrived to see the strange white man who had been pulled from the sea.

The scene in which I had found myself could not have been more idyllic, and had it not been for the circumstances, I could have stayed there forever. But the events that had led me to that point were impossible to put out of my mind, and I knew I needed to head back to the main island, Mahe, urgently. What had happened had been no accident, of that I was sure, and I needed to get back to Chris's house to check on Joe. Using young Edward as an interpreter, I spoke at length with the elder of the men, the one who had rescued me. Being the head of the village, he had the authority to make any important decisions. I told him I needed to get back to Mahe that day, an idea that he scoffed at first. But after some explanation that I had to inform my friends and family that I was okay, it seemed to gain some credence. There was a ferry leaving La Digue Island at 3:00 pm. that afternoon, which would arrive at Mahe at 5:00 pm. after making a stop at Praslin Island. I told Edward that I had to make that ferry no matter what.

But then it struck me that I had nothing to offer these simple islanders. Not a cent on me and not even a pair of shoes. However, I realized I could offer them the diving equipment. The mask, fins, aqualung, and regulator would suffice. At first, the old man refused and offered to give me the fare, but I insisted that it was the least I could do. The equipment would come in useful to the villagers. All I needed was the fare for the ferry, and I would take care of myself after that. One of the older women, a huge figure in an orange sarong, brought me a worn-out pair of rubber sandals to put on my sunburnt and wrinkled feet. At least that way, I would not look like a madman, barefoot and threadbare.

It was 1:30 pm. when finally the deal was made, and I was led out to a waiting ox-cart. Unlike the main islands of Mahe and Praslin, where cars were common, there were very few vehicles on La Digue, the main modes of transport being ox-carts and bicycles. Edward had arranged an umbrella to shield me from the blazing afternoon sun, something I would be eternally grateful for. Finally, with my strength at around 80%, I waved goodbye to my saviours and sat in the back of the wagon as it trundled off through the lush tropical jungle towards the south of the island and the port.

It was an hour later when we finally arrived, and I had spent most of that time sleeping on a pile of coconut husks. The tiny port was one of the most beautiful I had ever seen, nestled in a bay of perfectly blue water, surrounded by low hills of thick green vegetation. There was a serene sense of calm about the place, and even the pleasure boats seemed to relax in their moorings, only bobbing or moving occasionally when the breeze picked up. The ferry turned out to be a fairly modern vessel, and I paid for my ticket at a small rusted booth. The money I had been given by the old man was enough for the fare to the main island and perhaps enough to get a taxi up to Chris's house in the mountains. With my strength building by the minute, I did my best to put the horror of the past 34 hours out of my mind and focused on the task at hand. *This is a very serious situation, Green. What happened was no accident, and those men were responsible for murder. Make no mistake, they were behind it all. There is something on that sunken ship that is very important to them, important enough for them to want to kill. Fucking bastards!*

I settled down on a vinyl-covered seat near the wheelhouse of the ferry and sat there thinking as we made our way out of the port and southwest towards Praslin Island. The ocean was calm, and the passengers on the ferry were relaxed and chatty. I did get a few strange looks with my tatty attire and shell-shocked appearance, but everyone on board seemed cheerful and focused on their own business. It took less than an hour to reach the port at Praslin, and the stop lasted only 15 minutes before we set sail for Mahe. It came as a huge relief to see the towering peaks of the main island, something that until recently, I doubted I would ever see again. I got up and began pacing the deck, itching to get off the boat and make my way up to Chris's house. There was nothing else I could think of at that time, and I attributed this to my brain still being a bit fried from the horror I had just experienced.

As the sun was setting, the tyres of the battered old car I had hired crunched on the stones of Chris Fonseca's driveway, and I hurriedly handed the driver the cash. I watched as he drove away and rushed to the back door of the house. Racing through the hallway, I noticed with relief that there appeared to be nothing out of the ordinary—no disturbed furniture or smashed windows. Then, as I reached the sunken lounge facing the terrace, I saw Joe. He sat alone in his wheelchair on the decking, taking in the sunset and looking out to sea. Immediately, I felt a wave of relief, and I slowed down to a walk as I prepared what I would tell him. He appeared to be asleep, with his head to one side, and his right arm was outstretched exactly as it had been when I first laid eyes on him in Faro, Portugal.

"Joe..." I said as I approached him, "Joe, wake up!"

Joe Fonseca didn't move or respond at all. It was only when I walked around the front of him and looked at his face that I saw the neat bullet hole in the centre of his forehead. A stream of blackened, dried blood ran down the left side of his face, into his beard and onto the new shirt I had bought him only a few days ago. Suddenly, I was filled with immense sadness and a sense of guilt. I had brought him here and it was I, by my own stupid curiosity and propensity for finding danger, who had caused

his murder. Not only Joe, but his brother and Jimmy as well. Suddenly, my legs felt weak, and I dropped to my knees, holding his cold, dead hand in my own as tears welled up in my eyes.

"No, no, no, no..." I said quietly, in a shaking voice. "I'm so sorry, Joe. You didn't deserve this, my friend. None of you deserved this..."

I turned my head and stared out, unseeing, as the giant orb of the setting sun melted into the Indian Ocean. A warm breeze blew in and the fronds of the nearby palm trees rustled softly. The sea had turned a deep metallic orange, reflecting the wispy clouds that hung in the rapidly darkening sky. There was only one thing that was certain in my mind at that moment—the men responsible for this would pay. And it would not be in roubles or US dollars. They would pay with the only currency I would accept. They would pay with their lives...

CHAPTER SIXTY-THREE

I opened the door to my flat and stepped into the hallway. Although the events of the past 72 hours had been a complete blur, I was feeling somewhat rested from the sleep I had managed to get on the flight from Nairobi. After discovering Joe's body on the deck, I quickly attempted to remove any trace of my presence by cleaning all surfaces in my room and throughout the house. It pained me greatly to leave my friend as I had found him and not try to protect his dignity, but I knew that doing so would confuse any police investigation that would follow.

I found a late evening flight from Mahe Island to Nairobi and bought a connecting trip to London Heathrow afterwards. I quickly gathered up my belongings and called the same taxi driver who had brought me there from the harbour. I knew his old cab wasn't part of any computerized system, and although I could have taken one of Chris Fonseca's vehicles, I decided that doing so would hamper and confuse any investigation. Since Chris and Jimmy were nowhere to be seen, the fact that there was only one body at the house would likely trigger a lengthy investigation. I wasn't prepared to be part of that.

One thing I knew for certain was that the men were Wagner mercenaries from Russia and had likely arrived on the island using fake documents. The fact that they had used Chris's boat meant that their original vessel must have been unavailable. Another undeniable fact was that whatever was on The Pearl of Alexandria was valuable and important enough for them to murder four innocent people, or at least attempt to. It was only by the skin of my teeth that I had survived, and there was no way I would let them go unpunished. *No fucking way!*

I spent the journey down the mountain to the airport lost in deep thought and paid for the ride with cash. It was only after checking in and clearing security that I made an anonymous call to the local police station, reporting a murder. I provided the address and hung up when asked for my name. Before hanging up, I made sure the police operator recorded the correct address. There was a small comfort in knowing that Joe's body would be treated with respect from then on.

During the 3-hour flight to Nairobi, I fell into a coma-like sleep, and the same happened during my London connection. I knew I needed to get straight to work, but I took a shower upon arriving home. The visions of the nightmare I had endured at sea were still burned into my mind, and my skin was badly burned. The shower helped me freshen up somewhat, and I ordered takeout food to be delivered before settling down for a long night of searching.

Finally, I sat down with a pot of coffee percolating on the stove and got to work. My primary asset was the group of photographs I had secretly taken of the men during the initial exploratory dive. Little did I know that I would be sitting in my London flat, studying these photographs and knowing that the three men pictured were responsible for so much violence and murder. I created a series of images for each of the men, some zoomed in and some at a normal distance. I was grateful for the clear day and the excellent resolution of my phone's camera, as the images were perfect and as clear as day. In the end, I had amassed over 50 photographs, which I stored and backed up on multiple devices.

Next, I spent a good hour researching the ship, The Pearl of Alexandria. It came as no surprise to find that it had gone missing soon after the Second World War, but what astonished me was the fact that it had been rumoured to be carrying a wanted Nazi fugitive named Rudolf Baumann. This man had escaped the Allied forces and simply disappeared, along with a massive stash of gold stolen from prisoners at the death camps of Auschwitz and Birkenau in Poland. The disappearance of the ship had become a legend in maritime circles, as had the fact that so much gold had gone with it. *Those fuckers were after the gold, Green. There's your answer! The estimated amount of gold on board the Egyptian ship was five tons—five tons of pure gold! No wonder they were prepared to murder for it!*

There were numerous black-and-white pictures of the vessel, from its construction in England to various ports around the world. It was astonishing to think that I had swum under the bows of that very ship just a few days prior—a ship that had been missing and unseen for so many years, carrying an extremely valuable cargo.

Next, I delved into research on the Wagner Group itself. Although I was aware of its existence, I knew very little about its workings and owners. It turned out there was a wealth of information online about the group. The Wagner Group, also known as PMC Wagner or simply Wagner, is a private military company based in Russia, known for its involvement in various military conflicts, including Syria, Ukraine, and numerous African states. It is often linked to Yevgeny Prigozhin, a Russian businessman with close ties to Russian President Vladimir Putin. The company has been accused of carrying out covert operations on behalf of the Russian government, including supporting separatist rebels in eastern Ukraine. However, the exact nature and extent of Wagner's activities, as well as its ties to the Russian government, remain uncertain and subject to speculation and controversy.

I read several pieces written about the group, spending a good hour doing so. After taking a break to eat dinner, I returned to my laptop to attempt a reverse Google search using the images I had taken on the boat. I hoped that Google would recognize one of the images and reveal a similar one along with a possible name. There was no doubt that the names the men had used when they booked the boat were fake. These men were professionals and wouldn't take the risk of using their real names. Sadly, the search yielded no results, and I sat there stumped and rapidly fading from exhaustion and frayed nerves.

There were thousands of images to go through, but frustratingly, most were either blurry or showed the men wearing bandanas or scarves to hide their identities. This was true in all the countries where the Wagner Group operated, regardless of the weather. Many of the African countries they operated in were hot and humid, yet in nearly all the images of these mercenaries, the men wore bandanas or scarves covering their lower faces. It was a simple yet highly effective method of concealment.

What became clear to me was the extent of their brutality. These men were soldiers of fortune, paid much more than those in the standard Russian military. Since they worked for a private army, there was no direct link to the Russian state, and any suggestion of such involvement would be met with denials. *Fucking Russians can be caught red-handed, and they'll still deny involvement.* Several recent incidents came to mind, including the Novichok attack in Salisbury. It was a blatant chemical attack that had taken place on British soil, and the attackers had been identified. Yet, as usual, there were denials and extradition orders were flatly refused.

This was the standard modus operandi of the Russian state, and it wouldn't be any different in this case.

Had I stayed in Seychelles, there would have been a drawn-out and frustrating police investigation that would eventually lead to a dead end. It would take weeks, if not months, before any official conclusion would be reached, by which time any trail the Russians had left would have gone as cold as a Moscow winter. *No, Green. No one is gonna be of any help to you here. It's all on you.* But one thing was certain: those responsible for killing Joe, Chris, and Jimmy would pay, and pay dearly. No matter how long it took me or how far I had to go, I would see to it.

It was midnight when my vision began to blur, and I found myself nodding off to sleep at my keyboard. Despite hours of work, I had come up with nothing. *You need to sleep now, Green. You are wasting your fucking time forcing yourself like this, and you could easily miss something crucial. Sleep now and start again tomorrow.* Feeling like a dried-out husk of my former self, completely defeated, I made my way to bed. As I lay there, the faces of the men I had photographed flickered in my vision until I fell deeply asleep.

CHAPTER SIXTY-FOUR

Maxim Volkov walked briskly into the departure lounge at Sheremetyevo International Airport, located 29 km. south of Moscow. With a spring in his step, he headed straight for the nearest bar, eager to indulge in a double shot of Stolichnaya vodka. It had been four days since he committed the gruesome act of murdering, dismembering, and disposing of his wife, Ulyanka. Surprisingly, Volkov felt a sense of elation he hadn't experienced in years.

Everything was falling into place according to his meticulous plans. The two Wagner men, Yuri and Sergei, had already left the private military company and vanished into neighbouring Ukraine. He had given them clear instructions on what to do next. They were to find a hotel in the capital city of Kyiv, blend into the surroundings, and await a phone call with further directions. Volkov had paid them generously, providing enough funds for a month's stay in Kyiv, but he intended to expedite matters far more quickly than that.

The freedom he now enjoyed since abruptly resigning from the FSB was exhilarating beyond his wildest dreams. No longer was he confined to his desk in the rigid corridors of the Lubyanka building. No longer was he a subservient tool of the director and his colleagues. Maxim Volkov had finally become his own man, taking charge of his own destiny and breaking free from the chains of his previous career and his wife.

In his mind, the world appeared as an open oyster, brimming with abundant opportunities, waiting for him to seize them. A few minutes later, the announcement came over the loudspeaker that the Aeroflot flight to Paris was boarding. Volkov retrieved his business class boarding card from his top pocket, a smile playing across his face and proceeded towards the gate. Soon, he would be soaring away from the desolate frozen wasteland of Russia.

There would be a two-hour layover at Charles de Gaulle Airport before catching the non-stop flight to Miami. Volkov relished the thought of basking in the sun, enjoying the sea, and encountering beautiful American women. *Yes*, he thought to himself, this new chapter of his life held promise and adventure.

CHAPTER SIXTY-FIVE

I came awake with a start at 7:00 am. and for a moment, I didn't know where I was. Slowly, it all came back to me, and I sat up and rubbed my eyes as I perched on the edge of the bed. The images of the three Russians were still spinning through my mind, and I recalled the disappointment I had felt the previous night at being unable to identify any of them. *You're fishing in a very big sea here, Green. How can you expect to identify these men when they are probably among thousands of Wagner people? No, you are missing something here. Think!* I stood up, feeling my bones ache from the ordeal I had suffered at sea. At least the cuts on my ankles were healing, and my sunburnt skin was feeling less fried.

I made my way into the kitchenette and boiled the kettle to make coffee. Lifting the steaming mug I took it over to the curtains and pulled them open. It was still dark outside, with drizzle and wind lashing the window. Below me, the streets were bathed in the grimy yellow glow of the streetlights. I opened one of the windows slightly and gasped as I felt the outside temperature. I stood there, staring out at the urban landscape below, as I smoked the first cigarette of the day and drank the coffee. *Okay, what do you know here, Green? Three men, all Russian. One a lot older than the others. In other words, two soldiers and one boss man. All of them on a mission to find a sunken ship supposedly filled with gold bars. Nazi gold at that. Men who were prepared to murder to keep the discovery secret. Russian agents for sure. But what if they are simply Wagner people? What the fuck difference does it make? Wagner Group or the Russian state. Same deal. Think about it.*

There's no way you're going to discover who the two younger men were. Most pictures of Wagner mercenaries have men with bandanas covering their faces. No, Green. You've been searching for the wrong men. It's the older of the three you should be concentrating on. There's more chance of finding a picture of that man than the younger ones. He's the boss, the man in charge. He is the one you should be looking for.

I poured a second cup of coffee and sat down at my laptop with renewed energy. My search was now focused on senior Wagner operatives and Russian state officials only. No longer would I waste my time attempting to randomly stumble across pictures of the younger men. The problem was there were literally thousands of websites and even more photographs to go through. *There has to be a better way to tackle this, Green. How about working from a time scale? That man was in his sixties easily. Might have been older, but he was pretty sick when you took the pictures. You really need to start looking at pictures from around 1985 onwards. Fuck! This is gonna be a huge task with no guarantee that anything will turn up.* But I had no choice and made a light breakfast before making myself comfortable for what would be an undetermined and possibly lengthy period.

Once again, there were thousands upon thousands of grainy images dating from the mid-'80s onwards. I had decided to study those of the Russian state during that period, and by 10:00 am. my eyes were red and stinging from staring at the screen. It was around then that I became increasingly depressed, and I had half convinced myself that this was a task far bigger than me. *After all, you are dealing with a behemoth here, Green. This is 35 years of the Russian state. This is not gonna be a walk in the fucking park!* Feeling dejected and angry, I walked into the bathroom and washed my face. But it was when I stood up and stared into the mirror that I saw the sunburnt and shell-shocked face that stared back at me. *This is what those cunts did to you, Green. And what of Joe, Chris, and Jimmy? They didn't fare quite as well. Don't fucking give up. Ever!* So it was with this new conviction that I returned to my desk and continued my trawl through the mountain of archived photographs of nameless faces from the Russian state.

Around 11:30 am. I stumbled across an image that rang a bell. By then, I was flicking through the pictures so fast that it was amazing I didn't miss it. The era I was searching for was around the time of the dissolution of the Soviet Union, and the photograph in question had been taken on the 12th of June 1991 on the occasion of the election of Boris Yeltsin as president. The image was in colour and appeared to be from a Russian newspaper of the time. There were seven men in the image, but it was the face of the man on the far right that caught my attention. I immediately saved the image and brought it up in a new window. But upon zooming in, the image became blurred and useless. Feeling frustrated, I zoomed out once again and sat there, staring at the screen. *The hair is the right colour, although the style is different, and there was more of it. Could it be?* I sat there blinking as I stared at the screen, my mind playing tricks on me all the while. *Look at the bone structure, Green! It's the very same man!* I sat there, comparing the images in two separate windows for a good five minutes, my mind a frenzy of doubt and adrenaline.

Eventually, I decided to take a break and walked over to the window to smoke. But it was soon after lighting up that I crushed out the cigarette and returned to the laptop. The old photograph appeared to be a newspaper cutting. Underneath it was a section of printed words in Russian. More importantly, there was a list of names of the men in the image. I zoomed into the image slightly to read the name, and two words appeared: 'Maxim Volkov.' I sat there, staring at the screen, feeling unsure of myself. The resemblance was there, but the photograph was grainy and of poor quality. Scratching at my chin, I opened a new window and typed in the name on Google. There were very few results, but I clicked on the first one, which was from yet another Russian newspaper article. This time, the photograph was a lot clearer, and a cold chill ran up my spine as I stared at the face of the killer. There was no doubt in my mind.

This was the man who had hired the boat in the Seychelles. This was the man who sent his men to the seabed the following day, and the very same man I had clandestinely photographed. Although younger, his was a very recognizable face, and there was absolutely no mistaking the bushy blonde hair and ruggedly handsome features.

"Well, look at you," I whispered to myself. "Look at you, you son of a bitch..."

The other sites only served to confirm that I had indeed found my man. Using Google Translate, I found that he was a fairly low-level member of the Russian government, and that was pretty much all I could find out. I needed help, and there was only one person who could possibly assist in this situation. It was a long shot, but as I stared at the various images of the man, I picked up my phone and scrolled through the contacts until I found the number I needed.

I had known Detective Inspector Tracey Jones of the Met. Police for over 10 years. We had met during an insurance case I was handling that involved a particularly violent fraudster who had been subsequently jailed. Tracey had ensured the yob had been caged for as long as possible. We had dated for a short spell after the case, but the relationship had foundered due to pressure of work from both sides and the fact that she had teenage kids. There had been no bad feelings, and we had stayed in touch ever since as friends. She had helped me out on numerous occasions with my work over the years, something I was extremely grateful for. I rang the number, and she answered within two rings.

"Jason Green," she said quietly in her husky voice. "To what do I owe this pleasure?"

"I need your help, Tracey," I said. "This is important." I heard her sigh deeply before she spoke.

"Tell me," she said. "I have a pen ready."

"I need you to run a name for me," I replied. "Maxim Volkov. A Russian..."

"Don't tell me you're involved with the Russian mob, Jason!" she said with a chuckle.

"No," I replied. "But as I said, this is very important. And urgent."

"No problem," she said. "I'll get back to you shortly..."

CHAPTER SIXTY-SIX

The wide beach stretched out to the horizon, its blindingly white sand contrasting with the bright blue waters of the ocean. Volkov gazed at the picturesque view from his sea-facing room on the 25th floor of the luxurious Four Seasons Hotel in Fort Lauderdale, Florida. Below, on the pool deck, several young women were sunbathing and frolicking in the pool, arousing more than just his curiosity. However, he knew he had to postpone his investigation as he had an afternoon appointment with a company in nearby Lauderdale By The Sea.

The ten-hour flight in business class had been smooth, and he had consciously avoided consuming excessive amounts of vodka. Consequently, he felt refreshed and energetic. The newfound freedom he was experiencing since resigning from the FSB had been a revelation. It amazed him how naturally he adapted to this new phase of life, although it was also accompanied by the very welcome death of his wife. The afternoon sun pleasantly warmed his skin, prompting him to retreat into the luxurious comfort of his carpeted suite.

Arranging his visa had been a straightforward process, and it appeared that he was welcomed in the USA without any complications. There were no probing questions at the airport; he simply walked in with his luggage and credit card, ready for new experiences. Yuri and Sergei had kept in touch, following his instructions diligently. Once he concluded his business in Florida, he would reunite with the two former Wagner men and proceed with their project. Life was unfolding favourably and each day seemed better than the last.

No one had inquired about Ulyanka's whereabouts. Volkov dismissed any concerns about her absence, thinking that nobody would miss that woman. After all, she had never had any friends. Her absence was not something he worried about—she was gone and gone forever. His stomach had been behaving well lately, and since his resignation, he felt rejuvenated, as if he had shed ten years of age. The dark days of commuting to and from the imposing Lubyanka building in frozen Moscow were behind him. The future appeared bright and promising.

With a spring in his step, Volkov dressed in pastel cottons and left his suite, taking the elevator down to the exquisitely appointed reception area. As promised, his taxi waited outside and feeling like a millionaire, he strode out and settled into the air-conditioned comfort of the back seat. The driver, a middle-aged woman, greeted him with a New York accent.

"Good afternoon, sir," she said. "Where are we headed today?"

"I would like to visit a company called Alpha Marine," Maxim replied, glancing at his watch. "I believe they are located in Lauderdale By The Sea..."

CHAPTER SIXTY-SEVEN

" Jason, what the hell are you up to?" said Tracey Jones, her voice raised in alarm.

"That was quick," I said. "What do you mean?"

It had only been 10 minutes since I had called her asking for assistance with the name Maxim Volkov and she had clearly obtained some kind of result. I stood up from my desk and walked to the window to hear her out.

"This Volkov character is a bad egg, Jason," she said. "He recently retired from the Kremlin! What on earth are you doing that this man is of interest to you?"

I took a moment to think through my reply. The news that Volkov was linked to the Russian state came as no surprise, but I needed to be careful about what I said to Tracey, given that she was an active Met. Police officer.

"He's one of the names I'm checking up on in relation to an old fraud case," I said. "I know he's Russian, and that's about it."

"Jesus, Jason," she replied. "As soon as I typed it into the Interpol system, a number of red flags appeared. I got the fright of my life!"

"I'm sorry," I said quietly. "Rest assured, everything is fine with me. I'm not in any danger. What else can you tell me?"

"Well," she said, her voice somewhat calmer. "According to my database, this guy has recently retired after a lifetime's work for the FSB. That's the former KGB to you and me. It seems he was a fairly low-level operator, but there are suspected links to the Wagner Group. Have you heard about them?"

"Yeah, I think so..." I lied. "Mercenaries, right?"

"Correct," she said, "and they're a bloody nasty bunch!"

"You mentioned he recently retired?" I asked.

"That's right. Just days ago. If it hadn't been for that, there would have been questions to answer. You missed this by just days!"

"I'm sorry for raising red flags on your systems, Tracey," I said quietly. "Any chance you can keep me updated on his movements?"

There was a deep sigh on the other end of the line before she spoke again.

"His name will remain in our systems for another 10 years. The fact that he's now formally retired means I can do that for you, although I'm still feeling pretty uneasy about it, I can tell you!"

"Thank you, Tracey," I said. "As I mentioned, it's very important to me."

"Well," she said. "Your Maxim Volkov is currently enjoying some sunshine in Florida. He's checked in at the Four Seasons Hotel in Fort Lauderdale. It's costing him a fortune as well. Maybe I should have pursued a career with the FSB!"

"Can you monitor his movements going forward?" I asked.

"For now, yes, as long as he's out of Russia and keeps a low profile," she replied. "We have hundreds of current and former FSB personnel on our systems. Please don't ask me to search for anyone else. I don't need any questions being asked!"

"I won't, I promise," I said. "And thank you, Tracey. You're a star..."

CHAPTER SIXTY-EIGHT

The boatyard at Alpha Marine was unlike anything Maxim Volkov had ever seen. Spanning 25 sprawling acres, the state-of-the-art facility boasted nearly 300,000 square feet of covered manufacturing space. It was a place where dreams came to life. For many years, Alpha Marine had been renowned for producing the finest ocean-going motor yachts, catering to the world's elite, including well-known Russian oligarchs. Intrigued by this reputation, Maxim decided to visit the boatyard and express his interest in purchasing one of these extraordinary vessels. The young sales manager at Alpha Marine was more than willing to give him a tour of their vast facility and showcase the meticulous craftsmanship behind these bespoke creations. These massive luxury yachts were tailored to the exact specifications of their multimillionaire clients, leaving no desire unmet. Maxim found himself envisioning a life among the oligarchs he had long admired, indulging in the finest private boats in the world. Although he was spending his money in his mind before acquiring it, it hardly mattered to him. He revelled in the freedom he now possessed and eagerly explored the exquisite vessels, already imagining sailing into the Croatian port of Zadar and retiring aboard his chosen model. Nevertheless, Maxim still held affection for his current boat; however, the impending windfall would allow him to upgrade and savour the benefits of retirement to the fullest. After an hour-long tour of the boatyard, Maxim felt relieved as he entered the plush offices of Alpha Marine and took a seat across from the young sales manager. The conversation continued, accompanied by offerings of champagne and vodka, which Maxim gladly accepted. Eventually, they agreed that he would make a deposit for the Arianne model in a few months, initiating the construction of his dream boat. Maxim would eagerly await the call informing him of its completion, at which point he would arrange for a crew to sail it from Florida across the Atlantic to the Adriatic, where it would find its permanent home. With a firm handshake and gratitude, Maxim graciously accepted a ride back to his hotel from the company and settled into the vehicle, brimming with excitement and anticipation. He was finally living the life he had always dreamed of, joining the ranks of the men he had long envied.

He was finally free. Now, there remained the small task of retrieving one of the steel trunks from the ocean bed off Seychelles—an endeavour he believed he could accomplish within a month at most. From then on, it would be smooth sailing. Quite literally. The drive back to the hotel took a mere 20 minutes, and Maxim strode through the reception area, heading straight for the pool deck. Hoping to find the ladies he had spotted earlier from his balcony, he was ready for another drink. He planned to luxuriate in the lavish hotel for two nights before meeting Yuri and Sergei, and he was determined to make the most of that time. *Yes!* he thought, a smile spreading across his face. *Life is good!*

CHAPTER SIXTY-NINE

I emerged from the tall-ceilinged and extremely plush Fort Lauderdale airport and into the tropical heat of the Florida afternoon. Upon hearing that Volkov was there, I booked a late flight on United Airlines to Newark with a connection down to Florida. The flights had been long and uncomfortable, which had done nothing for my mood. Desperate for a cigarette, I found the nearest exit, which happened to be under an overhead traffic bypass. I removed my jacket and hung it on the pull handle of my small bag, which I had placed next to a large palm tree. Pulling cigarettes from my pocket, I lit up as a police car passed me slowly. The words 'Broward County Sheriff's Office' were emblazoned across the door, and I looked away in case I was in a non-smoking area. Thankfully, the police vehicle continued without slowing, and I lit up unhindered. Feeling a little less rattled, I made my way back into the building and sat on the edge of a marble flowerbed to summon an Uber. The short time in the heat had brought back memories of my time in the Seychelles, and most of those were bad. It turned out my Uber was only minutes away, and the journey to the hotel I had booked would only take 15 minutes.

Once again, I stepped outside the building and walked up to the taxi rank, which was a hundred yards away. The car was waiting, and I climbed in once I had confirmed the driver's name. The young man was chatty and friendly, but I was in no mood to talk. I was there for a reason, and a very serious one at that. The Blue Banana was a 34-room boutique hotel located in the cosy town of Lauderdale-By-The-Sea, steps away from the beach. I thanked the driver and headed through the blinding sunlight straight to the reception to check in and make payment. The young brunette hotel manager was friendly and welcomed me with a wide smile as I walked in. The formalities took less than five minutes, and I made my way past the pool and up a single set of stairs to my room. The late afternoon heat was oppressive, and it was a relief to step into the air-conditioned cool of the room. Basic as it was, it would serve my purpose. Feeling exhausted, I flopped down on the bed and stared at the stucco ceiling. *You're less than 15 minutes from that murdering fucker, Green. Pat yourself on the back. You found him, and now he will pay for what he did.*

Fighting the urge to fall asleep, I forced myself to sit up and get to work on my laptop.

The Four Seasons Hotel was situated on the beach, roughly 10 km. from where I was. Tracey had only been able to tell me where he was and give me occasional updates on his spending while there. His movements and travel plans were unknown, and this was a worry for me. Just why he would travel to Florida was a complete mystery to me, as was the reason that he had just resigned from his position in the Kremlin. *Fuck knows why, Green. But make no mistake, his time on this earth is about to end.*

Feeling the need to smoke, I went out on the balcony to light up. The hotel was situated a street back from the beach, near the popular tourist pier. In front of me was a street lined with other guest houses and hotels. The fact that Lauderdale-By-The-Sea was a small town and did not allow high-rise developments gave the place a small-town feel. The late afternoon sunshine was bright, and I watched a number of choppers and muscle cars go past with suntanned occupants blasting music. The scene reminded me of the old TV programme Miami Vice. I checked my watch to see it had just gone 4.30 pm. *Time to get moving, Green.* I knew that the cover of darkness would be an advantage when it came to monitoring and watching the hotel where Volkov was staying. The big problem I had was that I had no idea of his plans. This was a serious worry, especially since I had travelled so far to get to him. Still, there was nothing for it, so I had a quick shower and summoned another Uber. It was time to find Maxim Volkov.

CHAPTER SEVENTY

"Vodka, a double," said Volkov to the bartender on the pool deck.

"Certainly, sir," came the reply from the young man behind the bar.

The bartender maintained his usual smile, but deep down, he was growing concerned about the well-being and behaviour of this particular guest. The Russian man had been sitting at the pool deck bar since sunset, and it was now 8:00 pm. Initially, he had been quiet and unassuming, but with each sip of vodka, his demeanour had grown increasingly belligerent and lecherous towards the women present. As a result, several guests had left the pool deck in frustration. The departure of female guests had further angered the man, who was now extremely drunk and becoming aggressive.

Apart from mumbling to himself in Russian, the man had started bitterly complaining about everything related to the hotel. The professionalism that the bartender had honed over the years was now being severely tested by this unruly guest, who was starting to cause a scene. A discreet phone call had been made to reception, and the hotel manager had been alerted. Two security personnel had been dispatched and positioned themselves discreetly behind a flowerbed to monitor the situation.

Drunk guests were not uncommon in the hotel, but most were simply humoured and gently guided back to their rooms, where their well-stocked minibars awaited them. However, it seemed that this man had an insatiable appetite for Stolichnaya vodka and was quickly downing double shots every few minutes. Several new guests had arrived only to be greeted by the loud and tense exchanges at the bar, prompting them to quickly find tables at a safe distance from the disturbances. Apologies were quietly extended to them, and they did their best to relax despite the rising tension.

At 8:35 pm. the first glass was smashed. The man had reached for the crystal tumbler, but his grip was off-centre, causing the glass to fall and shatter on the tiled floor. The man simply grunted and ordered another drink. The staff promptly rushed to clean up the mess, but the ambience of the famous pool deck had been irreparably disrupted for the evening.

It was 9:00 pm. when the manager finally deemed it necessary to approach the man and calmly inquire about his well-being. Well-versed in handling such situations, the manager struck up a conversation with the Russian, asking unrelated questions and trying to divert the conversation away from the uncomfortable circumstances. Wide-eyed staff members watched on discreetly as the manager attempted to defuse the situation, but the heavily intoxicated man seemed oblivious to the manager's efforts.

Using well-practised techniques, the manager managed to establish a first-name basis with the man, learning that his name was Maxim. It became evident that Maxim was upset that the women had left earlier in the day and that none were currently present. The manager explained that most guests were enjoying dinner, accounting for their absence. It was quietly suggested that Maxim retire to his room to freshen up and as an appeasement, an offer of a complimentary bottle of vodka was extended in the hopes that he would drink himself into a stupor and sleep it off throughout the night.

However, it seemed that the man had an inexhaustible appetite for alcohol. By 9:00 pm. Maxim was visibly dribbling down his pastel-coloured shirt. It was then that the manager gave a curt nod to the two waiting security staff members positioned behind the flowerbed, signalling them to intervene. The two burly men stepped forward, while the manager continued to address the Russian by his first name in a calm voice.

"Let's both go up to your room, Maxim," said the manager. "We'll have more vodka waiting and perhaps we can come back down later when there are more guests around."

The arrival of the hotel security people seemed to infuriate the Russian further, causing him to shout and spit in rage as he was firmly held by both arms. The manager maintained the conversation as Maxim Volkov was lifted from his seat and guided towards the exit and the elevators. Another guard stood at the ready, directing guests away from the commotion and ensuring a clear path to the elevators.

Eventually, they managed to get the large man into the elevator and pressed the button for the 25th floor. Swiftly, the manager discreetly removed the keycard from Maxim's pocket. By this point, the staggering amount of alcohol consumed had taken its toll, causing Maxim's head to slump forward and his feet to drag heavily on the carpet. The manager rushed forward to open the door of the luxury suite, wasting no time in ushering the two men inside the bedroom. They gently laid Maxim face down on the bed where he immediately began snoring.

The three men stood there, observing the sleeping guest.

"I want you to remove all alcohol from this room," the manager said quietly. "This one will have to leave in the morning. We can't have guests causing scenes like that. See to it, will you?"

The two guards set about removing the contents of the minibar, while the manager shook his head and made his way to the door.

"Fucking Russians," he muttered to himself as he exited the room.

CHAPTER SEVENTY-ONE

The Uber arrived within five minutes and took me downtown in the warm glow of the Florida evening. My eyes were stinging from tiredness and I still felt dehydrated as I climbed into the cab. The journey took us south down the coastal road, past the endless hotels on the right and the immaculate white beaches to the left. The mood was calm, and it seemed the residents of Florida were all getting ready for the night as the streets were a lot quieter than when I had arrived not long before. Eventually, the grand facade of the Four Seasons Hotel loomed up in the distance to the right, and the driver pointed it out.

"Don't drive in," I said. "You can stop anywhere nearby. I think I'll take a walk on the beach first."

The knowledge that I was near the man who had caused so much pain and death awakened me, and I felt tingling in my arms and legs at the very thought. *You don't have a fucking plan, Green. What the fuck are you gonna do if and when you see him?* But I forced these thoughts from my mind as I handed the driver a $10 tip and made my way across the street. The sun had almost set behind the giant building, and I dodged a middle-aged lady on rollerblades as I stepped onto the sidewalk. She wore nothing but a skimpy bikini and said nothing as she raced past me. *Careful, Green. You're tired.* I made my way down the pavement until I found a bench near the entrance to the immaculate beach on my left. It was partially surrounded by lush green shrubbery and would offer a good vantage point from which to watch the entrance to the massive hotel. I took a seat and lit a cigarette as I watched and waited. But it was my total lack of any credible plan that bothered me. *You have flown across the Atlantic on a wild goose chase here, Green. You have no plan. You acted on impulse, and that was a mistake. You should have watched and waited rather than jump on a plane.* But the fact remained that this man was a Russian national, and although he had apparently retired from his position at the FSB, he was still well-known and clearly dangerous. *He might slip back into Russia, and then there would be no chance of ever tracking him down. You made the decision, Green. You are here now, so deal with it!*

Realizing I was exhausted and more than likely still suffering trauma from the ordeal I had endured at sea, I sat back and got myself comfortable on the bench. The sky was darkening above me, and already the lights in the buildings around me were illuminated. I yawned as I stood to crush out a cigarette and threw the butt into a nearby bin. The time was 6:30 pm. and I pulled my phone out from my pocket as I sat down once again. I dialled the number for the Four Seasons Hotel Fort Lauderdale and waited for the reception to answer.

"This is the Four Seasons. How can I help you?" said the bubbly female voice.

"Ah, good evening," I said. "Could you please tell me if Mr Volkov is still at the hotel?"

"Certainly, sir," came the reply. "Could you spell that for me?"

I did so, giving the Russian's first name as well.

"One moment, please..."

There was a brief pause, and then the receptionist came back on the line.

"Yes, sir," she said. "Mr Volkov is still a guest at the hotel. Would you like me to put you through to his room?"

"No, thanks," I said. "I'm a friend of his. I will contact him on his cellphone. Thanks very much..."

"A pleasure, sir. Have a great evening."

I thanked the lady, hung up, and placed the phone back in my pocket.

"Got you, you cunt..." I whispered to myself through gritted teeth as I stared across the street at the hotel.

By then, darkness was descending, and my eyes were stinging from lack of sleep. My brain was swirling with various scenarios and possible outcomes.

There was no doubt that if I got my hands on the man, his time on Earth would come to a sudden end. That was beyond question. But the fact remained that I knew very little of his current situation. *Was he alone, or was he in the company of others? What was he doing in Florida of all places?* A former Russian FSB man. None of it made any sense, and this was further compounded by my own exhaustion. I took a deep breath and sat back on the bench once again. *You just watch the hotel for now, Green. It's all you can do. Think things through and decide on a course of action. This is no time to make a mistake.*

CHAPTER SEVENTY-TWO

Maxim Volkov opened one eye and blinked repeatedly as his vision cleared. At first, he was unaware of where he was, but within a few seconds, it all came back to him. There had been a visit to the boatyard of Alpha Marine, followed by the journey back to the hotel. He frowned as he struggled to recall what had happened afterwards, but then the memory of the debacle at the pool deck returned. He had been angry and disappointed that the American women who were there had left soon after his arrival. He had been drinking fairly heavily afterwards and then his memory failed. With an audible groan, he lifted his head, and it was only then that the true severity of the hangover became clear. Suddenly, there was a thunderous pounding in his head, and a rush of bile reached his parched mouth from his stomach.

Maxim realized he was still fully clothed and had slept the entire night on top of his bed. There was no recollection of how he had gotten there, neither was there any memory of the events of the latter part of the evening. Slowly, and with great effort, he stood up and swayed on his feet as he brought his fingers to his temples to massage them. The fire in his belly rose suddenly, and he realized that he needed to be sick. Stumbling off towards the bathroom, Maxim Volkov retched and coughed, and it was by sheer luck that he reached the basin in time. Once there, a torrent of projectile vomit burst from his mouth, spraying the mirror and the surfaces surrounding the bowl. Again and again, it came until his tortured stomach was empty and the burning bile dribbled from his unshaven chin.

Slowly, and with great care, he removed his stained shirt and lay down on the cool tiles in a foetal position. He lay there for 20 minutes, falling asleep briefly until he awoke and glanced at his watch. It had just gone 7:45 am. and the Florida sunshine was streaming into the room behind him. Volkov got to his feet and kicked his shoes off, feeling the cool tiles under his feet. Then he dropped his cream slacks and walked naked into the shower. He stood there, groaning for 10 minutes, with the water streaming over his body and his head hung low. Finally, he stepped out of the shower wearing a white fluffy robe and searched his ablution bag for headache pills and antacids. Having found the required medication, he glanced down to where the mini bar had been, only to see it had since been removed. Whoever had done this had not even left a bottle of mineral water for him to drink.

"Yebat!" he shouted out loud. "Fuck!"

Still clutching his pills, and with his head pounding from the sudden outburst, he made his way into the vomit-splattered bathroom and filled a glass with tap water. He stood there, staring at himself as he swallowed the pills and drank the strange-tasting water. His face was pale and sweaty, and his eyes were red and sunken with dark, grey skin surrounding them. With another groan, he made his way back into the suite and carefully lay down on the crumpled bed. *Time*, he thought. *Time and silence, and you will be fine. You can still enjoy your final day in Florida.* But it was at exactly 8:30 am. as Maxim Volkov was just drifting off into a semi-comfortable sleep, that the bedside phone rang with a shrill electronic warble. The sound sent waves of aching pain through his brain, and his anger rose as he answered it.

"Yes," he said into the receiver.

The call was from the day manager of the hotel, and the news was not good at all. It turned out that his behaviour the previous night had been deemed unacceptable by management, and a decision had been made to ask him to leave the hotel immediately. A taxi had been called and was waiting for him near the lobby.

"Myagkiy chlen, amerikanskiye zasrantsy!" he screamed into the receiver. "Soft cock American assholes!"

But it was too late, and the fact that he had been thrown out of the flashy establishment only served to darken his mood and enrage him further.

"You will have to wait until I make other arrangements," he bellowed in English. "I will be leaving once that is done. Goodbye!"

Hungover, humiliated and seething with rage, Maxim Volkov made a few phone calls from his cell phone and began throwing his soiled clothes into his suitcase. He had secured a seat on the mid-morning flight to Paris and would be leaving American soil for good. The deposit on the yacht of his dreams had been paid, and there was nothing anyone could do to stop that purchase. *After all, there is work to do. Get the fuck out of here now, Maxim! European women are far better than these American pigs anyway!*

CHAPTER SEVENTY-THREE

S ometime around 11:30pm. exhaustion finally overtook me. A passing refuse truck had startled me from my seat on the bench. The night air was warm and humid, and the traffic had calmed down. Glancing at my watch, I realized I had dozed off. *This isn't helping you, Green. You need to get some rest.* I stood up, feeling my tired bones ache and stepped out from the darkness of the shrubs. I called an Uber and looked up at the massive hotel while waiting. *Mr Volkov, I know you're in there. I'll be back soon.* The Uber arrived and we took a short ride back to my hotel. I barely had the energy to take a shower, but I forced myself to do so. Exhausted, I collapsed on the bed with the damp towel still around my waist. As I drifted to sleep, my mind was filled with the haunting visions of the terrible events I had witnessed in Seychelles—events that seemed impossible to forget, even from halfway around the world.

I woke up abruptly at 6:00 am. and sat up rigidly in bed. Suddenly, everything rushed back to me, and I realized just how exhausted I must have been. The sleep had restored me well and my mind felt much clearer than the previous day. The morning sun seeped through a gap in the wide curtains, and hunger raged within me. I immediately decided that my first priority was to find some food, followed by formulating a plan. Mr Volkov was holed up in his luxury hotel, a mere 15 minutes away, and there was no way I was going to let him slip away. He would pay for what he did. That was certain. Wasting no time, I took a quick shower, then headed downstairs and out onto the street. I remembered that there was a tourist pier a few minutes' walk from the hotel, where I was sure to find restaurants and eateries serving breakfast. The morning air was warm and humid as I walked, passing by several typical Florida bungalows. I had learned from my brief research that Lauderdale-By-The-Sea was an historic town that prohibited high-rise developments, preserving its old-world charm amidst the billion-dollar developments surrounding it. Turning right at the stoplights, I took a short stroll toward the renowned pier. Day workers were busy cleaning up after what must have been a wild night of partying, but one restaurant was open and serving food. I took a seat at an outside table, perusing the menu placed before me. I ordered breakfast with coffee and ate heartily while carefully contemplating my situation.

You're here, just a stone's throw away from the man who killed your friends. You now know the motive behind their deaths—gold. A lost ship carrying a massive stash of gold bullion.

What you don't know is why this man, Volkov, resigned from his position at the Russian FSB. And it's unlikely you'll uncover that information. You flew here on a blind mission with one goal in mind: to exact justice upon this man. It's possible right now, but it could prove dangerous. You have no idea why he's here or who he's with. Those are the first things you need to establish, Green.

Glancing at my watch, I saw that it was just past 7:15 am. It's the middle of the night in the UK *you can't call Tracey now. What you must do is return to his hotel and start your investigation. Find out why he's here, who he's with and determine how you can reach him. Once you have that information, you can devise a credible and actionable plan. That's all, Green. Get to work!* I settled the bill, then walked to a nearby corner shop to purchase a newspaper. Afterwards, I hailed an Uber and stood in the morning sun, smoking a cigarette as I waited. The vehicle arrived within five minutes, and we embarked on the drive down the vibrant Florida coast toward the Four Seasons Hotel.

The morning traffic caused a slight delay, and it was 7:50 am. when the driver pulled up across from the hotel. I tipped him $10 and clambered out onto the sidewalk.

CHAPTER SEVENTY-FOUR

The phone rang for the second time as Maxim Volkov closed his case. The sound intensified his throbbing headache, causing the veins in his temples to pulse. With a furious mix of frustration and discomfort, he picked up the call.

"Your taxi is still waiting, sir," the manager informed him over the line.

"I will be there right away, you fucking swine!" Maxim shouted, his rage evident in his voice, before slamming the phone back on its cradle.

Maxim zipped up his case with trembling hands, his armpits damp with sweat. He cursed loudly, scanning the room for anything he might have forgotten. The nauseating sensation in his stomach grew, rising like a wave of fire in his throat. He let out a groan of distress, then stumbled his way back into the bathroom, which was still splattered with vomit, to gulp down another glass of water. Finally, he washed his face and tossed the towel onto the floor in frustration. He stared at his reflection in the mirror, woefully observing his pale and sickly appearance.

"You must try to cut back on the drinking, Maxim. It's really not good for you," he muttered to himself.

Gathering his composure, he returned to the room, gathered his bags and headed toward the elevator. While waiting, an elderly and seemingly affluent American couple joined him at the elevator doors.

"Good morning," the woman greeted him with a sweet smile.

Maxim grunted in response and closed his eyes, attempting to find a moment of calm amidst the chaos.

Finally, the elevator arrived, and Maxim ensured he was the first one to enter. The couple followed closely behind, and he pressed the button for the ground floor. The doors opened, revealing the spacious and elegantly furnished hotel reception area. Ignoring his elderly companions, Volkov forcefully exited the elevator and stormed towards the reception desk, where several managerial staff were nervously awaiting him.

CHAPTER SEVENTY-FIVE

The lobby of the hotel exuded a sense of grandeur, opulence and meticulous attention to detail. I glanced at the reception area before settling in a seating area near the elevators. Choosing a table on the far side, I positioned myself to have a clear view of both the lifts and the reception. The hotel buzzed with activity, as staff and guests moved about, and I was relieved that my arrival hadn't attracted any undue attention.

A waiter approached shortly after and I promptly ordered a pot of coffee for myself. When he asked for my room number, I informed him that I was waiting to meet a guest and would pay with my card. He accepted this without question, and I opened my newspaper, preparing for an unknown amount of waiting time. Sitting quietly, I absorbed the surroundings while discreetly watching from behind the newspaper.

Minutes later, the waiter returned, placing a cup and pot of coffee on the table before me. As he did so, I noticed the lift doors opening. There was no mistaking him—Maxim Volkov emerged from the elevator, stepping into the lobby. His face appeared pale, and a sheen of sweat covered his skin. Wet patches marked his armpits, and his complexion seemed sickly. My adrenaline surged as I watched him, leaning over in my seat to track his movements as he strode toward the reception desk.

In a flash, a tumultuous commotion erupted before my eyes. Shouting and protests filled the air as Volkov reached the reception area. Once again, I had to lean to my left to catch a glimpse of what was unfolding. The waiter, engrossed in pouring coffee, became alarmed by my reaction and spoke to me, but his words went unheard.

Volkov was dragging a bag and carrying luggage—clearly on his way out. *What now, Green? Something is not fucking right here!* The commotion at the reception seemed to subside, and I noticed several suited men guiding Volkov toward the hotel's exit. *Green, there's a problem—he's being thrown out!* Throwing the newspaper onto the nearby seat, I abruptly stood up, nearly knocking the coffee pot from the waiter's hand.

"I'll be right back," I declared as I raced toward the doors.

However, it was too late and the big man had already left the building. Aware that he would likely be picked up by a vehicle, I quickened my pace. Five suited staff members stood gathered at the doors, having escorted the Russian out. They stood like sentinels, protecting their domain. Pushing through them, I hurriedly excused myself, desperate to get a glimpse of what was happening outside. But it was futile. In the portico, a yellow cab with smoke billowing from its exhaust sat waiting. Seated in the back was the man I had travelled 6,000 miles to pursue. He appeared flustered and exceedingly unwell. As I made it through the doors, the vehicle pulled away, and I began running after it.

"Volkov!" I shouted at the top of my lungs.

Though the taxi was already halfway out of the raised portico, the Russian had heard me and turned in his seat, casting a brief but alarmed gaze in my direction. However, the distance between us was too far, and the taxi turned right, heading south on the coastal road. Its destination, a complete mystery. A terrible sinking feeling settled in my stomach as I retraced my steps toward the hotel doors, where the men who facilitated Volkov's departure awaited, displaying a mixture of relief and curiosity on their faces.

"Where did he go?" I asked desperately "Maxim Volkov. Where has he gone?"

CHAPTER SEVENTY-SIX

I shifted in my seat and adjusted the cushion behind me as I leaned towards the tripod that held my binoculars. The sleek, German-made Galleon 800 motor yacht sat, as it had done for the past 3 days, in its moorings in the picturesque harbour below. The sun was setting over my left shoulder and it cast a warm yellow glow over the many bobbing vessels floating in the cool, clear waters. My hotel room, in the famous old town, was specially chosen to give me an uninterrupted view of the harbour and the boat in question. I had spent 3 days quietly watching the expensive vessel from this room and observing the various comings and goings to and from it. The three men on board spent most of their time hidden from view in the cabins, but I had begun to see a pattern in their behaviour whenever they did venture out on deck. They did so at certain times of the day, in the early mornings, and then more frequently in the evenings, and their actions were as predictable as clockwork. The three men in question were Maxim Volkov and the two brutes who had dived the wreck in the Seychelles. The very same men who had murdered my friends and who had tried, but failed, to do the same to me. I cursed myself for the appalling blunder I had made at the entrance to the Four Seasons Hotel in Fort Lauderdale. I had realised that my actions were fuelled by raw emotion rather than common sense and it had been a grave mistake to call out after the departing taxi. The vision of Maxim Volkov as he stared back at me through the rear window of the taxi had haunted me ever since. *Had he really recognised me? Someone he believed to be long dead.* Our brief interactions in the Seychelles had been swift and business-like and I had no idea if he had put two and two together. I had to believe that the man was no fool. After all, until very recently he had been a high-ranking member of the Russian FSB. *Surely the man is no fool?*

Pretending to be a business associate, I had spoken briefly with the management of the hotel in Florida immediately after watching Volkov drive away. They were most professional and fairly guarded, but they had divulged that there had been an unfortunate incident the previous night involving excess liquor, and it had been decided that given the circumstances, Volkov should leave their establishment. My polite enquiries as to where he may have gone came up with zilch. The management had no idea where he was headed.

I had made my way back to my own hotel and spent the next few hours cursing my own stupidity. I had lost him in a fleeting moment and in the process, I had shown my face. If the man had any sense, he would have recognised me. It was a blunder I would never forgive myself for and one I would certainly not repeat. It had been 2:30 pm. that afternoon when finally I was able to get through to Tracey Jones in the UK. In the situation I had found myself in, she was my only hope of tracking the man. I knew full well that should he be heading back to Russia, I might have lost him forever. Tracey returned my call an hour later with a valuable update. Maxim Volkov had travelled to Florida to make a deposit on an extremely expensive motor yacht. The payment of $200,000.00 had been made the day before he had departed on a flight to Paris. There had also been a booking and payment made for a subsequent flight from Orly to Zadar, Croatia. Tracey had informed me that Volkov kept a motor yacht in the harbour of the small town and that she had naturally assumed that this was where he was headed. The name of the Zadar-based vessel, 'Krikun', was in memory of a Russian warship from the 1800s and translated into the English word 'Screamer'.

Still reeling from the guilt of my mistake in Florida, I caught a flight from Miami International to Rome, Italy. From there I boarded a city hopper to Zadar and had immediately taken a hotel with a view of the harbour where the 'Krikun' was moored. It had been in that room that I had spent the past three days watching and logging the activities on board the massive boat. During this time alone, I had gone through a thousand possible theories as to what the men were planning. Foremost of these theories was the huge amount of gold on board the sunken ship, The Pearl of Alexandria, which lay on the ocean bed 60 km east of La Digue island in Seychelles. These men had been prepared to kill for it and I could only assume that, given its value, retrieving it would be their main priority. *A hard-drinking ex-FSB man on the loose. Finally free from the constraints of his job. A man who has just made a deposit on an American-made superyacht the likes of which Russian oligarchs are so fond. You gotta put two and two together, Green. The fucker thinks he's about to come into a great deal of cash. Why else would he make such a bold move? They know the gold is there. They are going after it. Make no mistake.* The movements of the men on board the 'Krikun' had taught me a great deal in the past 3 days. During daylight hours, the younger Wagner men would come on deck on the hour, every hour.

Once there, they would perform a patrol of the vessel from the stern to the bow. This was repeated on both decks. It was after these patrols that each man would take a position on either side of the boat at the stern and at the bow. This was to allow them to smoke cigarettes. During the night, there would be only one man making these patrols. It was at midnight that the shift would change to allow one man to sleep. Their demeanour was that of men exercising extreme caution. The purpose of these hourly patrols was obviously to maintain security and told me that their boss, Volkov, was a worried man. If my hunch was right, it meant that I had indeed been recognized in Florida. It was only during the hours of darkness that Volkov showed his face. It was usually at around 9:00 pm. when he would emerge on the dimly lit lower deck at the stern of the vessel. Once there, he would spend a few hours in the jacuzzi sipping unknown drinks and eating takeout food that was delivered by moped to one of the Wagner men on the jetty. The food was usually McDonald's or pizza. I had noted the number plate of the scooter that delivered the food and had made several orders from the very same driver. It appeared the Uber Eats delivery service in the old town used the same driver for all deliveries. The scooter driver in question was a young Ukrainian man with bad skin and long greasy hair. I had taken my time to have a quiet word with him. Having no love lost for anyone of Russian origin, and in return for a crisp $100 bill, he had gladly supplied me with the phone number used to order the regular deliveries of food on the 'Krikun'. The men aboard the flashy vessel were in my sights and I had their phone number to boot. Exactly whose number it was, I had no idea, but I could only hope it was Volkov's. The patterns were the same each day and night and I had logged and observed it all in detail.

I turned my wrist to see my watch. It had just gone 4.45 pm. and my back was aching from the strain of the constant watch. I reached for the pack of cigarettes and lit one while staring out at the harbour below me. I took a deep draw of the cigarette and watched the smoke as it billowed out through the old wooden window frame in the gentle sea breeze. The pattern of activity on the boat had been the same for days. You could set your clock to it. But that night I would miss at least an hour of this activity. I had an appointment at 7.00 pm. A scheduled meeting in a bar in a seedy part of town on the outskirts of the city of Zadar. A place where no tourist would ever think of venturing.

I was due to pick up a piece of equipment that would ensure that the men in the boat below would never get their hands on the massive hoard of gold on the bed of the Indian Ocean. A piece of equipment that would ensure they paid the ultimate price for their heinous crimes.

"Oh yes," I whispered as I leaned forward to stare through the binoculars once again "Tonight is the night it ends for you all..."

CHAPTER SEVENTY-SEVEN

Maxim Volkov was a worried man. Although he was finally free from the job he had dedicated his life to and no longer encumbered by his nagging wife, he couldn't shake off his concerns. Despite having just made a deposit on his dream boat, a vessel that would allow him to retire in comfort and sail into the sunset. Despite arranging the charter salvage operation in the Indian Ocean to retrieve a crate of gold, he remained deeply troubled. It all started with a split-second encounter in a taxi as he left the hotel in Florida. Someone called his name, and when he turned to look, he saw a man whose face he never expected to see again—a man he believed to be dead. *Or was he really dead?* Maxim Volkov's own intuition had become unreliable, perhaps due to the severe hangover he had that morning. Could it have been his mind playing tricks on him? Maybe all his worrying was unfounded and a waste of time? He simply didn't know.

Since arriving in the coastal city of Zadar in Croatia, where his beloved vessel, the 'Krikun,' was docked, he had reunited with Yuri and Sergei and immediately implemented a strict security regime. Paranoia had consumed him, and the image of the man's face was etched in his mind. But perhaps it was all just an illusion, a product of an alcohol-addled mind suffering from jet lag? *Yes, that could be it!* To counteract this nagging paranoia, Maxim Volkov turned once again to the bottle. His daily consumption of vodka had tripled, and soon the stocks on his beloved 'Krikun' would be depleted. However, he maintained enough common sense to complete any necessary work before taking his first drink. That work ethic was ingrained in him.

In the past few days he had arranged and paid for a fully equipped salvage vessel in the port of Victoria on the island of Mahe, Seychelles. The charter vessel was owned by a Seychellois lowlife named Albert Pillay. Maxim had done thorough research and checked the man and his vessel extensively, without the knowledge of the Russian embassy in the Seychelles. The first exploratory trip had been conducted using false passports provided by the Russian state, but this time they would travel independently, using their own passports. This would be in 48 hours. The salvage operation was scheduled for the day after their arrival.

Once the steel crate was brought ashore, it would be swiftly moved to a secure location. Disposing of Albert Pillay and his crew discreetly would follow the same pattern as the owners of the dive charter. *But had they really been dealt with?* The nagging memory of the man chasing after the taxi haunted Maxim, driving him to pour another drink to calm his troubled thoughts. The smooth vodka burned his throat as it went down.

Maxim had repeatedly questioned both Yuri and Sergei, but their answers remained consistent. Everyone involved in the original exploratory charter had been taken care of—they were all dead, without a doubt. The Wagner men had assured him repeatedly. Their smirks and private jokes about Maxim's sanity only intensified as he kept asking. He overheard their conversations and laughter in their cabin aboard the 'Krikun.' However, the fear and worry persisted, refusing to dissipate no matter how much he drank. *Fuck those two meatheads!* he thought as he rose to pour another drink. *I'll kill them once I get the gold anyway.*

CHAPTER SEVENTY-EIGHT

The ancient flagstones that paved the narrow alleyways of the old city of Zadar were a rich brown colour and worn perfectly smooth from millennia of foot traffic. They resembled massive square slabs of toffee that had been partially sucked by giants. It was 5:00 pm. and I had left my hotel room, venturing out of the old city towards the parking lot located beyond the tall walls in the northern part. I had deliberately chosen this particular parking lot to avoid being seen near the harbour where the 'Krikun' was docked. Even in the gentle evening light, I felt exposed and somewhat vulnerable. The lights in numerous restaurants and bars had been illuminated with the staff preparing for the influx of tourists who would indulge in fine wines and feast on truffle pizzas. Eventually, I reached Five Wells Square and passed through it, ascending into the pleasant park beyond. Taking a left turn, I walked through the ancient archway that led out of the old city. The rental vehicle was parked just as I had left it, and without wasting any time, I climbed in and started the engine. I sat there in the dim twilight, consulting Google Maps on my phone. The bar I was about to visit lay south of the city of Zadar, nestled in a low-income area that rarely saw any tourist activity. It was frequented by gipsies and drug pedlars, so I needed to remain alert if I was to succeed in obtaining what I sought. The contact I was due to meet went by the name of Ivan. I had discovered him through an article on the dark web. Surprisingly, Ivan spoke fluent English despite being a former Yugoslav gangster. He was a dangerous criminal, best avoided if not for the fact that he possessed something I desperately needed. *Be careful, Green,* I reminded myself. I clicked 'Go' on my phone screen and pulled away into the darkening night.

The route took me inland from the old city, passing a roundabout near the airport. From there, the streets grew narrower, and the buildings became increasingly dilapidated, with peeling paint and potholed roads. Groups of skinny teenagers loitered on street corners, kicking footballs in the alleys. By the time I reached the designated bar, darkness had completely enveloped the surroundings. Following instructions, I parked the vehicle behind a dumpster near the entrance. A surge of adrenaline coursed through my arms and legs as I contemplated the possible consequences if the meeting were to go wrong.

I knew very little about this man named Ivan, apart from the information he had shared with me and the picture he had sent on WhatsApp. The image depicted a man in his early fifties, with close-cropped jet-black hair showing signs of greying, along with a beard. His eyes were black and cold, and I could tell he was an extremely unsavoury character from his picture alone. I patted the envelope in my pocket, which contained ten $100 bills. The WhatsApp instructions were to enter the bar, order a drink, hand my keys to the bartender, and take a seat near the toilet door. Once there, I was to wait until Ivan approached me and provided further instructions. Surveying the area surrounding the bar, mostly shrouded in darkness, I noticed an ageing yellow sign above the door that read 'Lambik Lounge.' One of the bulbs behind the perspex sign flickered repeatedly. Consulting my watch, I saw it was 6:00 pm. *Time to go, Green. Take it slow.* I took a deep breath and exited the car. The door of the 'Lambik Lounge' squeaked on its hinges as I entered. The room reeked of stale beer and cigarette smoke, and my shoes stuck to the carpet beneath me as I walked towards the bar. It was immediately evident that this establishment served as a haven for the city's undesirable elements. Drunkards clad in shiny tracksuits mingled with thin women sporting pinched faces and greasy hair. The sound system played an '80s rock song, "The Final Countdown" by the Swedish band Europe. The place matched my expectations of being dark and dingy. Ignoring the bewildered stares of the patrons, I made my way to the bar and ordered an Ožujsko beer. The rotund, bald man handed me a lukewarm bottle, and I slid my keys and a banknote towards him. Without a word, he took the money and keys, nodding towards a door on the right side of the room. Carrying my beer, I walked over to the door and settled onto a cheap vinyl chair with my back against the wall. Taking a sip, I scanned the room, relieved to see that the patrons had mostly resumed their conversations. A minute later, I observed the front door swing open, and I immediately recognized the man who entered as Ivan. Without pausing at the bar, he made his way towards me and spoke.

"Follow me," he said quietly, pushing open the door to the restroom.

Setting my beer on the table, I obeyed his instruction. The doorway led to a dimly lit corridor, permeated with the odour of urine and vomit.

Blinking in the darkness, I spotted the 'Gents' sign to my left. Pushing the door open, I found Ivan standing at the urinal with his back turned to me. The room was grimy and broken tiles and shattered mirrors adorned the filthy basins. Without turning his head, Ivan spoke.

"The money, please," he said, extending his right hand. I stepped forward and handed him the folded envelope.

"You will find your order in the trunk of your vehicle; the keys are in the ignition," he said quietly "Now, fuck off..."

CHAPTER SEVENTY-NINE

"**H**ave you noticed anything out of the ordinary, anything suspicious?" Maxim asked.

Yuri and Sergei exchanged smirks and shook their heads simultaneously. Their boss's paranoia permeated everything and to them, it seemed almost comical.

"No, sir," Yuri replied. "Everything is as it should be. There hasn't been anything unusual."

"Good, good," Maxim said as he poured a tumbler of vodka. "Well, I have a final briefing for both of you. Take a seat, let's get started."

The three men settled in the main cabin of the 'Krikun' as the briefing commenced. Their upcoming journey involved travelling to Zagreb the next morning in a rental car, followed by a commercial flight to Qatar and a connecting flight to Mahe in Seychelles. They would have one morning to acquire tools such as cutting torches and grinders, and the same afternoon to inspect the salvage vessel and interview the crew. The operation was scheduled for the following day. Every detail of their itinerary had been meticulously planned and double-checked. The diving gear and vehicles were prepared, and it was agreed upon that only two Seychellois crew members—the captain and a deckhand—would be aboard the salvage vessel to minimize risks. Once the steel trunk was delivered to Mahe's port, these two men would be eliminated. They had rented a 3-tonne truck equipped with a Hiab grab crane, which would transport the crate to their secluded beach house located to the north of the island. The house had high walls and a workshop area. If all went according to plan, they would open the crate that night and extract the gold bars. Maxim emphasized the weight and value of the gold, knowing it would ignite his men's enthusiasm. He went on to describe an elaborate plan to ship the bullion on a charter vessel to Mombasa, Kenya, making it easier to divide the spoils equally.

However, this last part was merely a fabrication, as Maxim Volkov had no intention of sharing the rewards with anyone. In fact, he had already acquired sleeping tablets, which he would use to drug Yuri and Sergei before killing them and disposing of their bodies in the ocean, shortly after the successful salvage operation. A wild celebration would take place, accompanied by copious amounts of vodka. Once the two Wagner men were unconscious from the powdered sleeping tablets, they would be eliminated. Every aspect of this intricate plan had been carefully considered and analysed numerous times. They were, as far as Maxim could determine, fully prepared to execute what would be the biggest payday of his life. If only it weren't for that nagging fear that persisted. It was the face of the man he had seen chasing after the taxi in Florida. The image haunted him, casting doubt on everything he had planned. Yet even that would not deter him. *No, Maxim Volkov would have his dues and secure his freedom forever*. That was the plan, at least.

CHAPTER EIGHTY

The narrow streets of the old town teemed with tourists, bustling around the various bars and restaurants. Following Ivan's instructions, I swiftly departed from our meeting at the 'Lambik Lounge.' I only paused momentarily to check the trunk of my car upon reaching the parking lot. As promised, a long green canvas bag awaited me there. Without inspecting its contents, I hurriedly made my way through the streets, past the church near the ruins of the Roman forum, and towards my hotel room overlooking the harbour. Although there was a distinct possibility of being ripped off, considering the dubious characters I had encountered at the seedy bar, I had decided to proceed and would soon find out the truth. The weight of the bag on my right shoulder provided some reassurance, but its contents remained a mystery until I reached my room.

Having spent the past few days confined to my room with binoculars as my only companion, I keenly felt the strange sensation of being exposed to the public eye. It almost made me yearn for the familiar isolation. However, as I walked through the dimly lit alley leading to the hotel entrance, my phone rang. It was Tracey Jones from London, calling with fresh information on Volkov's movements. Recognizing the importance of this information, yet unable to pause for a conversation, I requested her to send it via email for me to read upon my return. Aware that the men on the yacht had been confined like me for some time, I anticipated that they would soon make their move. These men would not simply idle away their time on their yacht in Zadar for the next two years. There was a sunken ship laden with gold bars awaiting them and leaving it unclaimed was out of the question. Knowing they had killed to protect their secret I was well aware that they were plotting something. Tracey agreed to send the email immediately and after thanking her, I continued towards the hotel.

The receptionist greeted me with a smile as I entered, and I climbed the three flights of red-carpeted stairs to my room overlooking the harbour. By the time I reached my room, beads of sweat had formed on my forehead and I was lightly panting. Placing the canvas bag on the dishevelled bed, I quickly grabbed the binoculars to check on the 'Krikun,' which remained exactly where I had left it. *Did you truly expect them to vanish so quickly, Green?*

Nevertheless, it was a relief to see it still there. Setting the binoculars down, I sat at the desk and opened my emails. True to her word, Tracey Jones had delivered. I clicked on her email to read the latest updates on Volkov's movements and purchases. The information I found was surprising but not entirely unexpected. Several payments had been made, the most significant being for three airfares to Seychelles the following day, an Airbnb reservation on the island of Mahe, and a substantial payment to a Seychelles company named Pillay Salvage Co. Nodding to myself as I read the details a second time, I muttered under my breath,

"You're on the move, Volkov, just as I knew you would be."

Next, I opened a new browser window and searched for Pillay Salvage Co. A shabby-looking website appeared, seemingly untouched for the past ten years. The displayed images showcased a 60-foot steel vessel equipped with standard cranes, compressors and marine salvage equipment. The boat, an unsightly red colour marred by rust and bird droppings, clearly indicated that its primary business involved small-scale recovery of abandoned engines and sports boats in Seychelles. It was evident that all my predictions were coming true.

There would be no delay in retrieving the gold; these men were prepared to return to the Indian Ocean to claim the lost treasure of the Pearl of Alexandria and I was determined to stop them. The news injected a fresh sense of urgency into my own mission. The murderers aboard the 'Krikun' were scheduled to depart the following morning, so Ivan's package needed to contain exactly what it claimed. Wasting no time, I walked over to the bed and unzipped the long canvas bag. My eyes widened as I scanned its contents.

"Well, well, Ivan," I whispered, "It seems you are a man of your word after all."

Procuring a weapon in the former Yugoslavia had proven relatively easy. The Dragunov SVD sniper rifle, a relic of the Soviet era, was designed in the 1960s to provide precise long-range engagement for troops armed only with the standard 7.62 by 39mm intermediate cartridge assault rifles issued within the Warsaw Pact.

The dismantled version lying in the green canvas bag before me was an older model, featuring a wooden handguard and gas tube cover, as well as a standard skeletonized stock. I was familiar with the weapon's effectiveness from my time in Africa. Although it was used, the rifle appeared to be in good condition, prompting me to swiftly assemble it. Equipped with the PSO-1 telescopic sights designed for military-designated marksmen and a standard bipod for enhanced stability during long-range engagements, it was an extremely potent and deadly piece of equipment. My heart sank when I picked up the curved magazine and realized it was empty. However, my disappointment faded as soon as I spotted the small cardboard box of bullets at the bottom of the bag. The final item, not a standard component by any means, was a brand new, heavy suppressor, manufactured by Brugger and Thomet. It served as both an effective silencer and flash hider. With the Dragunov and suppressor combined, I knew I had the perfect tools for the task at hand.

The lighting aboard the 'Krikun' was sufficient for me to take precise shots from the hotel window. Considering that the three men were set to depart for Seychelles the next day, it was crucial that I complete my mission that very night. The pressure was mounting, but I felt confident in my newfound equipment, courtesy of my encounter with the distinctly unsavoury Ivan. A glance at my watch told me that it was just past 7:00 pm. and perfect timing for their customary nocturnal excursions. I reckoned that their dinner would arrive, as usual, around 8:00 pm. and then it would be time. I needed to set everything up. Switching off the main lights and leaving only the bedside lamps on to mask my movements, I proceeded to position the rifle. I moved the desk well back from the window so that when the weapon was resting on it, it would be more difficult to see from outside. It reduced the field of fire but I did not need any width. As I gazed out at the 'Krikun,' I loaded the magazine with five rounds from the ammunition box. Five bullets would suffice for the job: two to calibrate the sights. With my preparations complete, I focused on selecting a target at a similar distance to the motor yacht. I found a suitable one in a cheap plastic mooring buoy, floating near a small pleasure boat from the 1970s. It rested close to a streetlight along the harbour walkway. The area appeared deserted, so the sound of a bullet striking the buoy or the water nearby would not raise any suspicion. It was perfect.

After a final check of the weapon and suppressor, I settled in to take the shot. I realized that this moment would be tense, as any failure on the suppressor's part would draw attention to my position.

Ideally, there would be zero muzzle flash and a barely audible sound when the weapon fired. The buoy, spherical and painted a bright red, had clearly been in place for quite some time, as algae growth was visible on its lower half through the scope. Lifting my head briefly to survey the surroundings and confirm the area was quiet, I then returned my focus to the sights, aiming for the buoy's centre where the streetlight cast its brightest glow. With controlled breathing, I fixed my sight on the target, exhaled slowly and squeezed the trigger. The rifle's recoil jolted my right shoulder, accompanied by a sound resembling a child's squib, and I observed the buoy's brief shudder. Without delay, I raised my gaze to the harbour below. There was no reaction whatsoever. Satisfied, I returned my attention to the scope, where the buoy remained clearly visible in the streetlight's glow. The bullet had penetrated the buoy three inches to the left of the centre where I had aimed and at the midway point above the waterline, leaving behind a tiny black hole that was barely discernible. *Good.*

For the next few minutes, I calibrated the sights to rectify the alignment, only then realizing that I was sweating heavily. I attributed it to the intense tension of the situation, especially considering the imminent departure of the Russians. Everything was happening rapidly and the weight of the task fell squarely on my shoulders. I had made a promise to a murdered friend, and I intended to honour it. The pressure was on. Once again, I quickly surveyed the surroundings, dropped my eyes to the scope, and aimed at the buoy. If my calculations were correct, the shot would strike within millimetres of the centre. I gently exhaled, squeezed the trigger and the Dragunov emitted its familiar pop and recoil. Without looking around, I immediately focused on the target. The bullet had struck within millimetres of my intended mark.

"Fucking bullseye," I whispered to myself as a bead of sweat dripped from my nose.

Leaving the rifle in position, I stood up and walked into the bathroom to wash my face and hands. Upon returning, I lit a cigarette and raised the binoculars to my eyes. Soon, the evening food delivery would arrive, and the Russians would appear on deck as usual.

"Oh, yes," I whispered, my eyes fixed on the vessel. "When night falls, the face of the wolf will be revealed."

CHAPTER EIGHTY-ONE

" **S** ergei!" Maxim shouted as he knocked on the cabin door of the Wagner man. "Where is dinner?"

The door promptly opened, revealing a towering figure in nothing but shorts. Sergei glanced at his phone before speaking.

"It has been ordered, boss," he said. "The driver is close by. I'll head to the jetty to await him now."

"Good," grunted Maxim. "Hurry up, I'm starving..."

Sergei nodded and went back into his cabin to put on a T-shirt, while Maxim returned to the main suite of the 'Krikun.' The routine had remained the same for days now. Takeout was ordered and delivered within an hour, always from the same delivery driver—a young Ukrainian university student. While Yuri and Sergei preferred pizza and salads, their boss seemed addicted to McDonald's food, often ordering two or three meals at a time, washed down with copious amounts of vodka. It was no wonder the man was cranky and sickly. Nonetheless, the mission would set them all up for life, and both Sergei and Yuri were determined to see it through. The fact that they had entertained treacherous thoughts, privately discussing killing Volkov after retrieving the gold, was a matter for later. For now, the most important thing was that the waiting was over, and they were scheduled to return to the Seychelles the following day. With funding and equipment secured, lifting the crate from the seabed would be child's play. Fully dressed now, Sergei slipped on his shoes and headed out of the cabin, taking a right toward the lower deck at the stern of the 'Krikun.' Passing the Jacuzzi, he leapt up to the concrete pier from the deck and hopped over a mooring line, making his way toward the designated arrival spot for the driver.

Overhead lights were positioned at ten-metre intervals along the jetty to ensure safe access to boats at night. As he walked, he checked the delivery app. on his phone and saw that the young Ukrainian driver was only two minutes away.

Good. I'm also starving, Sergei thought, oblivious to the fact that his every move was being scrutinized through the telescopic sights of a Soviet Dragunov sniper rifle.

The meeting with the delivery driver took place, as always, on the walkway near the old city walls. The large brown paper bag was removed from the thermal carrier and handed to him by the young Ukrainian. Wasting no time, Sergei thanked the young man and made his way back down the jetty toward the 'Krikun.' Once there, he jumped onto the lower deck and padded past the Jacuzzi, heading up to the living area where the men would dine and discuss their mission. Yuri and Maxim were patiently waiting at the dining table. Maxim, appearing drunk as usual, was eager to get his hands on the food. Fortunately, his paranoia seemed to have subsided somewhat, likely due to their impending departure for the Seychelles. The food arrived hot, and the three men ate in silence, save for Maxim's grunts and burps. When they finished, Sergei cleared the table and disposed of the food packaging in the galley.

"We need to thoroughly clean this boat tomorrow morning before we leave," Maxim declared as he rose from his seat. "That includes your cabins."

The two Wagner men nodded sullenly before retreating to their cabins to await the clock striking 9.00 pm. signalling the start of their routine security patrol. No one aboard the 'Krikun' had any inkling of the chaos that was about to unfold.

CHAPTER EIGHTY-TWO

There would only be one opportunity to get the job done cleanly. The routines I had observed over the past days had been precise and ran like clockwork. The Wagner men would come on deck on the hour, every hour. They would perform a walk-around patrol of the boat and then each man would take a position on either side of the boat at the bow and stern. Once there, they would both relax and smoke cigarettes for around 10 minutes before returning to their cabins. Volkov was a night owl and would usually appear on the lower deck at around 9:00 pm. Once there, he would spend an hour or so in the jacuzzi which was visible from my position at the window of my room. Three bullets were what I had allocated for these men. Three bullets that would need to find their targets in fairly quick succession. I had gone through it all a thousand times in my mind. First would be the man at the bow or front of the boat. The shot would be unheard and unseen and the others aboard would be totally oblivious of it. Next would be the Wagner man at the stern. I had watched and observed that this man would usually lean on the chrome rail at the rear of the lower deck as he smoked. This was below the line of sight of the jacuzzi in which Volkov would hopefully be sitting. With the two Wagner men eliminated, my next target would be Volkov himself. With any luck, he would be happily enjoying the warm bubbles of the jacuzzi when he died. It was a simple plan that I hoped would go smoothly. *No mess, no fuss. Three bullets to end it all.* But the pressure was beginning to affect me and I paced the room stopping every now and then to take a look at my watch and peer through the binoculars. It was 8:53 pm. when I sat down to take up the rifle and await the men on the deck of the 'Krikun'. I pulled my phone from my pocket and scrolled until I had the number I had been given by the Ukrainian delivery guy. With any luck, it would be Volkov's personal number and I would remind him of his sins before he died. I sat in silence with the binoculars to my face as I watched and waited. The seconds seemed to drag out into minutes and the minutes into eternities. *Focus, Green!* At 9:00 pm. exactly I saw the two Wagner men appear on the middle deck near the jacuzzi. I dropped the binoculars, wiped the sweat from my hands on my jeans and lifted the rifle. *Right, you fucking murderers. Your time has come.* As it had happened so many times before, both men did a patrol around the entire vessel, briefly going out of sight behind the streamlined cabins.

The crosshairs of the sights found them when they appeared once again and split up to take their positions at either end of the boat. *That's it, you carry on as usual. Where the fuck is Volkov?* The wait was agonizing but eventually, I saw him emerge from the cabins near the jacuzzi. With a thick white cotton towel around his waist, he appeared sluggish and uncoordinated. The warm glow of the middle deck lights gave his substantial paunch a creamy appearance as he dropped the towel, placed his phone and a glass on the side, and climbed clumsily into the jacuzzi. Everything began to appear as if it were happening in slow-motion. I paused while I watched Volkov lift the glass he had placed at the corner of the jacuzzi. In the crosshairs of the Dragunov sights I watched him bring it to his mouth and drink. My right forefinger itched on the trigger at the sight of it. *It's time now, Green! Do it. Now!* I brought the gun sights down to the right to see the one Wagner man had taken his position at the rear of the 'Krikun' on the lower deck. As usual, he was leaning on the chrome rail and had lit up a cigarette. *Good.* Next, I shifted my sights to the left along the length of the boat until I saw the second Wagner man at the bow. Yet to light up, he stood with one foot resting on the apex of the bow and appeared to be staring out into the dancing yellow reflections of the city lights in the rippling waters of the harbour. *He looks bored. Time to put him out of his misery, Green.* I took a deep breath and exhaled slowly while holding the crosshairs above the ear of the man. I squeezed the trigger and felt the kick of the Dragunov in my right shoulder. The report was exactly as it had been when I had calibrated the sights. Nothing more than the sound of a child's squib. I stared through the sights and for a split second, I thought I had missed my target. The man stood there as he had done and was unmoved. But it was then that I saw the tiny black hole above his ear appear as his body slumped forwards and fell silently into the blackness of the water below. There was no doubt, the Wagner man was dead. It had been a perfect shot and I felt the adrenalin coursing and tingling through my body. *You fuckin' beauty!* Next, I moved the sights to the right and focused on the middle deck and the jacuzzi. Volkov sat, as he had been in the warm water drinking clear liquid from his glass. The second Wagner man was in his usual position smoking while leaning on the chrome railing at the rear of the lower deck. But it was at that moment that I decided to take Volkov first. Both men were out of each other's line of vision. *Makes no difference who goes first.*

With my left hand, I lifted my phone and pressed 'Call' on the screen followed by the loudspeaker button. There was a brief pause as I placed the phone back on the desk and took aim at Volkov's head as I waited for the phone to ring.

"Say goodbye to the world you live in..." I whispered to myself as my finger tightened on the trigger.

At that moment I heard the phone ring and I waited for Volkov to react. A second passed and he sat there unmoved as it rang a third time. *What the fuck?* It was then that I heard the click of an answer and heard a voice speak on the line.

"Privet..." said the deep voice 'Hello...'

What the fuck? Volkov still sat happily in the jacuzzi. It was only then that I realised my mistake. Without waiting, I brought the gun sights down and to the right to see the Wagner man on the lower deck had stood up and was clutching his phone to his ear. All along I had assumed it was Volkov's number the delivery driver had given me. I had been badly mistaken. *Fuck!*

"Privet!" said the Wagner man, his voice betraying alarm "Kto eto?" 'Who is this?'

The man was standing facing the city walls below. His left hand was on his hip and I could see a frown of anger on his face. At that moment a thousand memories flashed through my mind. Images of my friend Joe smiling and the joy of his reunion with his brother, Chris. The happy-go-lucky Jimmy with his curly black hair blowing in the wind on the charter boat. All of them were dead. Murdered by the men in the harbour below. Then there were visions of the sharks. Terrible visions burned into my consciousness forever. Visions of Jimmy's young body being ripped to pieces underwater in clouds of red mist and shattered bone. Without thinking, I spoke.

"Look up..." I said. The Wagner man did exactly as instructed but his stare was directed at the next building. The crosshairs were trained on his forehead.

"Look to your right..." I said. It was then that he saw me and I watched his eyes widen in horror.

"Yes," I said before squeezing the trigger "It's me..."

The Dragunov kicked my right shoulder and I saw the hole appear below the man's left eye. The back of his head exploded in a spray of brain matter and shattered bone. The velocity of the bullet striking his cheekbone caused his neck to snap backwards and his upper body to be violently thrown back over the chrome railing. His flailing legs were the last thing I saw before his lifeless body fell into the blackness of the water below. Although there was a split second of satisfaction in the knowledge that the Wagner man had known he was about to die, there was still Volkov to take care of. *Two down, one to go.* But it was only as I moved the sights up and to the left that I realised my mistake. All along I had assumed that the lower deck was out of the line of sight from the jacuzzi on the middle deck. Sadly, I was wrong. Either that or Volkov had heard our exchange on the phone or the splash of the falling body. The big Russian stood hunched over in the jacuzzi, his body taught with alarm as he stared out over the lower deck.

I watched as his mouth shouted angrily and the tendons in his neck showed proud. Knowing there were precious seconds left to waste, I trained the crosshairs on Volkov's head and pulled the trigger. It turned out I was a split second too late. The Russian flung his body sideways and disappeared behind the jacuzzi. The bullet had missed and opened a divot in the shiny wooden deck beyond. *Fuck!* It had all turned to shit and I needed to act fast. I dropped the rifle and pulled the curved magazine from underneath it. *Fuck!* Wasting no time, I rammed another 5 rounds into it and jammed it once again into the rifle. Lifting the sights to my eyes, I scanned the middle deck of the 'Krikun' and waited. I knew that Volkov would be panicked now and would do anything to save his skin. A thousand thoughts raced through my mind at once. *He's trapped and he knows it. If he shows himself he'll catch a bullet. A rat in a cage. But what the fuck to do now? Will he raise the alarm? If so, to whom?* I knew that it would take me a good 5 minutes to physically get down to the boat. The only exit from the old city was through an archway halfway down the length of the harbour. *If you do that, Green, he could quite easily get away! No, you fucked up, you deal with it! Take him from where you are. He has to show himself!* With sweat running down my temples, I scanned the boat for any sign of movement. There was nothing for another 20 seconds until I saw his head pop up from where he had landed behind the jacuzzi. I pulled the trigger once again but once again, I was a split second too late. The bullet slammed into the rim of the jacuzzi sending shards of white fibreglass and enamel flying. *Fuck!* It was then that I saw Volkov's back briefly as he frantically crawled into the cabin. Then he was gone. *What the fuck will he do now? He knows he can't make a run for it down the jetty. He's trapped. You need to act fast, Green!* With my breathing now fast, and sweating profusely, I dropped the rifle and lifted the binoculars to get a wider view of the 'Krikun'. But it was then that I got my answer. It was as astonishing as it was predictable. It started with a series of lights suddenly illuminating atop the 'Krikun' and along the middle outer deck. This was soon followed by a swirl of frothing water at the rear of the vessel. *There's no fucking way! Surely not!* But it was happening. In a state of blind panic, Maxim Volkov had started the engines of the massive motor yacht and was preparing to force it out into the harbour from its moorings. I placed the binoculars on the desk and lifted the rifle once again. But the helmsman station was behind the sleek, blackened windows that surrounded the middle deck of the vessel. There was no way to see where exactly he was. Still, there was only one area where the wheel could be.

You gotta do it, Green. Pepper the wheelhouse with bullets! Wasting no time, I pulled the trigger 3 times, sending the last of the rounds in the magazine in a straight line across the wheelhouse. I watched as the frosted grey holes appeared in the blackened glass and prayed one of them had found my target. But they hadn't. I could only assume that Volkov would be taking cover somehow, perhaps crouching on his knees as he forced the throttle. In a state of disbelief, I watched the mooring ropes as they snapped under the force of the massive diesel engines and the 'Krikun' lurched forwards into the harbour. Once free of its tethers, the massive boat swung to the right, narrowly missing the lined-up vessels on the next jetty. From there it continued at speed for another 50 metres until it turned left and headed out into the darkness of the open ocean. Maxim Volkov was gone...

CHAPTER EIGHTY-THREE

The stinking confines of the lowest point of the bow of the salvage vessel were totally dark, cramped and stifling hot, even at 6:00 am. The air was thick with diesel fumes and a toxic mixture of oil and water sloshed around below my feet in the tiny steel compartment I had chosen to stow away in. I had found the spot two days earlier while on a nocturnal recce of the Pillay Salvage Co facilities in the very same harbour where Chris Fonseca had run his charter business. The fact that my hiding place was difficult to access was the only consolation for what I knew would be a long and extremely uncomfortable journey. I had found the hidden compartment deep within the hull behind two steel bulkheads which I had accessed from the engine room of the rusted old ship. At 24 metres long, the ancient vessel was on its last legs and was only really suitable for small-scale, shallow-water ocean salvage work. Still, it was fitted with two heavy-duty cranes and good rigging, and I had seen compressors, scuba equipment, and piles of flotation bags in the hold. My guess was the boat was primarily used for retrieving dropped engines and small leisure boats. Something that would be in demand in the tropical paradise of the Seychelles. My current location, however, was anything but idyllic. Perched on a narrow steel ledge with only the rusted hull to lean against, I could already feel my legs tingling from lack of blood. I shifted my body and attempted to bring my feet up on the ledge to get more comfortable. I sat in total and complete darkness, unable to see a thing. My head torch was the only source of light and it was to be used sparingly. I had arrived in the Seychelles four days ago having taken a flight from Zadar to London, then connecting to the Seychelles via Nairobi. I had dismantled and disposed of the Dragunov sniper rifle in Zadar and picked up extra surveillance equipment in London before my flight. I decided to make the move immediately rather than waiting for any information from Tracey Jones. By then I knew the kind of man Volkov was. Although he would be in a state of complete paranoia, I knew there was no way he would simply walk away from the vast fortune in gold that lay on the ocean bed. I knew he would return and I had been watching when he did. I had taken a guest house in the centre of the quaint town of Victoria, not far from the clock tower. From there it had been easy to enter the harbour and scout out the offices of the Pillay Salvage Co. I had done so in the dead of night and used the opportunity to place tiny pinhole cameras in both the offices and in and around the bridge of the salvage vessel.

Powered by compact lithium batteries, they would send high-quality audio and video whenever triggered by motion or sound. With a battery life of weeks, there was no fear of them failing. As it turned out, there was no need to have placed them in the offices as there was a broken old blackboard with both Volkov's cancelled and new booking chalked up on it. Only three words had been scrawled on the board. 'Russian, La Digue'. Volkov had arrived two days previously and had taken accommodation at new lodgings to the north of Victoria. I had been relaxing in my room when I watched his arrival late in the afternoon at the Pillay Salvage Co. As I had expected, he appeared nervous and looked rather sick in the view of my camera. The conversation had been recorded and it confirmed what I had seen on the blackboard.

Now short of two men, Volkov had requested only one diver and one deckhand only in addition to the captain, Mr Pillay himself. He had repeated this request twice in broken English before handing over a wad of cash. I had thought long and hard about simply informing the authorities about the discovery of The Pearl of Alexandria and allowing its precious cargo to be retrieved in the eyes of the world. There was no doubt, given its historical importance, it would make global headlines and would be done transparently. But doing so would alert Volkov and would almost certainly allow him to escape justice. The murderer would simply return to Russia and disappear. That was something I was not going to allow to happen. Although he had lost two of his men, I had to assume he was armed. The fact that he was dangerous was a given. Especially in his current state. My plan was to wait until he was at his most vulnerable before I took him. I would allow him to think that the gold was finally within his grasp before apprehending him and delivering him to the Seychelles police. The charge would be that of murder and it would be a fitting conclusion to know he would rot in a jail in paradise while the gold he coveted so much was retrieved by the authorities. I would wait until the salvage vessel was moored over the wreck of The Pearl of Alexandria and the diver had gone down to rig the first crate. That way there would be only 3 men on board when I made my surprise appearance. I would subdue and apprehend Volkov and return the salvage vessel to the harbour in Mahe where the police would be waiting. I had placed pinhole cameras in and around the bridge of the salvage vessel and I knew full well that Volkov would be in there for most of the operation. A strictly utilitarian boat, there was nowhere else aboard to sit apart from on rusted pieces of machinery in the full glare of the blazing sun.

From my hiding place deep within the hull, I would watch the men as they arrived on board and follow the progress of the ship until it reached the coordinates of the sunken vessel. I would listen to their conversations and watch the deck as they laid anchor in preparation to dive. The captain would no doubt be operating the crane while the deckhand handled the rigging for the diver. I would wait until all the men were occupied and then emerge from the engine room and surprise them. That was the plan, at least.

I first heard signs of life on the deck above me at exactly 6:03 am. I knew that the salvage charter was due to begin at that time so it came as no surprise. I pulled my phone from my pocket and waited until the spy camera in the bridge was activated and began transmitting. It was seconds later when it did. The first person to come into view was Pillay. A tall thin man of mixed race, his bushy afro was greying and he looked sleepy. My phone cast a blueish hue in the tight, dark space as I watched and saw the deckhand hand him a mug of coffee. There was a brief conversation in Creole and then both men disappeared from the bridge. 3 minutes later two men returned. I watched as Pillay walked in followed by Volkov. He wore a cheap Chinese copy of a Panama hat to save his skin from the fierce sun.

"Good morning..." I whispered to myself as I studied his face.

The man appeared pale and nervous. *That's to be expected, Green. Still, he will be excited because he thinks he is close to the prize. It's a distraction that will work to your advantage. Good.* There was some brief movement on the deck and then I saw and heard Pillay start the engine. The huge diesel groaned and heaved but eventually, it fired up and I found out then why my hiding place was so good. The hull vibrated and the sound was deafening. For a few moments, I worried that the space would be filled with carbon monoxide but thankfully the exhaust trunking was in good order. It was a minute later that I sensed we were moving and this was confirmed by the revving of the engine and the sound of water on the hull.

I checked the cameras once again and saw that the salvage vessel was towing a smaller boat. The fibreglass sports boat had a deep V-shaped hull and I watched it as it bobbed about in the wake. I could only assume the smaller vessel was used on salvage jobs where tricky manoeuvring was necessary. I knew the salvage vessel would be slow and the journey to the wreck site would be long and arduous. But nothing could have prepared me for the nightmare journey that I endured. It took 6 full hours of droning and heaving before I heard the engines slow and eventually come to a stop. By then I was half delirious from the heat, dripping with sweat and covered in a thick orange film of rust. I pulled the bottle of water from the small bag on my back and splashed my face after drinking some. A quick check of my watch told me it was 12:15pm. *Six fucking hours!* Just to be sure, I checked the coordinates on my GPS device. There was no doubt, we had arrived. It was then I heard the deckhand drop the bow anchor. The chain compartment must have been nearby as the clattering was deafening to the point I was sure my ears would be damaged. This was followed by the distant rattling of the stern anchor. The two anchors a feature of salvage boats essential to their stability while at work. Finally, there was some silence in the stinking heat of my steel coffin and I breathed a steamy sigh of relief. *Time to get busy, Green.* I pulled the phone from my pocket and took a look at what was going on in the bridge. Volkov was still sitting on the padded bench in the bridge but Pillay had ventured out on the stern deck. I switched cameras to check the deck and saw Pillay and the diver preparing the equipment. The diver was already in a wetsuit and was standing in the bright sunlight behind the bridge. It was then I saw Volkov come out to watch proceedings. Once again it struck me that the man looked ill. *Perhaps he can't handle open water? Seasick?* The good thing was he now appeared focused and a little less paranoid than when I had seen him earlier. I noticed the huge sweat stain on the back of his blue cotton shirt. *Still better than being stuck down here,* I thought. But it was then that I noticed the bulge at his waist. His sweating had made it more pronounced. There was no mistaking the outline of a holster. The man was armed. Although this was not unexpected, it posed a further danger for me and would be something I would have to deal with carefully and timeously. The deckhand appeared and began assisting the diver with his equipment while Volkov looked on.

The sound was muffled by the wind, but I could still make out some muted conversation.

I watched as Pillay moved off to the stern and began working on the crane controls. This was good news as it confirmed that the three men left on deck after the diver had gone down would be working behind the bridge. It would afford me some cover when I emerged from the engine room as their focus would be at the stern of the vessel around the crane. *Good.* I opened my bag and removed the powerful stun gun I had brought from London. I unclipped the safety and depressed the trigger. Instantly the dark interior was illuminated by a bright blue light and the air was filled with a loud electrical crackle. The device was fully charged and ready. It would render anyone who came in contact with the prongs incapacitated for five minutes at least. *Good.* Finally, I stretched my cramped legs and stood up with each foot on a steel rib above the stinking black water. Still in that position, I grabbed my phone and continued watching the proceedings on the deck above. The diver had strapped on his buoyancy compensator and aqualung and was about to roll on his neoprene hood when I saw Volkov remove some papers from his top pocket. He unfolded them and stepped up to the diver to speak to him. Although I could not hear what he was saying, I knew he was showing the diver photographs of the steel crate he wanted to be lifted from the seabed. As expected, he had held his cards to his chest until the very last moment. It was all playing out as I knew it would do. *Good.* The conversation lasted for a few minutes and I watched as Volkov repeatedly pointed at the photograph emphasising his points. The young diver nodded keenly then carried on with his hood and mask. It was then that I saw Pillay swing the crane around. He stepped down from the controls and lifted a heavy-duty swivel eye snap hook that was attached to the cable. Volkov stepped up and inspected it while nodding enthusiastically. I could see, from the sight of it, that the snap hook and cable would easily handle loads of up to five tons so there would be no problem lifting a compact steel box with a weight of just one tonne. The snap hook would easily fit over one of the handles of the crate and from there, it would be a simple job to raise it and lift it on board. I could almost feel the excitement building on the deck above me. With the equipment ready, I watched as Pillay tossed the snap hook over the side and released the cable barrel of the crane. I heard the clattering above as the barrel turned releasing the cable and hook to the depths below. It took less than a minute before the barrel stopped turning. The hook had reached the seabed. Next, Pillay stepped up to the diver who had donned his mask and was seated on the gunwale to the rear right of the bridge. Volkov stood nearby with his hands on his hips.

The gun and holster showed through the cotton of his shirt. After a brief conversation and a final check of his equipment, the diver placed the regulator in his mouth, gave the 'okay' signal, and fell backwards out of my line of sight into the ocean. The salvage job was on. I watched as the three remaining men gathered around the spot where the diver had entered the water. I knew that professional salvage divers wore helmets that carried closed-circuit video cameras. This was to allow surface teams to see what the diver was doing and be involved in inspection tasks. But here there was no such high-tech equipment and it remained to be seen how those on deck would know when to raise the cable. I could only assume the diver would surface when the snap hook had been attached to the first crate and give the signal to lift. There was also the possibility that the diver would send surface marker buoys up to give the go-ahead. Regardless, it was time to move and I clipped the stun gun to my belt in preparation to do just that. My bones ached as I climbed through the tiny oval door in the first bulkhead. My ears were still ringing from the hours of deafening noise from the engine. Once through, I stopped to check the activity on the deck. The men were still gathered around the spot where the diver had gone down. I knew it would take some time for the diver to descend to the wreck. Once there he would need to locate the first crate. This would be easy given Volkov had shown him numerous photographs of the wreck site. If all went smoothly, the first crate would be ready for lifting within 20 minutes. This would be the most nerve-wracking time for Volkov and his attention would be focussed on the water. It was then I saw Pillay move off and take his position near the controls for the crane. Volkov and the deckhand still stood near the gunwale, their attention firmly on the water. *Time to move, Green.* I pocketed my phone and quietly swung open the tiny steel door of the next bulkhead. Finally, there was now some natural light shining into the engine room from the loose hatch on the deck above. I turned off the head torch, removed it and placed it in my bag. Access to the engine room was from a hatch near the front of the bridge. To get to the hatch I would need to climb a 12-foot steel ladder and step onto a small platform. The engine room was greasy, dark, airless and unbelievably hot. I paused to wipe the sweat from my face and take a drink from the water bottle before climbing the ladder. The slippery steel rungs burnt my hands to the touch but the air became cooler as I ascended. Finally, I was able to breathe some fresh air and this was a tonic after the hours of hell I had endured in the dark bowels of the ship. I stopped upon reaching the platform and took another drink of water as I checked my phone to see what was happening on deck.

Pillay had moved from the controls of the crane and had taken shelter from the blazing sun on the bridge. I watched as he drank from a can of Coke, his attention squarely focused on the other two men who were still in the position where the diver had gone down.

I knew then that all on board would be seized with the moment. Their full attention would be on the task at hand and the last thing they would be expecting would be the sudden appearance of a stowaway. The diver had been down nearly 15 minutes and soon there would be some sort of signal to lift the first crate. *It's time to move, Green.* The engine hatch directly above me had been wedged open with a thick rectangular block of wood. I could only assume that this was to help with ventilation while the engine was running. It was fortuitous for me as it would allow access to the deck without having to open it. There was enough space for me to slide out onto the deck on my stomach. Once there I would be completely exposed, metres from the bridge and hopefully out of sight of Pillay who was cooling off inside. I took a final drink of water and checked my phone for any movement on deck. All the men were in the same positions. I took a deep breath and stood up, sliding the top half of my body under the hatch and into the sunlight. I wriggled my way out and silently crawled towards the front of the bridge where I would be hidden from view from inside it. Once there, I sat with my back to the wall of the bridge and removed the stun gun from my belt. Unaccustomed to the blinding light, I blinked repeatedly as I slowed my breathing and prepared to move. 20 seconds later I turned and moved into a kneeling position facing the bridge. With the stun gun in my right hand, I slowly stood up. The front windows of the bridge had been opened and raised on rusted hinges to allow the breeze to flow in. Pillay stood to the side of the wheel, inches from the window, completely oblivious with his back turned to me. His greying afro wobbled in the breeze. I glanced to the right to see Volkov and the deckhand still standing at the gunwale near the submerged cable. Their focus on the water and nothing else. I took a deep breath and reached forward through the window. Wasting no time, I depressed the trigger and jammed the prongs into Pillay's scrawny, coffee-coloured neck. There was a brief electronic buzzing sound and a whiff of singed hair followed by a dull thud as Pillay dropped unconscious to the floor. The remaining two men on deck were totally oblivious to this. *Good.* I quickly dropped to my knees and crawled along the front of the bridge to my left. The steel deck burned my hands as I did so but shortly, I rounded the corner and started towards the left rear of the bridge.

I knew this would be a dangerous moment and I said a silent prayer as I poked my head around to take a look. Volkov and the deckhand were still standing, staring at the water where the diver had gone down near the submerged cable. His cotton shirt was drenched with sweat and the pale skin of his arms had turned bright pink from the blazing sun. I paused as I tried to ascertain the make of the gun in the holster around his waist. *Looks like a Soviet Makarov pistol. Low recoil, and good stopping power. Depending on the version holds between 10 and 12 rounds. You better be quick, Green. Quiet and very quick!* It was then that the door at the rear of the bridge swung slightly in the breeze. I looked up to see there was a simple sliding Brenton bolt lock halfway up it. Ahead of me was the open deck with the crane to the rear. Standing with their backs to me were Volkov and the deckhand. In between us was a pile of rigging, a scuba tank rack, and a large steel toolbox that was bolted to the deck. Apart from the whisper of the breeze and the gentle lapping of the water on the hull, everything was quiet. I reached forward and slowly pulled the bridge door closed. It swung silently on its hinges. Once closed, I reached up and slid the bolt across, effectively locking the unconscious Pillay in the bridge. *One less person to deal with.* The tangled pile of rigging was made up of heavy straps, clasps and cables. It lay 6 feet from where I was crouched near the corner of the bridge. If my plan was to work, I would launch a sneak attack on the men while their attention was on the water. I would send the deckhand for a swim while immobilizing and restraining Volkov. This would mean I would need to get to the rigging which would give me some cover, then on to the toolbox and finally to the men. *So far, so good,*

Green. Keep it that way! Staying as low as I could, I crawled across the filthy deck towards the pile of rigging. I reached it without a problem and lowered my body onto the deck for cover as I arrived. Now there was only a space of 6 metres between Volkov and me. The deckhand stood with his left foot on the gunwale, his right hand clutching the cable that ran down from the boom tip of the crane above. A stream of sweat ran into my right eye. Mixed with grime from the depths of the ship, it stung fiercely and I brought my hand up to wipe it. But it was at that moment that the deckhand turned to look at the bridge. Out of the corner of his eye, he must have caught the movement. A frown formed on his forehead and he yelled out immediately, a mixture of panic and fear in his voice. For the big man that he was, Volkov moved with surprising speed. He spun around in a flash, his cold blue eyes scanning the deck behind him.

By then I was already on my way towards the large toolbox that stood between us. It was the only solid structure that would offer cover if the bullets started flying. My plan, which I had made in a split second, was to get to Volkov before he had the time to draw his weapon. As I went I grabbed a bunch of thick canvas strapping which I flung at the men to distract them. Attached to steel ratchets and hooks, the strapping flew in a tangled mess towards the men. But Volkov had anticipated this and had quickly ducked down out of the way, his right hand instinctively reaching for the pistol. The rigging hit the deckhand with a heavy hook striking his face. The young man went over the gunwale with a high-pitched screech and splashed unseen into the water below. I threw my body forward into a somersault roll and grazed my elbows deeply on the rusted deck as I did. But it was in doing this that I lost the stun gun which fell from my belt and rattled away on the deck. *Fuck!* It turned out I was just in time as I heard the first of the bullets slamming into the steel behind me.

"Koyzol!" screamed Volkov, his voice like the rasping bark of a wild animal. 'Motherfucker!'

I sat panting heavily with my back to the box as I counted the bullets. 3, 4, 5 of them clanged into the body of the box. Now I was in a lot of trouble with little at hand to mitigate the situation. But it was then that I saw the aqualung to my right. Clamped into a bracket to the rear of the toolbox, it was obviously a spare that would be put into use should the diver need it. I imagined there would be more of them and the thought of one exploding under gunfire crossed my mind. But there was no time to think and I quickly loosened it from its bracket and pulled it towards me using the pillar valve.

"Koyzol!" screamed Volkov again and I heard the crunch of his approaching footsteps on the deck.

By then I knew I was left with very little choice. There was only one weapon at hand and I needed to use it immediately.

With my back to the toolbox, I gripped the pillar valve in my right hand and readied myself. Another 6, 7, and 8 bullets slammed into the box and the deck near where I sat. A whizzing ricochet sent up a cloud of red dust inches from my head. I reached up and gripped the top of the toolbox with my left hand while lifting my body slightly. This gave me a peek over the top of the box. As expected, Volkov was on his way towards me, pistol raised, his face a pale mask of raging savagery. I ducked as yet another 2 bullets slammed into the top of the box above me. *That's 10 now.* It was time to play my last card. I swung the aqualung with all my might up and over the top of the toolbox. The effort of doing so ripped the tendons in my shoulder but the heavy missile flew true and fast. The base of the air-filled steel bottle struck Volkov squarely in the chest and I heard the wind as it was knocked out of him. This sound was followed by the clattering of the gun which had been knocked from his grasp. I stood up to see Volkov had dropped to his knees on the deck behind me, his hands on his chest as he fought to breathe. Wasting no time, I launched myself over the top of the toolbox and dived towards the kneeling man with outstretched arms. Our bodies connected at the shoulders and the force of my dive sent Volkov sprawling backwards towards the gunwale. But as he fell I heard the air return to his lungs in a great wheeze. As if by magic, the strength returned to the big man and I felt his arms fold around my back like bands of steel. With all my might, I forced my shoulders up and swung my right fist at the side of his head. It was as if I had struck a block of wood and bolts of pain shot up my arm into my shoulder. Again and again, I punched him in the side of his head but his frozen eyes never dulled. But it was then that I saw the man bare his teeth and I knew what was coming. Volkov growled like a wild animal and shot his head forward towards my own. The man was trying to bite me. *What the fuck?* I jerked my head to the side to avoid his teeth but he snarled and countered with another lunge, his cold blue eyes burning with white-hot rage. Then I saw his head turn to his right. Almost immediately, I was rolled over on my back with the weight of the man on top of me. It was clear to me that he was trying to get to the gun which lay on the deck 6 feet away. I planted another two blows to the side of his head while desperately trying to hold his face away from my own. The snarling and drooling continued and I began to wonder if the man was blessed with superhuman strength. Before I knew it, I was rolled over again and found myself on top of the man. His face turned to the right once again and his right hand lunged out for the gun.

I heard his fingernails screeching on the deck as he clawed his way towards it with me, seemingly helpless now, still atop him. *Can't let him get it, Green! Still 2 rounds left!* But it appeared that the man was unstoppable and I planted yet another blow to his right eye as he gripped the butt of the weapon. By then there was yelling from both the ocean behind the gunwale and from the bridge. Pillay had awoken from his sleep and was screaming in Creole from the window. The scene had become one of total mayhem and chaos, I was weakening and there was a strong possibility that I would be overcome. Seeing his hand had found the gun, I slammed my right elbow into his jaw and held it there to keep his head flat against the deck. As I did that I shot my left hand out and grabbed his wrist to prevent him from bringing the gun towards me. But my left arm was no match for the strength in his right, and slowly but surely, his gun hand scraped across the deck towards me. *You tried, Green. If it ends like this, at least you tried.* With my elbow and forearm pressed against his face, Volkov finally managed to bring the pistol to his side at stomach level. By then I was losing strength and I realised that my time in the hull of the salvage vessel had seriously depleted my energy levels. I was caught between a rock and a hard place knowing that if I removed my elbow, he would bite, and if I didn't, the gun would be brought up. The growling, panting and snarling continued as did the screaming from the bridge and the water. My heart sank as I felt his wrist twist and my left hand slipped from his. Volkov brought the pistol up at stomach level and forced it between our two bodies. In a last-ditch attempt to avoid the inevitable, I removed my right arm from his face and shoved it down between us. At that moment, the big man turned his head and lunged forward, sinking his teeth into the flesh of my right shoulder. I yelled out in agony as my right hand found the gun that was now sandwiched between our two bodies. With all of my might, I forced the barrel downwards and away from me, all the while expecting to hear and feel the shot. The shot came but the result was unexpected. Volkov gasped loudly in my ear as his teeth withdrew from my skin. Suddenly all of his strength was drained and his grip became weakened. It was then that I felt the warm pulsing of thick, sticky liquid around my midriff. Volkov froze and I watched his eyes widen as his mouth emitted a high-pitched wail. The sound reminded me of an opera singer. *What the fuck?* With my grip now firmly on the gun, I rolled off the man and lay there staring at the sun above, my chest heaving in great oxygen-starved wheezes. It was sometime later that I sat up and turned to look at the man who lay on the deck to my left. His mouth was open in an 'O' shape and his shaking hands clutched his crotch.

An ever-increasing patch of blood was mushrooming across his cotton slacks. Maxim Volkov had shot himself in the balls. Leaving him where he was, I staggered to my feet and stood there looking down at the man while swaying on my heels. He was going nowhere. Suddenly I became aware of shouting from the ocean beyond the gunwale. The diver had ascended and was now hanging on to the submerged cable with the deckhand. I pointed the pistol at them and spoke in between breaths.

"Get on board," I said "You try anything, I'll fucking kill you..."

Next, I walked over to the bridge and raised the pistol to point it directly at Pillay's face. The skinny old man cowered and whimpered in terror.

"I'm going to open this door now," I said "You will go to the crane and release the cable into the sea. You make a wrong move and I'll shoot you. Understood?"

Pillay nodded frantically as I released the Brenton bolt from the latch. I stood there catching my breath as I watched him scuttle over to the crane and release the cable. The barrel spun loosely and I watched as he used a spanner to undo the bolt that held it to the barrel. With a quiet whipping sound, the end of the cable flicked out of the boom tip of the crane and disappeared into the ocean. *The gold will stay where it is for now*. By then the diver and deckhand were back on deck and cowering together near the stern. Volkov had dragged himself into a sitting position and was leaning against the gunwale, his face pale and drawn. I pointed the gun once again at Pillay and spoke.

"Raise the anchors and start the engine," I said. "We are going back to the harbour."

It took several minutes for Pillay to get this done but he wasted no time doing so.

Finally, I felt the familiar vibration and droning of the engine and felt the breeze on my face as we got moving. I turned to look at Volkov once again. He sat there against the gunwale in an ever-increasing pool of his own blood. His face drained and his head hung low. Suddenly my thoughts went back to my friend, Joe Fonseca, his brother Chris and young Jimmy. All gone. Murdered by this man. *Is prison enough for him? Surely he should be made to feel the same fear as you did, Green? You can do better than that*. I walked over to the toolbox and sat down to think. Hanging from a rusted hook on the gunwale near Volkov was an old life ring. Its orange and white markings faded and chipped from exposure to the fierce sun. I paused for a while as I thought but my mind was already made up. To my left, the diver and deckhand sat quietly on the deck. The diver had removed his equipment and wore nothing but his shorts. I raised the gun once again and pointed it at them.

"Go to him," I said, motioning towards Volkov with my head "Go and lift him onto the side of the boat."

The two men got to their feet and walked over to where Volkov sat against the gunwale. They paused once they arrived and glanced nervously at me.

"Do it!" I shouted, gun still raised "Pick him up!"

The two men reached down and lifted Volkov from under his arms. Once more he let out a strange high-pitched wail as they placed his backside on the gunwale. I motioned the two men to return to the stern as I studied the man who had caused so much pain and death. *Do it, Green!* I turned my head to look at Pillay who was in the bridge looking back at us. His eyes were wide and his face filled with fear.

"You keep this boat moving!" I shouted.

Pillay nodded grimly as I got to my feet and walked quietly to where Volkov sat whimpering and clutching his blood-soaked groin. Reaching over to the left, I pulled the old life ring from its bracket and placed it over his head. Maxim Volkov lifted his gaze and I saw the undiluted hatred in his eyes.

"Good luck, Mr Volkov..." I said quietly as I reached forward and pushed him backwards over the gunwale.

With the Russian overboard, I walked back to the toolbox and sat down before calling Pillay to bring me some water. The engine had settled into a comfortable rhythm and the breeze was pleasant on my skin. It was several minutes later when I pulled the binoculars from my bag and looked out over the stern. It came as no surprise to see Volkov floating in the distance. What I hadn't expected was to hear the blood-curdling screams as I saw the two shiny black triangular fins that were slowly circling him.

CHAPTER EIGHTY-FOUR

London. Three weeks later

The early morning spring sunshine shone down on the sprawl of north London giving new life to the city after what had been a long and dreary winter. I stood at the open window of my 5th-floor flat and smoked the first cigarette of the day while sipping from a steaming mug of coffee. The events since I had left Mahe Island in the Seychelles had been swift and as expected, had caused an international sensation that was still grabbing global headlines. Reflecting on these developments, my mind went back to the events immediately after sending the Russian murderer, Maxim Volkov, for an afternoon swim. I had instructed Captain Pillay to make a course for the harbour at Mahe Island and had immediately destroyed his ship-to-shore radio. I had also thrown the crew's cell phones into the ocean so there would be no communication at all. It had been dusk when the salvage vessel had made sighting of Mahe island in the distance and I had then told Pillay to stop the engine and drop anchor. After that, I cut the fuel lines to the engine and poured seawater into the main tank. This was done to ensure that the crew of the salvage vessel would be stranded incommunicado for the night at least, giving me time to disappear. I knew full well that a passing vessel would see them and effect a rescue the following day by which time I would be long gone. I had fuelled up the small sports boat that had been towed behind the salvage vessel and sped back to Mahe, landing after dark on an isolated beach to the south of Victoria. Once there,

I cleaned myself up as best as I could and caught an Uber back to my lodgings. After treating my wounds, I booked an early morning flight on Qatar Airways to Abu Dhabi and on to London. Once back, I sent out an anonymous press release to every major news channel informing them of the discovery of the famous ship, The Pearl of Alexandria. This had been copied to the Seychelles Maritime Authority and all major television networks including National Geographic and Discovery. My own pictures of the wreck had gone viral on Twitter and other social media channels and continued to be the source of wild curiosity and excitement. The fact that the wreck had been found in international waters, and the unusual and uncertain circumstances regarding who had actually found it had caused great debate as to ownership. Given the fact that the fortune in bullion on board the sunken ship had been Nazi gold stolen from Jews during the Second World War, it was now widely expected that the ownership and any subsequent proceeds from the gold would go to the Auschwitz-Birkenau State Museum in Poland.

For me, this was an outcome far better than it falling into the hands of the Russian state or worse still, to a crazed wannabe oligarch. An international team of salvage divers would soon retrieve the gold, streamed live and under the scrutiny of multiple agencies ensuring complete transparency for the entire process. Numerous documentaries were now in the works and very soon, the entire process would be beamed to the world via the internet and various television channels. My mind went back to the brief time of joy and happiness when I had arrived in the Seychelles with my friend, Joe. His reunion with his brother and the laughter and good times we had shared. Good times that had been so brutally and unexpectedly ended. There was some satisfaction in the knowledge that those responsible for that period of horror had been dealt with accordingly. Even given the fact that I had nearly lost my own life in doing so. It was with a feeling of dull melancholy that I crushed out the cigarette and walked over to my desk to check my emails and take a look at my work schedule with the insurance firm for the rest of the week. *Another day, another dollar, Green. Another day, another dollar...*

The End

Dear reader. I guess if you're seeing this message, you have finished this book. If so, I really hope you enjoyed it. If you have a spare minute, I would greatly appreciate it if you could leave a review on Amazon and Goodreads. Reviews REALLY help me reach new readers. There are many other books in The Jason Green Series which you can find at this link. https://geni.us/QCVsT24 . Please visit my Facebook page and say hello. I love hearing from readers. Thanks again, and rest assured. Jason Green will return soon...

Printed in Great Britain
by Amazon

36660880R00182